"We must flee!" Chiun said.

"The Bunji must make her stand here," said Lobsang from the door.

"She will die," Chiun said firmly.

"If she dies, it is the will of the gods. The people will hear of this and rise up."

"The Bunji is under the protection of the House of Sinanju. Her death would bring shame on my House. I will not have it."

Squirrelly stamped a bare foot. "Don't I get some say here?"

"You are the Bunji," said Kula, bowing his head in Squirrelly's direction. "Of course we will obey your merest whim."

"Fine. My whim is that we—"

The Master of Sinanju slipped up and touched the back of Squirrelly Chicane's neck. Her mouth kept moving but no words issued forth. She tried coughing. It only made her throat raw. Not a syllable came out.

Created by
# WARREN MURPHY
## and RICHARD SAPIR

---

# THE Destroyer

---

## HIGH PRIESTESS

A GOLD EAGLE BOOK FROM
# WORLDWIDE ®

TORONTO • NEW YORK • LONDON
AMSTERDAM • PARIS • SYDNEY • HAMBURG
STOCKHOLM • ATHENS • TOKYO • MILAN
MADRID • WARSAW • BUDAPEST • AUCKLAND

First edition May 1994

ISBN 0-373-63210-X

Special thanks and acknowledgment to
Will Murray for his contribution to this work.

HIGH PRIESTESS

Printed in U.S.A.

For John Godin, friend of the old days.
And for the Glorious House of Sinanju,
P.O. Box 2505, Quincy, MA 02269

# AN IMPORTANT EXPLANATION FROM CHIUN, MASTER OF SINANJU

*"You fired the publisher?"* Warren Murphy wailed upon learning of my actions.

"Their gold was too slow, indolent one," I told Murphy.

"Their gold keeps me in beer and skittles," Murphy complained. "Maybe we can go back to Pinnacle," he added ruefully.

"Pinnacle? I instructed Remo to destroy their house utterly, and sow salt on the ground where it formerly stood."

"Somebody bought the name," said Murphy.

This news shocked me. "Remo left the name standing?"

Murphy shrugged. "Nobody's perfect."

"He takes after you," I pointed out.

"So what do we do?" asked the white wretch who has lived off my glory for more than twenty winters.

"I am finished with American publishers," I announced. "The House of Sinanju, which existed long before this tawdry nation, will have nothing to do with any of their flint-skinned ilk."

"That leaves only Gold Eagle."

"Gold—?"

"They've been publishing the Executioner like there's no tomorrow."

"What! Pendleton lives, too?"

"He bailed out of Pinnacle long before you had Remo wreck the place. Anyway, Gold Eagle's up in Toronto."

"Quickly! Speak to me of exotic Toronto, Land of Golden Eagles," I cried. "What are their customs? Are their emperors renowned for their generosity?"

Murphy pondered this question in the dull-witted way typical of sub-Koreans. "All I can remember are the squirrels."

"Even the squirrels are of gold?"

"No," said Murphy. "They're kind of a reddish-black."

"And?"

"That's all I remember. I got off the plane, saw that the squirrels were a sinister color, and spent the rest of my vacation barricaded in the airport saloon, trying to blot out the memory."

"You have frittered your entire life away in saloons," I retorted. "But I have made up my mind. We will work for the publisher whose eagles are of gold."

"It's just a name," said Murphy.

"Be certain they understand that if their gold is not promptly delivered to Castle Sinanju on the wings of the swiftest eagles, not only will their lives be forfeit, but their very name will not be left standing."

"That should propel negotiations along," said Murphy. "We're trying to sell the series to them, you know."

"In that case," I said triumphantly, "inform the Guild of the Gold Eagle that they have 48 hours to make us a handsome offer or no mercy will be shown to their chieftains."

"They're called publishers."

"If they consent to publish my glorious adventures," I told Murphy, "they will be elevated to chieftains in the eyes of an envious world."

One day later, Murphy called from storied Toronto.

"We got a deal. They loved the chieftains bit."

"White vanity is like clay, heavy and wet, but easily molded," I said.

"But they don't want to make any changes."

"My name will not go above the title?"

"They insist we keep the Destroyer name and the numbering system, or it's no deal."

"Have you examined their gold stores, as I instructed?"

"Yeah. The gold takes perfect teeth marks."

"Inform them that we have a deal."

"One more thing—they want you to write an introduction reassuring the readers that nothing's gonna change."

"I will do this subject to one condition," I told Murphy.

"What's that?"

"That you return with exotic Torontonian rodents perched on each of your slothful shoulders, whistling 'Hail to the Chieftains.'"

"Who's whistling—me or the squirrels?"

"All three of you. In harmony."

Murphy made a strange sound which I took to be assent, and so I am compelled to write the following:

## A GUARANTEE

I, Chiun, Reigning Master of Sinanju, warrant that the book you hold in your hand has not been tampered with by the new publishing chieftains of Gold

Eagle. It will be as wretchedly written as all previous books in this inept series have been.

Remo Williams, my pupil, will continue to be foisted off as star of these books, even though all intelligent persons know that I richly deserve that accolade.

It will be riddled with lies, distortions and anti-Korean slurs, as always.

The same illiterate scribbler will continue to write them. I have even allowed that dauber, Hector Garrido, to continue painting the covers even though he stubbornly draws the awesome magnificence that is Chiun with a mustache, because his wife, a long-suffering woman who is too good for him, assures me that he will get it right this time.

If you are dissatisfied with this book, do not inundate me with unworthy complaints. It has been written by Americans and published by Canadians. You should not expect excellence. Be thankful if the vowels do not fall out when the book is opened.

> With moderate tolerance
> for you, I am—
> Chi n,
> Re gn ng Mast r of
> S n nj.

# PROLOGUE

The Bunji Lama lay dying.

It was the second month of the Tibetan Year of the Fire Dog. Within the stone walls of the meditation cell whose Tibetan name translated as "Prayerful Refuge from the Temptations of the Sensual World," Gedun Tsering, forty-sixth Bunji Lama and the third Living Buddha, lingered as his regents fretted and paced the lamasery corridors in their boots of chewed yak hide.

On the lamasery roof, the howling winds spun the prayer wheels to no avail. The skies would not accept their whirling entreaties. Yak-butter lamps guttered before the altar of Buddha Maitreya, and other lamps flickered in the cramped unglazed windows of the simple houses of the village. The Bunji Lama was destined to die on this day. All Tibet knew this. There was a single communications line that stretched out of the Himalayan village called Bunji-Kiang through the trackless snows and impassable mountain passes, and the wind-whipped line crackled with Morse code carrying the grim tidings to the dead Dalai Lama's regents in Lhasa and the living Panchen Lama in Peiping.

No one knew that the Bunji Lama had been poisoned. No one, that is, except the regents who had engineered the wicked deed and their victim, Gedun Tsering, the forty-sixth Bunji Lama, three weeks short of his fifteenth birthday.

As he lay in the chill of the meditation chamber, his slight body growing cool even as his stomach burned like a coal, the Bunji Lama's dying thoughts were of home. Burang. The village in which he was born, where he had played with his brothers and sisters, the son of a simple yak herder. Until the council of regents had come and stripped the cloth from his left arm, showing the birthmark that had pitted the shoulder of every Bunji Lama since the first. They had dangled the jade rosary of the previous Bunji Lama before his curious child's eyes, and when he reached for it, they proclaimed to the gullible that he had recognized a relic of his previous life. No one could deny them, for they were priests.

They bore Gedun Tsering away on a palanquin of gilt emblazoned with thunderbolts of bronze. It was a great honor. His mother wept, of course, but his father had beamed with pride. They were not allowed to visit him throughout the years in which he learned the five lesser and higher subjects, absorbed the tantras, studied the sutras and prepared to assume the exalted office of Bunji Lama, living incarnation of Champa, Buddha of the future.

As the day he was to be enshrined approached, the council of regents revealed him to the terrible hidden truths: that the previous Dalai Lama had been a weakling unworthy of the Lion Throne on which he had sat and that the Panchen Lama was a tool of the wicked Chinese who gnawed at Tibet's sacred borders like greedy rodents.

One day, he was told, it would be his destiny to unseat the next Dalai Lama, who had yet to be discovered, and cast out the Panchen Lama, who was a puppet of the Chinese. Only then would Tibet prosper. Thus had spoken the oracles, the regents had said.

The Bunji Lama had accepted none of this. The abbots stank of worldly ambition. Even he, still yearning for the humble village he had left behind, could see that they were but slaves of the sensual world.

So when he had refused their entreaties to denounce the rival lamas, and set the stage for assuming primacy over them, the regents had scolded him, argued and even threatened. Their worst threat had been to return him to the squalor of Burang. And when they saw in the Bunji Lama's eyes that he wished to go home more than anything else, they grew very still and locked him in his meditation room.

Finally, realizing they could not control their creation, they had poisoned his food.

Somewhere, they knew, would be found a child who could be molded into the forty-seventh Bunji Lama. It would only postpone their evil ambitions, not cancel them.

Thinking of that nameless unsuspecting child, ordained to be born in the exact moment of his own death, the forty-sixth Bunji Lama raised his voice. "Attend me, followers of the virtuous way! For I have seen a vision."

The ironbound teak door creaked open, and they padded in, resplendent in their scarlet-and-gold robes. They surrounded him, already laid out in his funeral robes of gold brocade in a long box lined with salt so that the embalmed husk of the Bunji Lama could lie in state, preserved, until his successor was brought to this lamasery in the mountains.

"The inexorable Wheel of Time turns," prophesied the Bunji Lama, "and I must drop this unworthy body for another. These are troubled times, for the fourteenth Dalai Lama has not yet been discovered and the need for my divine guidance is great. And so a vision has been revealed to me, one that will allow the faithful to locate my next body with utmost dispatch."

The abbots pressed closer, eagerness on their long faces. They believed. All save Lungten Drub, the high regent whose sour countenance curdled like day-old buttered tea.

The Bunji Lama let the words tumble out of him. "The next body that I shall reside in will have hair that is the hue of flame and will not remember this life," he said, "nor any of the trappings of it. No trapping of this body will stir recollection in me."

The abbots gasped. "But how will we recognize you, or you us, Presence?" one asked.

"You will know this body because in my next incarnation I will possess a golden joss with no face."

The abbots looked to one another. None had ever heard of such a figurine.

"This defaced joss will wield a sword and will be found in a place distant from here. By these signs, and others, will you know me, and I you."

"We will not rest until we find you again, O Presence," the abbots vowed.

And closing his eyes, the Bunji Lama smiled thinly—which the abbots took for an expression of his forbearance in the face of pain. In his heart he was glad. For there had been no vision. The faceless golden joss was a figment of his imagination. No such joss was to be discovered in all the world or any other world. Of this the Bunji Lama was certain.

He died in the next instant, secure in the knowledge that no innocent child would fall into the ambitious clutches of Lungten Drub and his council of regents, and that his cycle of reincarnations was at last over. Nirvana was his.

The winds howled down from the mountains, tearing the flimsy prayer flags from their anchorage. Conch shells were blown. The white flags of mourning went up, and all Tibet was desolated.

And in that exact moment, an incalculable distance from the meditation cell whose name meant "Prayerful Refuge from the Temptations of the Sensual World," a red-haired infant was born.

On the next morning, the search for the next Bunji Lama began.

It would go on for a very long time.

**1**

The Most Holy Lobsang Drom Rinpoche sat naked in the cave that was his home high in the Himalayas. The winds that had howled around the snowcapped peaks relentlessly for the sixty years since the Fire Dog Year blew snowdrifts deep into the cave. Yet the stone floor in a circle around Lobsang Drom was moist with melted snow. It was as if his scrawny body were a human coal, giving off rays of warmth that defeated the accumulating flakes.

He did not shiver under the lash of the elements even though he ate but once a day and then only five grains of parched barley washed down by melted snow.

Distantly there was thunder. Not high above, in the howling sky, but far below, in the purplish black valley. The thunder came again. It climbed toward the sky, its echoes rebounding off the granite peaks. Somewhere a snow leopard growled.

Lobsang Drom listened to the thunder, knowing that it was not thunder but Chinese artillery. Below, Tibet was in revolt against the harsh rule of the oppressors from Beijing. It was painful to the ears, but there was many a painful thing in the world. Such as failure.

For all of his forty-three years, Lobsang Drom had endured the yoke of Chinese rule. It was a bitter thing, but the Chinese had placed their heels on the necks of the Tibetan people more than once in centuries past. Sometimes they themselves had staggered under a Tibetan yoke, as well. So turned the Wheel of Destiny, inexorably.

The combat would pass. The guns would fall silent. The Chinese dead would be shipped to their home provinces, and the Tibetan dead would be given sky burial. But Lobsang Drom's bitterness would go on the remainder of his days. For he had failed in his sacred duty, as had his father, Lungten Drub, high regent for the Bunji Lama, before him.

For the Bunji Lama, reincarnation of the Buddha of the Future, had become lost in the translation between incarnations. This had never before happened. It was not known what had gone awry, for the previous Bunji Lama had rendered a great prophecy to Lobsang Drom's father, foretelling certain events.

Lungten Drub had scoured Tibet for the forty-seventh Bunji Lama but found no redheaded boys. Nor any golden joss lacking a face but possessing a sword. He was forced to venture beyond inner Tibet. Nepal was searched, as was Bhutan, Sikkim, and even both sides of the Di-Chu, Ghost River, on the border of Tibet and China. India, cradle of Buddhism, was scoured, as well, before the Worshipful Nameless Ones in the Dark Who See the Light That is Coming—of whom his father had been first among equals—were forced to give up their sacred quest.

For China had made her long-feared lunge and absorbed Tibet. The new Dalai Lama, now grown to manhood, fled into exile. The Panchen Lama remained, a servile tool of the Chinese, as Lobsang Drom's father had predicted. It was the perfect hour for the return of the Bunji Lama, who would have been a young man by that time, but the Bunji Lama remained unfindable.

It was the year of the Iron Tiger, called 1950 in the West.

Finally the day came when the regents were dragged off by the People's Liberation Army, and Lobsang Drom was left alone. At first Lobsang hid in a high lamasery that had escaped Chinese notice, where he studied to be a monk. Upon taking his vows, he was spirited to outlying towns where he could resume the great search. He was the last of the Worshipful Nameless Ones in the Dark Who See the Light That is Coming and while he greatly feared the Chinese troops, his duty was stronger than his fear.

The day at last came when hope ran out. All Tibet whispered of the missing Much Sought for Red-haired Boy who Would Save Tibet. He could not be found. Perhaps he did not wish to be found.

Broken in spirit, Lobsang Drom retired to a cave high in the mountains to meditate, subsisting on barley and bitterness.

His meditations were broken but once a year, when a trustworthy farmer climbed the narrow footpaths to leave an offering of barley and announce tidings of supreme import.

"O Most Holy," said the barley farmer one year. "The Panchen Lama is dead."

"The Panchen Lama is a tool of the Chinese, so my father told me," Lobsang Drom had replied.

"It is said that the Chinese poisoned him. The search is on for the new incarnation."

"Let them search," said Lobsang Drom. "The next one will be no less unworthy."

That was in the Fire Hog Year. By that time Lobsang Drom had lost track of the passing years. In the Earth Hare Year, the same farmer reappeared to speak tearful words.

"There is word from the West that the exiled Dalai Lama speaks of eventual surrender to fate. He mouths words that are impossible to accept, predicting that he is destined to be the last Dalai Lama, and there will be no more after him."

"The Dalai Lama has been corrupted by the West," intoned Lobsang Drom. "It is no more or less than my honorable father warned."

"There is only the Bunji Lama left. Will you not seek him out, Most Holy?"

Lobsang Drom shook his shaved head. "He does not wish to be found."

"Then Tibet is forevermore a vassal of China."

"It is the fault of Tibetan mothers, who refuse to bear flame-haired children, or surrender them if they do."

But that was the past.

It was now the Year of the Earth Dog, but Lobsang Drom had no way of knowing this. He sat in a puddle of melted snow practicing the art known as Tumo, which kept his naked body warm without benefit of sheepskin garments, listening to the thunder that was not thunder when, in a lull between peals, a snow leopard growled.

The growl was long and low and was answered by the nervous whinny of a pony. Having had no entertainment in many years, Lobsang Drom lifted his low-hanging head and cocked it to one side.

The snow leopard growled anew. Abruptly its sound was stifled. There had been no other sound. It was as if the leopard had been conquered by a magician.

Presently the soft squeaking of desultory hooves in snow approached the cave where Lobsang Drom nursed his bitterness.

"A thousandfold fruitful blessings upon you, traveler," Lobsang Drom called in greeting.

The one who approached replied only with the squeakings of his coming.

"If you are a Chinese soldier," Lobsang Drom added, "I am not afraid to die."

"If I were a Chinese soldier," a brassy voice called back, "you should not be a man unless you strangled me with your bare hands."

"I am a monk. Violence is not my way."

A thick shadow stepped into view, leading a pony by its reins.

"You are a failure, Lobsang Drom," the shadow accused.

"With those words, I have no quarrel," admitted Lobsang Drom.

The man stepped into the cave, and Lobsang saw that his face was like a flat gong of brass set on a tree-stump neck. Not Tibetan. A Mongol. He wore the black leather vest and quilted riding pants of a horse Mongol. A dagger hung from his waist by a silver chain. Across the wooden saddle of his war pony was slung the ghost-gray shape of a dead snow leopard, its pristine pelt unflecked by blood.

"How did you slay that?" Lobsang asked.

"I spit in his eye," laughed the Mongol. "He is only a cat and so he died. Where I come from, the suckling wolf cubs would tear him to rags in play."

But Lobsang saw the Mongol's pole lasso hanging from the pony's saddle and understood that the snow leopard had been snared and strangled in one expert cast.

"Why come you here, Mongol?" asked Lobsang Drom curiously.

"I was dispatched by Boldbator Khan to seek out your lazy bones."

"Why?" wondered Lobsang, not taking offense.

"The new Panchen Lama has been found."

Lobsang Drom spit into the snow by way of answer.

"Well, have you nothing more to say?"

"The Panchen Lama is not worth the breath required to curse his name," said Lobsang Drom.

"And you are unworthy of even living in a cave," grunted the Mongol, planting one boot on Lobsang Drom's chest and giving a hard push. Lobsang Drom was sent sprawling into his pile of barley.

Calmly the Mongol pulled the dead snow leopard off his mount and, taking his dagger from his belt, began to skin it.

"What are you doing, Mongol?" demanded Lobsang Drom, sitting up again.

"Wasting a perfectly good pelt," growled the Mongol, who then proceeded to cut the magnificent silver-gray pelt into bolts and strips of fur.

When he was done, Lobsang saw that he had fashioned a crude robe, which landed at the Tibetan's naked feet. It steamed with the dead animal's fading warmth.

"Put that on," the Mongol commanded.

"Why?"

"So that I am not offended by your nakedness during the long journey that lies before us."

"I cannot leave this cave until I have proven to the Bunji Lama by my iron will that I am worthy to be his discoverer."

The Mongol's eyes narrowed at that, and when he spoke again, there was a hint of respect in his tone.

"You cannot obtain the Bunji Lama's respect unless from his very lips. Come, I will take you to him."

Lobsang Drom blinked. "You know where he is to be found?"

"No, but there is one who, among men, can find him if anyone can."

"How can that be? I am the last of the Worshipful Nameless Ones in the Dark Who See the Light That is Coming."

"Which is why I am about to dishonor my fine pony by letting you mount him, unwashed one," returned the Mongol. "Now hurry. We have only fourteen or fifteen years to find the Bunji Lama. Otherwise, the damned Panchen Lama will ascend to the Lion Throne, and the thrice-damned Chinese will control Tibet until the Kali Yug comes."

Striding stiffly because he was unaccustomed to walking and not due to the bitter cold that had long ago settled into his bones, Lobsang Drom donned the rich snow-leopard pelt. It steamed as if cooking, and felt comfortingly warm against his wind-dried skin.

Mounting the wooden saddle chased with silver filigree, Lobsang Drom struggled to retain his balance as the Tibetan led the pony around in a circle and started down the precarious two-foot-wide mountain pass.

"Mongol, what is your name?" he asked after a time.

"I am called Kula."

"And who is this person who will locate the long-lost Bunji Lama when the Worshipful Nameless Ones in the Dark Who See the Light That is Coming, of which I am the last, have all failed?"

"He is the Master of Sinanju," said Kula the Mongol over the cannonading of Chinese artillery. "And if there is enough gold in the bargain, he will find the moon in a blizzard."

"It is a long trek to Korea, where the Master of Sinanju dwells. All of it through Chinese territory."

"It is even longer journey to America, where the Master of Sinanju will be found."

"The Master of Sinanju is an exile, too?"

"Hush, Priest. You will need your breath and all of your strength if you are to negotiate the Karo La Pass."

By that, Lobsang Drom knew that the Mongol sought to escape into India.

"There is a mighty ocean between India and America," he said. "How are we to cross it with only one horse?"

"In my *namdu*," he said unconcernedly.

Hearing this, Lobsang Drom could not help but ask, "What manner of Mongol owns a skyboat?"

At that, the Mongol Kula only laughed. He said no more as they picked their way down the mountainside.

It was the Earth Dog Year. Exactly five astrological cycles had transpired since the Fire Dog Year. The wind howled, the snows of the Himalayas cut into the lines of the Most Holy Lobsang Drom Rinpoche's weathered features, and he refused to believe that the Bunji Lama would be found at the end of the long journey before him.

For to hold hope in his embittered heart was to risk having his spirit crushed forever.

**2**

His name was Remo, and he was trying to remember how to spell Buttafuoco.

He stood before the automatic teller machine in the Plexiglas-enclosed outer lobby of the neighborhood bank in the seaside Massachusetts town he called home. It was night, so the green letters on the ATM screen were like jade on fire.

They read: "Hello Mr./Mrs. XXXXXXXXXX, please spell your last name."

"Damn," muttered Remo, staring at the huge, piano-sized keyboard. Streetlights reflecting off the clear Lucite picked up his lean-featured face with its grimly humorous mouth. Shadows pooling in the hollows of his deep-set eyes suggested a skull, with skin stretched drum tight over high cheekbones. It was not a happy face. It had never been a happy face. It would never be a happy face, but at least, after many plastic surgeries, it was pretty much the face he had been born with.

His high forehead wrinkled as he struggled with his problem.

It was a new wrinkle in ATM security. Four-digit password numbers were no longer enough. A customer had to correctly input his last name before accessing his account.

It had not been a problem last night, when Remo withdrew a hundred dollars as Remo Brown, or the night before, when he pulled fifty out of the checking account he had under the name Remo Black, or the night before that, when he was Remo Green. He could spell those names.

Remo really hoped he would be held up before he had to play the Buttafuoco card. But it was his own fault, he realized. After all, he was the one who picked the last-name aliases so Upstairs could provide phony driver's licenses, credit cards and ATM cards. There was, as he saw it, no problem being Remo Buttafuoco whenever he needed a quick hundred bucks.

Until the banking industry, run ragged by a proliferation of ATM-based scams, decided four-digit pass numbers weren't secure enough.

Remo stared at the screen, wondering if the number of glowing green *X*'s corresponded to the number of letters in Buttafuoco. He hoped so. It would help a lot. He punched in the letters *BUTT.* That was easy. Simple word association.

He saw that the string of green *X*'s became "BUTTXXXXXX."

Next, he tried an *E.* So far so, good. Five *X*'s left. How hard could it be?

But when he punched in the letters *FUOCO* and pressed Enter, the machine displayed "you are an imposter" and ate his ATM card.

"Hey! Don't I get a second chance?" Remo complained.

A new screen came up. It was dense with fine print. Remo was reading how in the interest of customer-account security the ATM machine was programmed to shut down in the event of a misspelling.

It apologized for the inconvenience, but pointed out that bank security was important, too. Besides, customers should know how to spell their own last names.

"Not if it's Buttafuoco," said Remo, whose real last name, in the days when he was a good citizen and not a dead man, had been Williams. "Nobody can spell Buttafuoco right on the first try!"

Remo was so upset he almost forgot about the ATM bandit who had been waylaying after-hours customers as they walked from area banks with their withdrawals. He had been striking on random nights. So far nobody had been hurt, but a few people had been roughed up, including a nun from the church across the street.

Remo had a soft spot in his heart for nuns. He had been raised in a Catholic orphanage.

When he'd read about the crimes in the newspaper, Remo decided to do something about it. It wasn't the kind of crime that ordinarily got his attention, but this was his neighborhood now and his bank—even if he did have four different accounts under four different aliases, and not one teller had ever noticed and he wasn't about to let some lowlife ruin it for everyone else.

He stormed out of the bank lobby and almost walked into the shiny blue .357 Magnum revolver. Almost but not quite. The second he exited the sense-deadening Plexiglas enclosure, he knew someone was lurking in the shadows. His nose picked up the sweat stink of fear. His ears heard a heart beating erratically.

Automatically he pretended not to notice the lurker. Just as automatically he changed direction so he could pretend to walk into him.

"Right there!" a raspy voice warned.

There wasn't much to the man holding the revolver. He had dead gray skin and the emaciated aspect of a drug addict—all bone and sinew, with nerve endings jangling like wind chimes. The only thing about him that stuck out was his weapon.

Remo allowed his eyes to rest upon the well-crafted pistol. In his previous life, the sight of a .357 bore pointed at his solar plexus would have started the adrenaline flowing. Instead, Remo simply relaxed.

Where once he would have been intimidated by the precision steel and smoothly fitting parts designed to inflict massive internal injury to human flesh and bone and organs, Remo saw the weapon for what it was—a crude, almost medieval device.

Chiefly it was a conglomeration of the most primitive of man-made tools—the wheel, the lever and the hammer. After all, the trigger was just a lever designed to trip the hammer, the action of both actuating the bullet-bearing cylinder, which was really a form of wheel.

As these idle thoughts passed through the remarkably calm brain of Remo Williams, the gunman growled, "Give me your money." He pulled back on the hammer. The thick wheel turned with all the smoothness of a windlass, bringing a bullet into line with the barrel, which was the most primitive of tools—a hollow tube. It happened in the blink of an eye, but to Remo's heightened senses, the action had all the subtlety of a drawbridge clanking into the raised position.

"You the one that's been holding people up?" asked Remo in the cool, unruffled voice which, like his body language, was calculated to relax the target.

Nonthreatening was better. They never saw it coming.

"No, I'm the one who's holding *you* up," the gunman snapped.

And while he was snapping out the words, Remo's right hand, dangling loosely at the end of an unusually thick wrist, came up. One finger went into the gun barrel like a long cork.

The gunman looked at Remo as if he were crazy. He didn't fire. Remo knew he wouldn't. If Remo had tried to run away or fight or yell for help, he would have fired. All the gunman wanted was Remo's money.

He didn't expect his victim to do something as stupid as trying to stop a bullet with his finger.

"What're you, on drugs or something?" the gunman demanded in an indignant voice.

"That's right," said Remo, holding his finger steady because it would hold the Magnum steady.

The gunman squinted at Remo in the yellowish haze of a nearby streetlight.

"Yeah?" he asked curiously. "What is it? Crystal meth? Crank? Acid?"

"Sinanju," said Remo.

"That's a new one on me," the gunman muttered. "What kinda high do you get from it?"

"The ultimate high. It teaches you to breathe with your whole body, think with every part of your brain and not the ten percent most people use—in your case, two percent—and become at one with the universe."

"Sounds like acid," the gunman said in a disappointed voice. "You trippin' on acid, man? Acid ain't new."

"No," returned Remo. "But this is."

And holding the .357 Magnum steady with his right index finger, Remo used the stiff, steel-hard fingers of his right hand to spank the heavy cylinder out of the frame.

The cylinder flew a short distance and bounced off the Plexiglas door, scattering soft-nosed bullets on the walk.

The gunman's reflexes weren't bad. He was pulling the trigger at the first loud sound. He never saw Remo's hand or felt the cylinder jump off its sheared pins. He was reacting to the impact of the cylinder against the door, never realizing he was dropping the hammer on thin air.

The gun went click. The gunman blinked. Remo let a cool, insolent smile touch his thin lips. His dark eyes, set deep in his skull, grew grimly humorous.

The gunman kept pulling the trigger and getting noisy ineffectual clickings.

Removing his index finger, Remo brought the precision-machined weapon up and turned it sideways so that the gunman could see the square aperture where the cylinder had been. For an instant in eternity the gunman saw it for what it actually was—a crude contraption of steel.

Then it turned lethal again as Remo's hands drove the shiny barrel up and back into the gunman's surprised brain.

Remo left him jittering on the sidewalk, the maimed weapon sticking out of his shattered forehead, gun hand frozen on the grip as if he had lain down preparatory to putting a bullet in his own brain.

The next morning, when the police found him there, they would run a check on fingerprints found at the crime scene. When all was said and done, every set would be accounted for, and every possible suspect questioned and released. Except one set: Remo's. The police never found that set in any fingerprint file on record.

They had no way of knowing the file on Remo Williams had been pulled two decades ago. After he was pronounced dead.

As he walked home, whistling, Remo didn't think of himself as dead. He felt very much alive. The night wind was blowing the cool salt tang of the Atlantic Ocean inland. A sea gull perched on top of the street lamp, cyeing the ground for scraps.

As he walked, Remo thought that he was a long way from the orphanage of his earliest memories, from the jungles of Vietnam, where he had been a Marine, from the Ironbound section of Newark, New Jersey, where as Patrolman Remo Williams, he had tried to protect honest citizens from the kind of criminal scum who changed only their tactics, and from death row in Newark State Prison, where he had lived out his last days. He was home.

It had taken a year to come to think of Quincy, Massachusetts, as home. Not that it was a bad place to live. It was fine—a residential suburb of Boston with a nice beach busy with cormorants and sea gulls, sand you could sit on and calm blue water you could swim in when the fecal coliform bacteria count was safe. Usually twice a year.

It was convenient to Logan Airport when work called him to travel and handy to the Weymouth Naval Air Station when a national emergency required flying at taxpayers' expense. You could be on the Southeast Expressway within five minutes of starting the car—not that you ever really wanted to be in Boston traffic—and except for the odd convenience-store robbery and night burglary, it was pretty quiet.

No, the problem with getting used to Quincy, Massachusetts, was not in thinking of it as home, but in thinking of the house where Remo lived as home.

As he turned off Hancock Street and came within sight of the high school, Remo was reminded why he had had such trouble adjusting.

There it was, a warm golden brown in the light of the street lamps, tucked behind the high school. Once it had been a Congregational church. According to neighborhood legend, it had served as a Sikh temple after the church fathers had sold it. Then, at the height of the condo craze, a real estate developer had condoized it into its current state.

Technically it was still a condo. There were sixteen units, but only Remo and the man who taught him Sinanju, which was not a drug but a way of life, lived there. But it looked like some mad cross between a church and a Tudor castle.

It was ugly. The peaked roof had been built up to form a third floor with rows of closely spaced dormer windows. The outer walls were fieldstone and set with Tudor-style decorative panels high up in the eaves, and the concrete foundation had been painted beige. Here and there a few jewellike stained-glass windows remained.

Still, it was home. Remo was used to it now. The crenellated tower was like a lighthouse shedding an amber glow that called him home.

Yes, it was a long way from his past life, where he had been Patrolman Remo Williams, veteran, honest citizen and patsy. It had not been a great life. What child who couldn't remember his parents could say he had enjoyed a great life? But the nuns at St. Theresa's orphanage had raised him right, the Marine Corps had made him a man, and in police work he had found something he could believe in.

Until the detectives came to arrest him.

It was easy to fall into the trap of thinking a mistake had been made. Remo had been an honest cop. But his badge had been found next to the pusher's body lying in an alley on his beat. No cop would have gone to trial on such circumstantial evidence, but Remo Williams had. No cop would have been convicted. But Remo Williams was.

By the time he found himself on death row, Remo still hadn't stopped believing in the American justice system. But he had begun to wonder if he was being railroaded because he was honest.

He still wondered who among his higher-ups had hung him out to dry when the Capuchin monk came to deliver the last rights. The monk had slipped him a black pill and whispered instructions to bite down when they pulled the knife-blade switch that sent current to the electric chair. Then they took him to the death house of Newark State Prison.

He had bitten down on the black pill just as the first jolt ripped through his shaking body.

When he'd woken up, Remo had a new face, no last name and two options, neither one good. No higher-up had framed Patrolman Remo Williams. His own government had set him up. His name had been on file ever since a one-handed spook of a CIA agent had noticed his cool, methodical ability to kill Vietcong snipers with a bolt-action Garand rifle. The file had been pulled, and as a result Remo Williams became a living dead man. Officially in his grave, file closed, end of freaking story.

But the grave, Remo was told, could be opened at any time and he could be dumped into it, his body cooked by electrocution, if he chose not to cooperate.

Remo chose to cooperate. And so became the sole enforcement arm for CURE, a supersecret government organization created in the early 1960s by a United States President who would not live to see the experiment he had launched come to fruition. Because in those dark days, the American flirtation with democracy was close to the breaking point. Organized crime was reaching high into the government. Laws designed to protect the lawful instead shielded the lawless from simple justice. The young, idealistic President faced two choices—suspend the Constitution and admit that democracy was a dead end, or set in place a secret agency to bridge the gap.

Thus CURE. Not an acronym, but a code name. It represented a remedy for America's social ills. And when CURE, working quietly behind the scenes, reached the point where its anonymous brand of justice was not enough, the director of CURE reached out and chose honest, patriotic but lethal Remo Williams to be the assassin sanctioned to destroy a struggling country's enemies, foreign and domestic. The Destroyer.

It had been so long ago that Remo had all but forgotten the early days when he had been retrained in weapons handling, exotic poisons and other deadly arts that became instantly obsolete once he was introduced to the elderly Korean who was the Master of Sinanju, a discipline that people who thought kung fu was something special would call a martial art.

If Sinanju was a martial art, it was the original martial art. The ultimate system of attack and defense. It was practiced by the greatest house of assassins in human history, taught to only one man in a generation and never taught to anyone who was not born in the obscure Korean fishing village of Sinanju—until the American government asked the last living Master of Sinanju to train a white man in the forbidden discipline. Remo Williams.

Now Remo would no sooner carry a gun than wear a gorilla for a hat. The sight of a firearm no longer triggered his survival instincts. And he walked the earth, one hundred fifty-five pounds of lean muscle and perfectly coordinated bone, the most remorseless and implacable killer since Tyrannosaurus rex.

It felt good. It always felt good. His blood surged through his circulatory system pure and untainted by chemicals or drugs, and his lungs processed oxygen with such efficiency that every cell in his body worked like a miniature furnace. Whatever the human body was capable of at its maximum potential, Remo could do on his off days. And more.

Across the night came a strange haunting sound.

"Aummm...."

It came again. "Aummm...."

Then Remo saw the unfamiliar silhouette in the north window of the square tower.

He ran, shifting from an easy, efficient walk to a graceful run that looked slow but covered space like a ray of light.

He hit the front door and went up the stairs. Every sense was operating. He smelled death. And unfamiliar living bodies. Not Americans. No American had such a buttery smoky odor.

At the top of the stairs, his reflexes carried him over the scattered luggage without thinking, and he hit the door to the tower room.

In the center of the square room, squatting in a lotus position, sat an Asian in a saffron robe. His head was shaved close to his skull, and his face was as smooth as soaked tissue paper.

His mouth was parted and out came a mournful sound.

"Aummm..."

Then, noticing he was not alone, he stuck his tongue out in Remo's direction as far as it would go.

"Who the hell are you?" Remo demanded.

Behind him, down the stairs, a door banged open and a pungent human scent came to Remo's sensitive nostrils. He was in the act of turning when a booming voice cried, "Ho, White Tiger! I bring you death. Catch it if you can!"

And the unmistakable sound of a knife whizzing toward his exposed back came to Remo's ears.

**3**

The skills that Remo Williams had learned under the tutelage of Chiun, the last Master of Sinanju, were so ingrained that his reactions to danger were automatic.

All thrown blades make a specific sound. Remo had learned to differentiate among these sounds in the long-ago days of his early Sinanju training when the Master of Sinanju would pluck assorted dull knives, daggers and even scissors from his wide sleeves and send them arrowing toward Remo's back.

Remo acquired numerous bruises and minor nicks, but had learned to move first and think later whenever his ears told his brain that a deadly instrument was zipping toward him. As his training progressed, these weapons were sharpened finer and finer with a whetstone. Chiun made Remo sharpen them himself.

"You're trying to kill me, aren't you?" Remo had said one day.

"Yes," the Master of Sinanju had replied blandly.

"You admit it, huh?"

The Master of Sinanju had shrugged carelessly. "I admit it. For your enemies will attempt to kill you in earnest. If I am to instill in you the reflexes that will save your life, I must do my best to motivate them in like earnestness. That is why you must sharpen these tools yourself, so that your dull white senses fully comprehend the danger you face."

And Remo had. The training progressed from bruises to punctures and the occasional scar. Then it was second nature to twist out of the way. When no blade could catch him unawares, Remo was taken to the next level. Turning the weapon against his attacker.

Now, as the dagger neared his back, Remo slid off to one side, pivoting. His hands, impelled by chemical reactions in his brain he no longer thought about, swept around and clasped the dagger—he knew it was a dagger before he saw it because they sounded heavier in flight than a stiletto or a bowie knife—capturing it. Its momentum, redirected, became a part of Remo's pivoting until he let go.

Still in motion, the dagger spun around and returned to the one who had thrown it, point first. It was called "Returning the Angry Coin."

The blade buried itself in a wall with a heavy *thunk*.

And under its quivering bone hilt, a crouching man boomed out joyful laughter.

"Very good, White Tiger! Very good indeed!"

The attacker straightened, his face a beaming brazen gong in which dark almond eyes twinkled with good humor.

"Kula! What are you doing here!"

Kula the Mongol surged up the stairs and threw out his great arms in welcome.

Fading off to one side, Remo ducked the bear hug.

"Where's Chiun?" he demanded, keeping a safe distance. Mongols ate and drank things that caused their pores to leak unpleasant odors Remo would rather not inhale.

"Preparing our tea, as a good host should." The Mongol squinted. "Are you not pleased to see me?"

Remo wasn't sure if he was or he wasn't. He didn't like company. He never had company, as a matter of fact. And every time Chiun had company, trouble usually followed.

"Chiun never mentioned that you were coming," Remo pointed out.

"How could he? He did not know."

"Then how'd you find us?"

"I called the magic number and the secret address was revealed to me by the Master of Sinanju's servant, Pullyang."

"What magic number?"

"1-800-SINANJU."

"Chiun has a toll-free number!"

"Does not everyone these days?"

"You, too?"

Kula nodded. "1-800-PILLAGE. What is your magic number?"

"I don't have one."

"Ah, you have not earned the right. I see." Kula tried to give Remo a reassuring clap on the back, but ended up smacking himself in the face. Remo wasn't there when the hand reached his back. He was suddenly to Kula's right. "Do not worry, White Tiger, you will receive your magic number when you are deemed worthy. I was given mine by Boldbator Khan himself. His magic number is 1-800-GENGHIS."

"Look, in America call me Remo. Okay?"

Kula the Mongol looked injured. "You have forgotten the days when you and I harried Chinese soldiers—you the White Tiger and I your strong right arm?"

"I haven't forgotten it. I just put that stuff behind me."

"There is a statue celebrating your glory in the lobby of the Hotel Genghis Khan in Ulan Bator."

"There is?" said Remo, brightening.

"Truly. It commemorates your mighty deeds. Of course, we gave you Mongolian eyes so as not to frighten our children with your fearsome round eyes."

"Good move," said Remo. "Now, where's Chiun?"

"He is below, communing with the Bunji Lama."

"Who's the Bunji Lama?"

"A great man, alas."

"Why is that 'alas'?"

"You will know why when you come face-to-face with the Bunji Lama."

Remo cocked a thumb at the open door where the shaved-headed man sat serenely. "Then who's that rude guy in there?"

"He is the Most Holy Lobsang Drom Rinpoche, who is destined to find the lost Bunji Lama."

"How can the Bunji Lama be lost if he's downstairs with Chiun?"

"You will see with your own eyes."

"Why don't I do that?" said Remo. "Wait here."

Kula folded his burly arms. "I have waited all my life for the Bunji Lama. I can wait a little longer."

"Right," said Remo, starting down the stairs. His happy mood had evaporated. He had met Kula years ago in a Mongolian tavern.

Back then Kula had been a bandit chief, and Remo had hired him to help track down the Master of Sinanju, who had disappeared into the wild steppes of Outer Mongolia in search of the lost treasure of

Genghis Khan. The treasure had been found and divided between the Master of Sinanju and Boldbator Khan, who had mustered an army of Mongols to fight off an attempt by Chinese troops to claim the booty for Beijing.

It had been a very difficult trek for Remo, who in addition to everything else had received none of the treasure.

Remo found the Master of Sinanju in the first-floor kitchen.

Remo noticed that Chiun wore one of his heavy brocaded kimonos usually reserved for meeting with heads of state. This one was a deep blue. It sat on his frail-looking shoulders like a lap rug supported by a clutch of sticks.

The Master of Sinanju didn't look like the deadliest assassin on earth. He stood approximately five feet tall. He weighed about as much as a hollow tree. There was no hair on his head other than the tufts of wispy white floating over the tips of his tiny ears. As he moved about the stove, his wrinkled features came into view. A tendril of stiff hair that barely passed for a beard stood out against the dark ivory of his parchment face.

He looked, not old, but ancient. But he moved with a quick, birdlike grace that put Remo's lean economy of movement to shame. The old Korean pretended not to be aware of Remo's presence. But his quick hazel eyes stole appraising glances as he moved about the kitchen.

Chiun was puttering over the stove, Remo saw, brewing tea. But the smell of tea was overpowered by a musty stench that reminded Remo of a tomb.

"What're you cooking, Little Father?" he asked. "Yak?"

"I am brewing tea for our illustrious guests," replied Chiun in a voice that was distinctly squeaky.

Remo frowned. "Smells like yak. What's going on?"

"We have guests."

"So my nose tells me," said Remo, looking around. The smell wasn't coming from the stove. It seemed to be emanating from a large black steamer trunk that sat on one end in a corner of the kitchen.

"What's that?"

"The Bunji Lama's trunk."

"It must be really old to smell like that," said Remo, going to the trunk.

"Remo! Do not disturb it."

"Okay, I won't."

"If you promise to do so carefully, you may have the honor of carrying the Bunji Lama's trunk up to the meditation room."

"Not until you explain what this is all about."

"What is anything of importance about?" Chiun asked carelessly.

Remo gave that a second's thought, reminded himself that it was Chiun asking the question and said, "Gold?"

Chiun nodded. "Gold. Good. You are learning."

"So help me, Chiun, if you've taken to renting out the other units to your friends for pocket money, I'm moving out."

"This is agreeable. Your room will fetch a good price."

"Get stuffed."

"I will carry the tea if you will carry the trunk of the Bunji Lama."

"Will carrying the trunk get me straight answers faster?"

"It will."

"Deal."

Remo used both hands to lift the trunk. As a result, it almost went crashing into the ceiling. It looked heavy but weighed next to nothing. Remo had been caught off guard. He got the awkward container under control.

"Remo! You will anger the Bunji Lama."

"Sorry." Remo started up the stairs, Chiun following and wearing a silver tray laden with celadon tea-cups and hot water in a brass kettle. "Where is the Bunji Lama anyway? Kula said he was with you."

"He was. Now he is with you."

"Huh?"

"He is in the trunk that you carry, and take care not to drop him or his wrath will be upon you like black hailstones."

"The Bunji Lama is inside this trunk?" Remo demanded.

"The old Bunji Lama, yes."

"He must be really old to smell this bad," said Remo, reaching the top of the stairs.

Remo set the trunk down in the center of the meditation room. The shaved-headed man continued to sit on the floor with the serenity of a contented bullfrog. Kula was laying tatami mats in a circle around the trunk as Chiun set down the tea, crossed his legs at the ankles and scissored onto his personal mat. He began pouring at once.

Remo pointed to the trunk and asked, "Is the Bunji Lama really in this thing?"

"The old Bunji Lama," Kula corrected.

"Guess he flew economy class," said Remo, knocking on the trunk. "Time to stretch your legs, pal."

"It is not time," said the Master of Sinanju. "We must bargain first."

The tea was passed around. Remo took his place, sitting as far from the colorful personal odors of Chiun's guests as possible.

Kula took his cup and swallowed it all in one greedy gulp and offered the empty cup for more. Chiun obligingly poured.

The shaved-headed Asian accepted his tea, looked deep into the cup and spoke up. "No yak butter?"

The Master of Sinanju bestowed his pupil with a reproving glare. "Remo, did you forget to churn the yak butter this morning?"

"I must've. Silly me."

Chiun addressed the shaved-headed man. "I apologize for the inefficient white help, Most Holy, but you will have to drink your tea without yak butter."

"It is good tea," boomed Kula, offering his drained cup for the third time.

When all the cups were refilled, Remo whispered to Chiun, "Yak butter?"

"The Most Holy Lobsang Drom is a Tibetan. They put yak butter in their tea," Chiun confided.

"Is that why he smells so bad?"

"Tibetans have many beliefs you would find strange. Bathing regularly is not among them."

"I don't know what smells worse, him or that trunk. Smells like it was stored in a musty cellar."

"It was. Since before you were born."

Remo settled down as tea was imbibed in silence for some time.

At length the Tibetan spoke up. "I am the Most Holy Lobsang Drom Rinpoche. Rinpoche means 'treasured one.' I seek the Light That is Coming. What is your name?" he asked Remo.

"Remo."

"Re-mo?"

"Yeah," said Remo.

"It is a strange name."

"My last name's Buttafuoco."

"Butt-a-fu—"

Remo nodded. "It means 'lies through teeth with head up ass,'" he said with a straight face.

Lobsang Drom nodded somberly. "It is a worthy name."

"For a white," inserted Chiun.

"For a white, it is a perfect name!" roared Kula.

Everyone except Remo laughed and drank to that.

Remo waited for the hilarity to settle down, then asked, "So what's this about?"

"The Bunji Lama," said Chiun, his hands disappearing into the brocaded sleeves of his kimono and the sleeves coming together to form a tube.

"He is lost," said Kula.

"I thought he was in the trunk," said Remo.

"That is the old Bunji Lama," said Kula. "We seek the new Bunji Lama."

"So if you're looking for the new Bunji Lama, why'd you drag the old Bunji Lama all this way?"

Everyone looked at Remo as if he had just asked why they exhaled after each intake of breath.

"The nuns who raised me had a saying—there's no such thing as a stupid question," Remo said.

"These nuns were white, too?" asked Kula.

"Yeah."

"Buddhist nuns?" asked Lobsang Drom.

Chiun answered that: "Christian."

Kula and the Most Holy Lobsang Drom grew wide of eye.

"I have beaten the Christianity out of him," Chiun said hastily. "Most of it. Some remains." He shrugged.

"He is white," Kula pointed out.

"He cannot help being white," Lobsang Drom added.

Everyone agreed that Remo couldn't help being white and if the Master of Sinanju continued beating him regularly, he would renounce the last lingering delusions of Christianity in due time.

Remo sighed. His eyes kept going to the steamer trunk.

"I'm still waiting for the answer to my question," he said. He was ignored.

Instead, Lobsang Drom said, "We have come a great distance to acquire your services, great one whose hands are like swords."

"I cannot help you," Chiun told his visitors sadly.

Kula started. Lobsang Drom slumped where he sat.

"For I serve the white emperor of America who is named Smith," Chiun said, one clawlike hand emerging. His fingernails, like bone blades, flashed in the room's mellow light.

"A simple smith rules this land?" Lobsang Drom asked in surprise.

"Why not?" said Kula. "Lord Genghis was born Temujin, a name which means 'ironworker,' and he grew up to found a great empire."

"Of plunderers and murderers," said Remo.

"Who told you those lies?" Kula demanded.

"The history books," said Remo.

"Christian histories?"

"No, American ones."

"Hah! You are well named, Remo Buttafuoco, for you speak lies even without an ass on your head."

"That's 'head up my ass,'" corrected Remo.

Kula nodded, and, his point made, addressed the Master of Sinanju.

"Why can you not help us, Master of Sinanju? Does the emperor of America fear the return of the Bunji Lama?"

"I do not know if he does or does not," said Chiun, "but while I enjoy his gold, I can work for no other, for my contract is with him."

"We will pay more gold."

"How much?"

Kula extracted a yak-hide bag from his vest. Untying the drawstring, he emptied out shapeless nuggets of gold.

Chiun made a face, as Remo knew he would. "Not enough."

Grumbling, Kula removed another bag, and the pile of gold was doubled.

Chiun's eyes grew veiled and his voice thin. "The gold of Smith would fill this room three times over," he pointed out.

Kula the Mongol threw his gaze about the room, avoiding Chiun's hazel orbs. "For how many years of service?" he asked aridly.

"One."

"We ask only for help finding the Bunji Lama."

"Which could take one year or twenty," returned Chiun.

"We have less than ten years, for the Panchen Lama has been found."

Chiun nodded wisely. "I read of this. A Chinese, discovered dwelling in America. Never has a *tulku* been discovered so far from Tibet."

"Since the Dalai Lama sits spineless in exile, the Panchen Lama is next in line to the Lion Throne of Lhasa and will claim it when he comes of age. Unless the Bunji Lama can be found."

"It is a bad thing," Chiun agreed. "But I cannot risk angering my emperor for less than a roomful of gold."

"A roomful of gold would earn how much service?" Kula asked.

"For a roomful of gold, I would search the entire West for the Bunji Lama until he was found or my last breath was spent."

"The West! Why the West?"

"It is simple. The East has been scoured to no avail. No flame-headed one bearing the true birthmark has been found. Nor any faceless joss holding a sword. There can be but one conclusion. The Bunji Lama was born in the West."

Kula the Mongol and Lobsang Drom exchanged startled glances. Remo sat there and looked confused.

"It is impossible," Lobsang Drom spit.

"If the Panchen Lama has been found in the West, why not the Bunji Lama?" Chiun countered. "Clearly the Panchen Lama chose to be born in the West to evade Chinese oppression. Might not the Bunji Lama have foreseen the coming of the oppressors and elected to be born here in the West, so that his next body would not be imperiled?"

Kula leaned across and muttered to Lobsang Drom, "He speaks sense."

"He's conning you both," Remo said.

Chiun spanked the floor with his heel. The overhead light rattled. "Silence, Christian! Do not interfere."

"Blow it out your ass," Remo hissed.

"I must consult with Boldbator Khan before I can agree to your terms, Master of Sinanju," said Kula. "For he authorized me to offer no more than six bags of gold."

The Master of Sinanju said, "Remo, bring our honored guests a telephone."

"Want me to dial 1-800-GENGHIS for them, too?" he said acidly.

"Yes," said Kula.

Frowning, Remo returned with the phone. He sat down and punched out the numbers, but only because he wanted to see if the 800 number really existed. There was a brief clicking of overseas relays, and a musical voice said, *"Sain Baina."*

"Sounds like Outer Mongolia to me," muttered Remo, who recognized the traditional Mongolian greeting.

Kula took the phone. In his native tongue, he spoke in low whispers, listening often. Chiun feigned disinterest, but Remo knew that the old Korean was following every word of both sides of the conversation.

At length Kula clapped a beefy hand over the receiver and said, "Boldbator Khan, Khan of Khans,

Future Overlord of Mankind, has instructed me to tell you that he will agree to pay you a roomful of gold for your services upon one condition."

"Name it," said Chiun.

"That you permit the gold to be shipped on your Federal Express account number."

"Done," said Chiun, clapping his hands.

"Since when did you get a Federal Express number?" Remo demanded of Chiun.

"It was a stipulation of my last agreement with Emperor Smith," said Chiun.

By that Remo knew Chiun meant Harold W. Smith, director of CURE, whom Chiun called emperor because it kept up appearances. His ancestors, the past Masters of Sinanju, had slain in the service of history's kings and emperors, and Chiun, who hoped to go down in the histories of the House of Sinanju as Chiun the Great, could not admit to serving anything less than a caliph.

As they waited, Kula finished his long-distance conversation and hung up.

"It is done," he boomed. "We have an agreement."

"We have an agreement," said Chiun. "Now it is time to consult the oracle."

"What oracle?" asked Remo.

"That one," said Chiun.

All eyes followed the Master of Sinanju's indicating finger.

It was pointing toward a big-screen TV in one corner of the great square room.

**4**

"It is a fearsome-looking oracle," intoned Lobsang Drom.

"It's a freaking TV," said Remo.

"Yes, it is a freaking TV," said Kula. "Now that we have thrown off the yoke of communism, there are freaking TVs just like that one in every town and *ger* in Mongolia. I myself have thirty such devices so that I may watch every program at once without having to change channels."

"It is no ordinary television," said Chiun. "It is an enchanted television."

"Enchanted television, my Buttafuoco," said Remo. "It's Japanese."

The others looked closely and saw the brand name: Nishitsu.

"Truly it is a Japanese TV, as well as a freaking one," muttered Kula.

"Is it a Zen oracle?" Lobsang Drom asked. "I cannot accept visions from an oracle that is Zen."

The Master of Sinanju shook his head sagely. "It is not Zen. And it will show us the new Bunji Lama if he lives."

"The Bunji Lama always lives," said Lobsang Drom.

"Not for long if you don't let him out of his trunk," said Remo.

Abruptly the Master of Sinanju clapped his hands together. "In order to consult the oracle, we must first consult the guide," he proclaimed. "Remo, fetch the mystic guide."

"What guide?"

"The guide to the oracle, witless one," Chiun hissed. "Are your ears filled with hardened wax?"

"No, but my nose is clogged from the stink of whatever's in that freaking trunk."

"I did not know it was a freaking trunk," muttered Kula.

"The guide is always kept in a place of honor atop the oracle so that it will not be misplaced by careless servants," Chiun said pointedly. "Now, bring it to us."

"Oh, *that* guide," said Remo. He padded over to the TV set and brought back the current week's issue. Chiun accepted it and turned it around so that the others could see the cover clearly.

"I cannot read those English characters," said Lobsang Drom, squinting.

"I can," said Kula. "The red shape forms the words, *TV Guide.* The Master speaks truly. It is the legendary *TV Guide.* Very rare to find a copy in this land of America."

"One shape makes two words?" said Lobsang Drom in wonderment.

"You should talk about another person's language," said Remo.

Lobsang Drom leaned closer, squinting at the cover. "Is that a *dugpa* I see?"

Remo looked. He didn't know what a *dugpa* was, but he figured it was as good a name for Roseanne Arnold as any.

"She is the most feared *dugpa* on American television," he assured the Tibetan.

"I do not know this word, *tel-a-vish-on,*" said Lobsang Drom slowly.

Remo asked, "Where have you been living—in a cave?"

"Yes."

Remo blinked. Then Chiun began consulting the guide to the oracle.

"I vote for 'The Twilight Zone,'" Remo whispered. "Rod Serling's usually good for putting things in perspective."

"Hush!" Chiun hissed. "I seek an augury of the Bunji Lama's fate in this guide."

"And if you find it?" asked Lobsang Drom.

"It will foretell the most auspicious time to consult the oracle on the fate of the Bunji Lama, which will be revealed to us on the dark screen of glass."

Lobsang Drom nodded. It was strange magic but not much stranger than a Tibetan oracle. Perhaps there was hope after all.

Remo noticed that Chiun was consulting the evening listings.

"If you find the Bunji Lama in there," he whispered, "I'll eat whatever's in that trunk."

His face tightening like a spiderweb whose anchorings were stretched taut, the Master of Sinanju ran a long-nailed forefinger down the listings.

"According to the guide to the oracle," he announced solemnly, "the Bunji Lama will be revealed to us at midnight."

Remo closed his eyes. His mind told him that midnight was less than an hour away. He hadn't needed a watch in years. He always knew what time it was. He just didn't know how he knew.

"I have lived for this moment most of my life," said Lobsang Drom, his voice trembling.

"This is a great moment," agreed Kula.

"This is a great big scam," Remo muttered.

"Scam?" said Lobsang Drom.

"It is American slang," said Chiun quickly. "It means a glorious occurrence."

"Yes, it is a great scam we are on the brink of," said Kula. And they drank tea in silence as they waited for the hour of midnight to strike.

"Anyone for opening the trunk?" Remo asked at one point.

Chiun shook his aged head. "It is not yet time."

"So what do we do—sit here telling camp-fire stories?" Remo snapped.

"I will build a fire," Kula said, starting to rise.

"No fire is necessary for those of us who sit in the presence of the Worshipful Nameless Ones in the Dark Who See the Light That is Coming," said Chiun in a magnanimous voice.

Seeing that the old Korean meant Lobsang Drom, Remo said, "Him? It's not dark, he told us his name and besides, he stuck his tongue out the moment he first laid eyes on me."

"Then you should be honored," said Chiun.

"Why should I be honored?" said Remo.

"In Tibet to display the tongue is to give greetings."

"And you a *chiling,*" added Kula.

Remo looked his question.

"A foreigner," explained Kula.

"Foreigner? This is *my* country, not his."

"Now," said Kula.

"What do you mean—now?"

"The Khan of Khans talks of following in the war boots of Lord Genghis, may his praises be sung forever. At the proper moment, he intends to topple the citified Mongols who govern in Ulan Bator. Once that is done, China, Russia and other lands will follow. Korea will be spared, of course."

"I do not care what happens to South Korea, as long as no unpleasant sounds reach my village," said Chiun dismissively.

"Considerate of you," said Remo.

"North Korea will be spared," resumed Kula the Mongol. "Europe will fall in time, and then perhaps this country, if there is sufficient booty and the women are compliant."

"American women are about as compliant as mules," Remo said.

Kula grinned broadly. "I will be happy to tame these American mules."

"A lot of them are diseased. You could catch leprosy or something worse."

"I do not fear their diseases, for American women now have condoms of their very own. Their condoms will protect Mongol men from their diseases."

"Just try to get an American woman to wear one," Remo growled.

Kula leaned over to Remo and confided, "I have heard that they squeak like mice in bed."

"I never heard a woman squeak in bed in my life."

"I meant the condom."

"Let's just change the subject," said Remo, rolling his eyes. "You're a Mongol. Why are you so worried about Tibet?"

"The Chinese think Tibet is Chinese. The Tibetans know they are Tibetan. They are fighting now, which is good. Tibetans do not fight as much as they should, and so they are conquered often. At least once every second century."

"But we are fighting now," said Lobsang Drom.

Kula nodded. "Now you fight. It is a good thing."

"I hear they're getting the crap kicked out of them," said Remo.

"Should they lose, and Tibet become a slave of China forever," said Kula, "the Chinese who think they rule Inner Mongolia will turn their eyes upon Outer Mongolia. This should not happen too soon, before Boldbator Khan unites all of Mongolia. Otherwise, Mongols might lose. And then we will never own the world. Excepting North Korea, of course," he added for Chiun's benefit.

"I do not care about all of North Korea," Chiun said. "Only my village of Sinanju."

Kula brightened. "You would not object if we sack Pyongyang?"

"Pyongyang is yours if the wailing of the vanquished does not keep innocent Sinanju babies awake at night."

"It is agreed. There will be no unseemly wailing. Any so inconsiderate as to wail will be beheaded without mercy."

"Before you divide up the whole world," Remo inserted, "let's stay on the subject. Where does the Bunji Lama fit into this?"

"We Mongols have always followed the Bunji Lama. This is well-known, White Tiger."

Chiun said, "Remo must be forgiven, for he is an orphan and raised by virgins."

"You Mongols are Buddhists?" Remo blurted.

"Of course. This is well-known, too."

"I thought Buddhists were pacifists."

Kula laughed roughly. "Tibetan Buddhists are pacifists. Not Mongol Buddhists. We are fighting Buddhists, proud to slay and conquer in the name of the Buddha of Infinite Compassion, knowing that those who die will be reincarnated anyway, so that Mongols can conquer and slay them all over again. It is a very good system. There is always something to do."

"In times past, Mongols were the protectors of Tibet," said Lobsang Drom.

"So why are you running around looking for the Bunji Lama instead of fighting to free Tibet?" wondered Remo.

"If Mongolia enters the fighting openly, there will be war between Mongolia and China. The Chinese would lose, of course. They only outnumber us five hundred soldiers to one Mongol horseman. But it will take time to defeat China. Better if the Chinese are demoralized by a Tibetan people led by the new Bunji Lama. Then when we strike, they will surrender without resistance, for they will know if they cannot defeat peaceful Tibetans, what chance have they against the new Golden Horde?"

"Fighting Buddhists, huh?" said Remo.

"We also worship ancestors," said Kula.

"Ancestor worship is a good thing," spoke Chiun.

"Do you worship your ancestors?" Kula asked Remo.

"No," said Remo.

Remo found himself the recipient of thin almond gazes that might have accused him of breaking wind loudly.

"He is an orphan," Chiun explained. "He does not know his ancestors and therefore cannot worship them. If he knew who they were, he would make offerings to them nightly."

"It is a sad thing to be an orphan," clucked Kula.

"And Christian, too," murmured Lobsang Drom, shaking his shaved head.

Remo rolled his eyes and prayed to his nameless ancestors for midnight to hurry up.

AT MIDNIGHT the Master of Sinanju closed his eyes and began to chant in Korean. Neither Kula nor Lobsang Drom spoke Korean, so only Remo knew that Chiun was heaping abuse, recriminations and dire warnings of what pain would be inflicted on him if he again spoke out of turn and jeopardized Chiun's promised roomful of gold.

Remo sat quietly, not saying anything when the old Korean began making passes in the air before the TV with his right hand while surreptitiously activating the remote control hidden in the folds of his lap with the left.

The set winked on.

Lobsang Drom gasped in surprise. Kula's eyes narrowed, and he leaned forward on his mat.

"We will behold the Bunji Lama with our own eyes," he hissed.

Remo bit his tongue.

Happy-sounding music emerged from the speaker while the set warmed up. The brightening colors on the screen resolved into a free-spirited black woman dancing in and out of a free-floating graphic that read, "The Poopi Silverfish Show."

"Is that a sorcerer?" asked Lobsang Drom.

"It is Poopi Silverfish," said Chiun. "A famous wizard of this land."

"Her skin is as black as a corpse, and her hair hangs in mats," Lobsang muttered. "I have never see the like of it."

"Wasn't her show cancelled last year?" Remo asked.

"I told you this was a magic television," said Chiun.

"Or a rerun," grumbled Remo.

The credits faded, and the happy music segued to wind chimes. The picture became a darkened living room where Poopi Silverfish lounged on an over-stuffed couch catercorner with a settee on which a redheaded figure sat sprawled.

The camera moved in closer.

And the voice of the Master of Sinanju lifted to proclaim, "Behold! Behold the long-lost Bunji Lama."

Gasps came from the lips of Lobsang Drom and Kula the Mongol.

"It cannot be!" the Tibetan gasped.

"If you do not trust your eyes, Tibetan, then listen well with your ears."

"So, tell me," Poopi Silverfish was saying in a voice like a smoky cat's purr, "exactly how many lives *have* you lived?"

And the answer brought the eyes bugging out of Lobsang Drom's head.

"If you count the Moovian princess and the time I shared a Siamese soul with Mae West, thirty-two. I don't know why I keep coming back to this world, Poopi, but there must be a good reason.''

"Maybe there's something you really need to do on this earth that you can't remember," suggested Poopi.

"That's exactly what my last guru told me!"

The Most Holy Lobsang Drom Rinpoche wrenched his stricken eyes from the screen. "Master of Sinanju," he said thickly, "how can this be?"

**5**

"Wait a minute!" Remo blurted. "You know who that is? Squirrelly Chicane! She's a professional fruitcake."

Kula demanded, "You know this flame-haired woman, White Tiger?"

"Not personally. She's an actress. She also writes books about her life."

"More than one book?"

Remo shrugged. "She's got in her head that she's lived more than one life. And people eat it up."

Kula nodded somberly. "She is spreading the Buddha's teaching. That is a sign she has found the true path, even though she has had the misfortune to be born white."

Lobsang Drom wore a drained expression. "But she is a female," he said. "The Bunji Lama would not come back as a woman."

"Do not question the oracle," said the Master of Sinanju in a loud voice. "Watch and learn. Listen and believe, for the words spoken by the flame-haired incarnation of the Buddha to come will convince you with their sweet grace and forcefulness."

"Laying it on a little thick, aren't you, Little Father?" whispered Remo.

The Master of Sinanju reached over to take his incorrigible pupil by the hand and squeezed a wrist nerve that would test his ability to withstand pain.

Remo gritted his teeth and tried to pull away. Chiun exerted greater force. Remo squeezed his eyes shut but emitted no dishonorable sounds of surrender.

When he was satisfied that his willful white pupil would neither succumb to the overwhelming temptation to shout out his pain nor speak out of turn after it abated, Chiun released him.

Thereafter Remo sat quietly and watched the screen.

"I never heard of a Siamese soul," said Poopi Silverfish, shaking her head so her dreadlocks seemed to rattle. With her high cheekbones, very white teeth and animated eyes, she resembled a human marionette swayed by the tug of unseen strings.

"I may be the first human being in history to evolve a Siamese soul," said Squirrelly Chicane. "I think it's because my soul was searching for something important and knew it needed two bodies to do it."

"Do you know what it was, this important thing?"

"No. And frankly, Poopi, I'm becoming worried. I turn—dare I say it—sixty pretty soon. My Mae West body is dead, and now this one is getting a little frayed around the edges."

"Oh, don't say that! You look great. And you're still the best hoofer in the business."

"Hoofer?" said Kula.

Remo swallowed the urge to crack that the speaker was half-yak.

Squirrelly Chicane beamed, and mischievous gleams came into her blue eyes. "Why, thank you for saying so, Poopi. But on the cosmic scale, I have only a twinkling of time left in this body. I'm afraid I'll have to wait for my next incarnation and I start the search all over again. Whatever it is.''

"It is the Bunji Lama," breathed Kula.

"No, no," said Lobsang, shaking his head stubbornly. "It cannot be. She is white."

Kula frowned. "The age is correct. By her own words, she has seen nearly sixty yak-foaling seasons. The last Bunji Lama has been missing for that span. And her hair is like a flame."

"No, no, it cannot be. The Bunji Lama is fated to lead Tibet to greatness. That person is communing with a creature that might have climbed out of Hell itself.''

"No argument there," said Remo.

"I do not see the joss without a face," said Lobsang.

"No doubt it is kept on a sacred altar that we must locate," Kula said firmly.

"Listen closely," said Chiun. "The words of the new Bunji Lama will unveil the truth if only you heed them.''

The program continued. The Master of Sinanju pretended to watch as intently as the others, but he was actually observing the actions of his guests. Their faces, in the shifting glow of the television screen, were tight with concentration. The Mongol, Kula, wore the rapt expression of an accepting child. But Lobsang Drom contorted his long face with every sentence that reached his ears. From his saffron robe, he extracted a Buddhist rosary of tiny jade skulls and fingered them nervously.

"How do you come up with all these past lives, Squirl?" Poopi Silverfish was saying. "I mean, do they come to you in dreams or something?"

"Past-life regressions. My guru taught me how to invoke the buried memories. But we broke up. Now I do it all myself."

Poopi Silverfish rolled her eyes, and her dark face broke out in a smile that managed to be beatific and goofy at the same time. "You know, sometimes I like to think I was the Queen of Sheba about a million years ago."

"I was a princess in the lost continent of Moo twenty million years ago. My name was Tooma-zooma."

"How did it turn out?"

"Moo sank and I drowned. To this day my heart pounds uncontrollably whenever I slip into the Jacuzzi."

"I'm that way about showers ever since *Psycho.*"

Kula muttered, "I do not understand much of her words, therefore she is very wise."

"No doubt her guru was a very wise man," suggested Chiun in a bland voice.

No one challenged this statement. Least of all Remo.

As the program wound down, the Most Holy Lobsang Drom Rinpoche remained unconvinced.

"That is not the Bunji Lama," he said bitterly.

"Do you distrust what your lazy eyes have seen, Priest?" Kula demanded. "Or what your ears have heard? It is the incarnation, the *tulku,* the Light That is Coming, himself."

"Herself," Remo inserted.

"Is her hair not flame?" Kula went on. "Does she not speak of many past lives?"

Lobsang Drom hardened his eyes. "I refuse to accept this."

"But we must go to the Bunji Lama and prove it or disprove it ourselves. The Master of Sinanju would not lie."

Chiun cast a warning glance in Remo's direction, then came to his feet like a pillar of blue smoke.

"There is one who can convince you," he said firmly.

"How?" said Lobsang.

"The old Bunji Lama. We will consult him."

All eyes went to the closed steamer trunk, including Remo's.

Chiun waved toward it, saying, "Remo, you will have the honor of opening the trunk."

"Pass," said Remo, making a face.

They looked at him as if he had spoken a filthy word.

"It is a great honor," Chiun chided.

"All right, all right." Remo walked over to the trunk. It was not locked. The brass hasps opened easily enough. Remo forced the two halves apart and stepped back from what was revealed with sudden haste.

It was not the sight of the thing in the trunk that caused him to step back. It was the smell. The interior of the trunk was lined with salt to retard decomposition and hold the odor of decay inside.

For the trunk contained a mummy. Seated in a lotus position, hands cupped in a lap that was covered by a faded and moth-eaten robe of gold, the Bunji Lama wore lichens and mold where his face should be. His eyes were black pits, and his teeth were exposed between lips that had long ago dried and withered. In his hands lay a bronze object that might have been a very ornate dumbbell.

"Looks like a midget," Remo said.

"The Bunji Lama was not yet fifteen when he dropped that body."

Remo made a face. "Don't you people believe in a proper burial?"

Lobsang Drom said, "When a Tibetan dies, he is given sky burial. The *ragyabas* take the corpse to a proper place, and after its bones have been picked clean by vultures, they are interred."

"Must save a lot of space down at the ol' boneyard," Remo said dryly. "Not to mention entertaining the kiddies."

Lobsang Drom regarded him thinly. "How do you bury *your* dead?"

"They go into a wood box, and that goes into the ground."

"Your barley must taste like corpses," said Lobsang Drom.

Remo looked blank.

Kula said, "The Bunji Lama always sits in state until his next body is discovered, with his face turned to the south, which is the direction of long life. This is a form of respect for the old body, and there have been times when the old body will help point the way to the new."

"It is said that the body of the previous Dalai Lama turned his dead face to the northeast after he had been in state for ten days," offered Lobsang. "And it was to the northeast that the new Dalai Lama was discovered."

"Imagine that," said Remo.

"We will ask the Bunji Lama if the oracle has truly revealed his present body," announced Chiun.

The others came to their feet. Remo watched carefully.

Lobsang Drom faced the mummified remains of the forty-sixth Bunji Lama and said, "O, Light That Was. If the oracle reveals to us the Light That is Coming, as the Master of Sinanju has said, give us a sign, Thrice-Blessed One."

The old Bunji Lama sat mutely, the shifting colored light from the TV set making shadows crawl in his hollow eye sockets.

From the TV came the voice of Squirrelly Chicane, "My guru told me that I have a better chance of discovering my true mission in life after I turn sixty."

"Why is that, child?" asked Poopi Silverfish.

"Because sixty is the age when a woman becomes a crone."

"You mean like a *witch?*"

"That's just superstition. Throughout history the crone has been a symbol of female wisdom. Upon my sixtieth birthday, I will become wise."

"Honey," laughed Poopi, "if you look as good then as you do now, they're going to have to put a whole new picture next to the word 'crone' in the dictionaries!"

And covered by the laughter emanating from the TV, the Master of Sinanju surreptitiously swept a hand into the black steamer trunk and swept it out again.

The head of the Bunji Lama toppled off his dried stalk of a neck and rolled across the floor to come to a rest under the television set just as Poopi Silverfish said, "Squirrelly Chicane! Girl, I do believe you're gonna find your mission in life."

"Hark well," cried the Master of Sinanju, "the Bunji Lama has spoken."

"The Bunji Lama on the screen or the Bunji Lama whose head is on the floor?" asked Remo.

"Both," cried Chiun. "By rolling his head on the floor, the last Bunji Lama has revealed the long-hidden truth to the incredulous."

"Incredulous is right," said Remo.

Quivering from head to toe, Lobsang Drom faced Chiun, bowed once deeply and said, "Master of Sinanju, I should never have doubted you."

And the Master of Sinanju bowed back, the better to conceal his beaming face of triumph. Tibetans were so gullible.

"This is a great scam," Kula said reverently, brushing at a tear. "Perhaps the greatest of my life."

"No argument there," muttered Remo.

## 6

The next morning Remo Williams awoke with the sun.

He rolled off his sleeping mat, stretched his limbs and went to his walk-in clothes closet. The T-shirts were up on wooden hangers on one side, and his pants on the other. They all looked brand-new, which they were. When one of his T-shirts got dirty, Remo threw it away—if it was a white one. If it was black, he might save it for a rainy day. He only wore black or white T-shirts. Plain. No dippy sayings or decorations.

His pants occupied the other half of the walk-in closet. Remo wore chinos almost exclusively with a preference for tan, gray or black, although the black ones tended to pick up lint and therefore, unlike the black T-shirts, were usually thrown out after a day's use.

Remo selected a white T-shirt and a fresh pair of black chinos. Remembering that before he had turned in for the night, Chiun had announced that they would seek out the living Bunji Lama on the morrow, he switched to a black T-shirt and gray chinos. No telling when they'd be back, and Remo didn't feel like packing for what might turn out to be only a day trip.

Clothes on his arm, he walked across the hall to his private bathroom. From behind the closed door came the sound of someone moving around.

Remo knocked and asked, "Who's in there?"

A boisterous voice cried, "It is I—Kula!"

"Water warm enough for you?"

"It is wonderfully cold."

"You shower cold?"

"I was speaking of the well water. It is very cold and sweet when one plunges one's face in it."

"For an extra thrill, pull the silver handle," said Remo, annoyed that his private bathroom had been usurped. Still, there were sixteen units and each had a bathroom. Finding an unoccupied shower wouldn't be hard.

Scraping sounds came from the next bathroom. The door was open and Remo peered in.

Inside, the Most Holy Lobsang Drom Rinpoche was seated beside the bathtub, stark naked, using one of Remo's spare toothbrushes to abrade caked dirt off the skull and shoulders of the dead Bunji Lama.

"What the hell are you doing?"

Lobsang Drom stuck out his tongue at Remo in greeting and said, "I am making the old Bunji Lama presentable so that he may meet the new."

"After you're done, don't forget to clean the tub."

The Tibetan looked injured. "You are the servant here, not me."

"Fine. I'll clean the tub if you agree to bathe."

"I will bathe when the proper time comes."

"When will that be?"

"When the new Bunji Lama sits on the Lion Throne. For I took a vow that I would not bathe until that glorious day arrives."

"You took a vow of nonbathing?"

"Yes. What do devout Christians do?"

"Oh, the usual. Mass. Fasting. Celibacy. Bingo."

"I too have taken a vow of celibacy."

"When you stop bathing, celibacy stops being optional," said Remo, moving on to the next bathroom.

From the downstairs kitchen came the sound of Chiun puttering around, and Remo decided his shower could wait. On the way down the stairs he climbed into his clothes.

The Master of Sinanju did not turn at his approach. Instead, he sniffed the air, wearing a disagreeable expression on his parchment countenance.

"I see you have not showered this morning," he said in an arid tone.

"So call me a filthy Tibetan."

"You are worse than an unbathed Tibetan. You are insolent. I can stand the way you reek, but not your braying."

"Look, these people are your friends. How can you con them with this Bunji Lama mumbo jumbo?"

Chiun whirled. "Remo! How can you ask a question like that of me? The one who raised you up from the muck of this backward white land and made you into what no white has ever been?"

"I meant no disrespect, Little Father—"

"I do what I must do so that the babies of my humble village are properly fed and want for nothing. If my emperor tells me that an enemy of his waxes great in strength and must be dispatched, do I ask if this enemy truly deserves death? No. I go to the place where he dwells and although it is an unpleasant thing, I do this. For it is the obligation I took upon my frail shoulders when I assumed full Masterhood, as you one day must do. For if we fail in our obligation, no more gold will go to the barren shores of Sinanju, and the people, who cannot fish because the waters of the bay are too cold and cannot plant because the ground is always hard and untillable, will be forced to send the babies home to the sea, which is another way of drowning them so they do not suffer from privation."

"Look, I know this story by heart."

Chiun cocked his birdlike head to one side curiously. "And do you believe it?"

"Not completely."

"No! What part do you not believe?"

Remo thought a moment. "All of it."

"All?"

"Yeah. I don't think the babies have been in danger of being sent home to the sea in centuries. Maybe they never were. Maybe it's just a story your ancestors told themselves because they did things that were hard to stomach. Besides, you've got so much treasure back at the Masters of the House that you could feed all of Korea on the gold alone."

Remo waited for Chiun to explode.

"That is what you truly think?" he asked coldly.

Remo folded his bare, lean arms in quiet defiance. "Yeah. Sorry. But that's the way I figure it."

Chiun cocked his head the other way and clucked, "You are learning more quickly than I had imagined you would."

Remo blinked. "So answer my question. Why are you conning your friends? They take this Bunji Lama stuff very seriously. It's their religion."

"I do this for a very simple reason."

"Yeah?"

Chiun lifted a wise finger. "They have turned to the Master of Sinanju for help—"

"And—?"

"And they offered a roomful of gold!" said Chiun, raising both fists to the sky so fast his wide kimono sleeves dropped back to reveal bony pipe-stem arms.

"I should have known," said Remo. "Look, how about I stay home for this outing?"

"You would let your adopted father travel across this country in the company of strangers, unescorted?"

"You just want me to carry your trunks, and you know it."

"Kula will carry my trunks."

"What do I carry?"

"You," said Chiun, returning to his pot of rice, "will carry the burden of making an honored guest of this house carry my trunks."

TWO HOURS LATER, Remo was carrying Chiun's steamer trunks to the rental limousine idling in the condo parking lot. Since it was a day trip, Chiun had not insisted on bringing all fourteen. He had wanted Remo to carry five, but Remo had put his foot down.

"There's room in that trunk for maybe four trunks, and that's it," Remo had pointed out.

"Then I will make do with only four," Chiun had allowed.

Remo got the fourth one into the spacious trunk and locked it.

"Why did you lock the trunk?" asked Kula when Remo started back to the house.

"Because it's full."

"What about the Bunji Lama's trunk?"

"Damn! I forgot about that."

"How could you forget the Bunji Lama?"

"Believe me, it wasn't easy. But there's no room for him in the trunk."

"Then he will ride with us."

"I'll give it a second look. You never know."

"No, it is only fitting that the Bunji Lama ride with us."

Remo thought fast and said, "How about if I ride up front?"

"That is agreeable," said Kula.

"Good," said Remo, who hoped the glass partition between the driver's compartment and the back was airtight.

It turned out to be completely airtight. It also turned out that when the Master of Sinanju heard that Remo had insisted on sitting up front, he had dismissed the expensive rental driver so Remo could drive, and personally placed the trunk containing the Bunji Lama in the front passenger seat.

Remo found this out when he slid behind the wheel and almost gagged. He rolled down the windows, got in again and glared at the Master of Sinanju in the rearview mirror.

Chiun looked his blandest.

Remo started the limo, and soon they were humming along the Southeast Expressway, north to Logan Airport. It was normally called the Southeast Distressway, but this morning traffic was flowing smoothly.

Kula's voice boomed over the passenger intercom.

"There is no fermented mare's milk in the refrigerator."

"Remind me to give the limo company people a severe scolding when we get back," Remo said.

"You live in a very uncivilized country, White Tiger."

"No argument there."

"But do not worry. There will be plenty of fermented mare's milk in my personal skyboat."

Remo blinked. "You have your own plane?"

"How did you think I came to this country—on horseback?"

And everyone laughed at the foolish white dolt whom the Master of Sinanju had kindly taken under his wing in the hope that he would one day become Korean, or close to Korean.

THE PLANE WAS a pristine sky blue with a silver stripe running along the windows on both sides. It was a 747 and it might have belonged to some exotic airline, except there was no company name and on the tail was the silhouette of a heavy wheel mounted on a pole, from which dangled nine horsetails. Remo knew it was a representation of the nine-horsetail standard of Genghis Khan.

The pilot and copilot stood at attention at either side of the door. They wore the traditional *del* of the Mongol nomad and bowed when the Master of Sinanju, Kula and Lobsang Drom stepped from the parked limousine.

As Remo got the trunks, the pilots yelled at him to hurry up.

"Hold your horsetails," muttered Remo, carrying Chiun's trunks to the open cargo bay. Once they were stowed, he brought the Bunji Lama's trunk into the cabin.

Inside it was dark. From the outside there had been the usual rows of windows. Inside, the walls were hung with colorful Mongol tapestries, which also covered the windows. There were no seats, just piles of overlapping rugs on the floor. Here and there were low taborets and chests.

Remo had been in Mongol felt tents before. They looked exactly like this, except they were round and spacious, with a stove in the center and a stovepipe leading to an open smoke hole in the ceiling.

There was no stove here, and the ceiling was intact, but otherwise it looked exactly like the interior of a very long *ger*.

"Place the Bunji Lama in the spot of honor," Kula called, indicating a gorgeous Oriental rug.

"And close the door after you," called the pilot from up front.

Remo did both and found a place on the floor.

"I'm glad to see you haven't let all that treasure spoil you, Kula," Remo told the Mongol.

Kula beamed. "You like my skyboat? It has every modern convenience. There is a microwave oven, and through that door behind you there is a flying well."

"Where are the stewardesses?" Remo asked.

Kula looked blank.

"He means the slave girls," said Chiun.

Kula scowled. "We do not allow Mongol women to fly. Otherwise, they will give birth to two-headed babies and other freaks. Only warriors are allowed to fly."

"Do American women fly?" asked Lobsang Drom.

"All the time," said Remo.

"And what is done with the babies that are born with two heads?" he asked in a puzzled voice.

"Oh, usually the mother picks the head she likes best and chops off the other one," said Remo.

"American women are very clever," said Kula.

"Perhaps the American woman with flame for hair is the Bunji Lama after all," muttered Lobsang Drom as the jet's engines began screaming, setting the wall hangings to shaking and shivering.

They were airborne a moment later. The rugs and chests shifted until the plane leveled out.

Lobsang Drom immediately closed his eyes and began moaning one word over and over.

"Aummm."

In one hand he spun something that looked to Remo like a wooden cat-food can on a stick. The turquoise-studded teak can spun and spun. Other than a creaky whirring, it made no noise.

"How long does this go on?" Remo muttered.

"It is a prayer wheel," Kula explained. "One writes his prayer on a strip of paper and places it in the wheel. Each time it spins, the prayer goes forth, earning much merit."

Remo groaned. "This is going to be a long flight."

Kula blinked. "How many marches to this land called California?"

"Marches?"

"It is less than five hours," announced Chiun.

"On horse?"

"By air," said Chiun.

Lobsang Drom's eyes came open instantly. He and Kula exchanged startled glances.

"So wide as that?" Lobsang said.

"It is a very great country in size," said Chiun. "Not so great in culture."

Frowning, Kula flung aside a tapestry and pressed his flat nose to a window. He squinted.

"I see no yak herds."

"They have no yaks," said Chiun.

"Not one?"

"Perhaps a few underfed buffalo," Chiun allowed.

"Not enough to reimburse the invasion army," added Remo.

Kula's scowl darkened. "Then we will bring yaks with us. As a peace offering. To lull the white man into thinking that we bring peace."

"You're pretty open with your master invasion plan," said Remo. "You don't expect to just ride into every city and town from Outer Mongolia to L.A. and announce you're now in charge."

Kula scooted away from the window. "Of course not."

"So how do you figure to pull it off?"

"It is simple. Japan has purchased many places in America and other citified lands."

"True."

"When they have bought up most of the world, we will take over Japan. Struck numb with fear, the rest will fall into place."

"Sounds like a long-term project to me."

"Rome was not sacked in a day," Kula said unconcernedly.

"You meant Rome wasn't *built* in a day," corrected Remo.

"Do you think one can simply sack an empire in an afternoon?"

"I got news for you. The American people will fight back."

"I will show you something," Kula said, digging a thick leather-bound book from an ornate chest. He opened it to a certain page and presented it to Remo.

Remo took it and saw that the book was open to the entry on Genghis Khan. Kula's thick finger pointed to the final paragraph.

> In the past unsympathetic Persian, Chinese and Arab writers condemned Genghis as a ruthless and cruel destroyer, but his terrorism was in reality calculated psychological warfare. He never set out to annihilate a people, like Hitler, or a social class, like Stalin and Mao. Although Genghis did destroy some centers of culture, his administration was generally very tolerant in religious matters and toward ethnic minorities. Today China champions and Russia condemns him, while in Mongolia he is venerated as a symbol of Mongolian nationhood.

"What idiot wrote this?" Remo demanded.

"It is from a very wise and famous American book called the Encyclopedia," said Kula proudly.

Remo looked. He was holding an encyclopedia, all right. One found on the shelves of every library, school and university in the nation.

"This takes political correctness to new lows," he muttered, surrendering the book.

Kula beamed. "Boldbator Khan has made a study of Western thinking. As long as we slay and pillage without regard for race, creed or color, no one will condemn us. And of course we will be merciful in our conquests. If a city submits to us without resistance, only the adult males will be put to the sword."

"You are too kind to us poor backward Americans," said Remo.

"Pax Mongolia is the wave of the future," said Kula, beaming.

"It will be a good thing," said Chiun, "to bring Eastern culture to this benighted land."

Remo looked at him and demanded, "You mean to tell me that when the Mongol cavalry rides in, you're just going to watch? What about the gold America pays you?"

"The gold of Emperor Smith reserves the services of Sinanju for the express purpose of disposing of America's enemies upon demand," said Chiun. "Not in preventing possible invasions. If Emperor Smith decrees Boldbator Khan an enemy to be slain, I will slay him. With regret, of course," he added for Kula's benefit.

"And if you slay my Khan, I will be forced to seek your illustrious head in revenge," returned Kula. "Although it will pain me to lop it off."

"If the Wheel of the Inexorable decrees these events," inserted Lobsang, "what mortal hand can stay them?"

"We will all be reincarnated anyway," Kula said, laughing. "Except the White Tiger, who, being Christian, is disqualified from rebirth."

"I don't want to be reincarnated," muttered Remo. "So there."

"Remo means that he does not wish to be reincarnated as a Christian," said Chiun.

"Bulldooky," said Remo. He got up to get a glass of water from the washroom sink. When he came back, both Kula and Lobsang looked at the paper cup in his hand with horrified expressions.

"What?" said Remo.

"You do not know enough not to drink water intended for washing the hands?" Kula said.

Remo emptied the paper cup in one satisfied gulp, saying, "Well water doesn't agree with me."

7

On the morning of her sixtieth birthday, Squirrelly
Chicane awoke, expecting wisdom.

She flung off her sleeping mask and blinked blue
eyes at the California sunshine flooding in through the
windows. Outside, the surging Pacific gnashed at her
private Malibu beachfront.

"I'm sixty!" she cried, sitting up. Her hair was the
color and texture of carrot shavings. "I'm a crone.
The wisdom that comes to every woman in her rightful time is mine!"

There was no wisdom in the sunshine. It hurt her
eyes. The pounding of the ocean made her head throb
in sympathy.

"Gotta align my chakras," she muttered, closing
her dancing blue eyes.

But her chakras wouldn't align. Especially the yellow one. It was being stubborn again.

The phone rang.

"Squirl, baby-doll. How goes it?"

"Wonderfully, Julius."

"Great. Great. Listen, you read that Mamet script
yet?"

"Three pages of it. Gotta say no."

"No! Why not? It's perfect for you. Free-spirited
woman decides to have a baby at fifty, goes to a sperm

bank and ten years later figures out it was her long-lost high school sweetheart's sperm. She sets out to find the brat's father, they fall in love, but something's not copacetic. Turns out it's the guy's twin brother, and the real guy, the father, he's been dead for years. So your character decides to raise the brat without a father. It's the perfect love story for the nineties woman. She gets laid all over the place and still has her freedom. It's very *Bridges of Madison County*ish."

"The clothes are the same as my last picture."

"Clothes-shmothes! We'll hold out for a bigger wardrobe budget, which you get to keep because, after all, it's you."

"That's sweet of you, Julius, but I'm turning a new leaf today. No more ditzy roles."

"But you're the queen of ditz. And glitz, of course."

"I'm sick of ditz. Just like I got sick of being called kooky, loopy, daffy, dizzy, free spirited and every other ditz synonym the trades could think of. You know, they didn't stop calling me a gamin-faced starlet until I was past forty."

"Don't knock it. You project youth. That's very important in this biz."

"From now on, I project crone."

"Crone! Baby-cakes, I'm third generation. My Yiddish goes only skin-deep. What's this crone?"

"A crone is what I am—a vital, brilliant, mature sixty-year-old woman."

"Sixty! When'd you turn sixty?"

"This morning. I'm a new me, Julius. Throw out all the scripts the majors have been sending you. That's the old Squirrelly Chicane. Get me the kind of scripts that Jessica Tandy gets."

"Jessica Tandy! No offense to Jessica. A lovely woman. But I think she took advantage of a special discount on predeceased embalming. She looks positively pickled."

"Jessica Tandy. But I'll settle for Barbra Streisand."

"Squirrelly, doll. Listen, boobala. If you want to flush your career down the john, that's your business, but don't take your ever-loving agent with you. I got kids."

"My way or the highway, Julius. Get me all the crone scripts that are out there. Remember, I can always write another book."

"Okay, okay, I'll do what I can. But I'm not loving this. And this turning-sixty thing? Don't breathe it to anyone, not even your mother."

"I'm going to shout it from the rooftops. I'm sixty. I'm beyond men and sex and all those unevolved things."

Squirrelly hung up. Almost immediately she picked up the receiver and dialed a long-distance number.

"Hello, Bev. Squirrelly. Just great. It's my birthday! I'm sixty! Isn't that a kick? Listen, I just had a brainstorm. Another self-help book. Different angle this time. Here's the title—*Squirrelly: Sixty and Sexellent.*"

A prim voice at the other end said, "I don't think that's exactly what your readers want to read."

"Don't be silly. My readers will buy any book with my name on it. They always have."

"We need a media tie-in. Do you have anything happening?"

"You know I'm *always* happening."

There was a long silence at the other end of the line.

"I don't suppose you've uncovered any more past lives?"

"Did I tell you I was a scullery maid in the days of Henry VIII and he kept hitting on me?"

"Doesn't sound racy enough for a whole book."

"What do you want from a scullery maid? Upward mobility hadn't been invented back then."

"Well, if you get something publishable, give me a call."

The line went dead, and Squirrelly Chicane stared at the holes where the dial tone was coming from.

"What's with everybody today? You'd think I'd contracted the plague. I haven't had the plague since— well, whenever that awful time was."

Squirrelly lay back and stared at the ceiling. It was pink. So were the bedroom walls. Not to mention the bed, the covers and everything else that would take paint.

"Okay," she said slowly. "I'm having an off day." She corrected herself. "A bad *birthday*. It was bound to happen sometime. I've had such wonderful karma up till now. It'll pass."

She closed her eyes and focused on her chakras. Once she got them lined up, the day would fall into place.

But they refused to align, and the day wasn't getting any younger.

"What I need," she told herself, sitting up, "is a good old-fashioned past-life regression."

Scooting around on the spacious heart-shaped bed, Squirrelly took a pair of silver chopsticks from the night table and used them to extract a cake of brownish material from a turquoise box. She placed the cake in the brass bowl of the silver-filigreed hookah that dominated the night table. The cake crumbled to powder under the rapping of the chopsticks, and a Zippo brought the bit of coal under the bowl to smoldering.

The pipe began bubbling, and Squirrelly Chicane took up the pipe with its amber mouthpiece. She took a hit, held it in her lungs and exhaled it with studied langour.

It felt good. In fact, it felt great. She took another hit, slid back under the pink satin covers and smoked contentedly. It was good *bhang*. Very excellent. It mellowed her right out.

As she sank deeper into a fog of smoke, Squirrelly thought that she was a long way from the sleepy Virginia town where she had been born.

The *bhang* brought back her most treasured memories. It was hard to believe it was sixty years ago.

"Sixty years," she murmured. "Sixty years. Two hundred forty seasons. Forty-three pictures. Twenty-eight plays and musicals. Six autobiographies and one self-actualization book. Thirty-two past lives—so far. One flop TV comedy, true, but a gal's gotta eat."

It had, Squirrelly Chicane decided, been a very fulfilling sixty years. She had traveled everywhere. And everywhere she went, she was recognized and feted. It's true the Peruvian authorities had tossed her out of their country for insisting that saucer men had built the Inca pyramids. And there were those unfortunate run-ins with customs over some inconsequential amounts of recreational hallucinogens. But the best was yet to come. She could feel it in her bones. After all, she was a Taurus.

Once she felt loose and relaxed and ready to take on the world, Squirrelly laid aside the pipe and started to rise.

She got her head clear of the pillow when she heard a distinct crack in the area of her lower spine. Then she fell back.

"What's wrong with my back?" she muttered.

She tried rolling over. It was an effort.

"Imelda! Bring me my healing crystals. Quick!"

But the healing crystals failed to work after her trusted Philippina maid had rubbed them up and down her bumpy spine.

"I will call doctor, Miss Squirrelly."

"No way. Doctors are old-fashioned."

"But you cannot get out of the bed."

"It'll pass. It's probably just a crick from the cold. Close all the windows and get a good fire going. That'll warm up my wise old bones."

"I think that is a good idea," Imelda said, replacing the covers.

"Good."

"Heat is good for arthritis."

"Arthritis?"

"My poor mother had it just like you got it, Miss Squirrelly. On damp mornings she could not even turn over."

"Arthritis! It can't be. I eat smart. I do my yoga. And I'm a Taurus."

"You are not a young woman anymore."

And the maid slipped from the room to start the great fireplace going.

Squirrelly Chicane lay on her pink silk sheets, her disordered mop of red hair on the pink satin pillow, and stared at the pink ceiling with troubled blue eyes.

"I'm sixty and I'm falling apart," she moaned. "Why me? Why now?"

**8**

At LAX, Lobsang Drom and Kula the Mongol looked to Remo Williams with expectation writ large on their faces.

"Which way lies the Bunji Lama, White Tiger?" asked Kula.

"What are you looking at me for?" Remo replied.

"This is your land," said Kula. "Do you not know your own neighbors?"

"We just crossed the entire freaking country."

"We must consult another oracle," announced Chiun.

They looked around the airport. Video monitors were mounted at several locations.

"But which one?" asked Lobsang. "There are so many."

"We will each seek the answer, and good fortune smile upon him who discovers the truth first," proclaimed Chiun.

Kula and Lobsang stood before different monitors, attracting rude stares.

"Quick, Remo!" Chiun urged. "We must discover where Squirrelly Chicane lives, or I will forfeit my Mongol gold!"

"Couldn't you have thought of that before we left?"

"What is a pilgrimage without uncertainty?"

"Over with quicker," said Remo. "Look, let's call Smith. He's got every useless piece of trivia that ever was stored on those computers of his."

"No, not Smith."

"Why not?"

"If you ask Smith for Squirrelly Chicane's address, he will want to know why you wish this knowledge. I do not want him to know that I am sunlighting."

Remo sighed. "The word is 'moonlighting.' And have it your way."

Chiun clapped his hands abruptly. "Remo has had a revelation," he called out. "We must do as he says."

The others returned and regarded Remo with narrowed eyes.

"I say we rent a car to start," said Remo.

Reluctantly Kula and Lobsang followed Remo and Chiun to a car-rental counter. Seeing that it was staffed by a woman, Kula said suddenly, "I demand the honor of renting the vehicle that will transport us to our destiny."

When no one else claimed the honor, Kula whispered, "Remo, teach me the honeyed words American men use to impress their women with their virility and yaks. I wish to practice wooing your women so that when America writhes under our merciful heel, no woman will go unsatisfied."

" 'I have herpes' is a pretty arresting opening line," said Remo.

Purposefully Kula marched up to the counter and, slapping down his gold card, announced, "I am Kula the Mongol, owner of many yaks. I also have herpes in plenty, unlike your weak American men."

A minute later Kula came back with the rental keys in his hand and a broad smile on his face.

"She was very impressed. Her face paled in surprise, and her eyes went exceedingly round in her head."

"Would I steer you wrong?" said Remo.

The rental had a cellular phone, and once they were in traffic, Remo dialed directory assistance, breathing through his mouth because the smell emanating from the old Bunji Lama's trunk in the seat beside him hadn't improved any. Opening the windows didn't help, either. The stench of pollution smelled almost as bad.

"Give me the numbers of the Hollywood tour-bus services," he asked. "All of them."

"Do you have a pencil handy?" asked the operator.

"Don't need one," said Remo, and held up the phone so the Master of Sinanju could absorb the numbers when they emerged from the receiver.

One by one Chiun repeated the telephone numbers back to Remo, who then dialed and asked whoever answered, "Does your tour go by Squirrelly Chicane's place?"

When he got a yes, Remo asked for the tour company address and they drove there.

They were in luck. As soon as they pulled up, a tour bus was pulling out, and Remo got behind it.

The bus led them to the seaside community of Malibu, and they listened for the amplified voice of the driver to announce Squirrelly Chicane's residence.

Over the sound of the bus's engine, the driver started to say, "And just up the road ahead is the home of the multitalented Squirrelly—"

The caterwauling of an ambulance overtook them, forcing Remo to pull over. The bus got out of the way, too, and the white-and-orange ambulance roared up the road marked Private.

"Uh-oh," said Remo.

"What is it?" asked Lobsang, his voice stricken. "What means that awful sound?"

"It is an ambulance," explained Chiun, tight of voice. "In this land it serves but two purposes—to fetch the sick to a doctor and to carry off the dead."

"It is going to the place where the Bunji Lama dwells," muttered Kula uneasily.

Lobsang swallowed hard. "If she has died, we must begin the search anew."

"Quickly, Remo!" squeaked Chiun. "We must save the Bunji Lama from death, else our quest will go on for years to come."

And Remo, trying to keep the dead smell of the old Bunji Lama out of his lungs, floored the accelerator.

SQUIRRELLY CHICANE LAY on a throw rug before her environmentally correct fireplace with her eyes closed, trying to align her chakras. Maybe if she got them lined up, her spine would fall into place. It was a good theory and it might have worked, but for some reason she was seeing double. Even with her eyes closed. Maybe it was the *bhang*.

She opened her eyes. She was still seeing double. The flames were dancing in stereo just inches away from her pink-nailed toes. Their crackling was as loud as a California brushfire.

"This is great *bhang*," she said aloud. Everything was repeated, from her twenty—no, make that forty— toes, to her various Obies, Tonys, Oscars, Emmys and

Grammys ranked upon the mantelpiece. She tried to remember how many Oscars she had won. Three, or was it four? It was hard to tell. She kept spares in every home she owned, from her Parisian pied-à-terre to her London flat.

She lay back, her vertebrae popping audibly with her every move.

"Maybe I should try a chiropractor," she told the high, white ceiling.

The phone rang. Imelda immediately brought it in and held the receiver to her face so Squirrelly needn't sit up and risk dislocating her spine.

"Hello?" she said through gritted capped teeth.

A low, ingratiating voice said, "Hello. How's my favorite sixty-year-old nymphet?"

"Warren! You remembered my birthday! How sweet."

"How could I forget?" The pause on the line was awkward. "So, now that you're sixty, wanna make it with me?"

"Warren! For God sakes, I'm your sister!"

"Yeah, but you're the only actress left in Hollywood I haven't slept with."

"Sue me, you satyr."

"Is that a no?"

"Yes."

"Is that a yes?"

"No."

"So, you'll think about it?"

"Hang up, Imelda," said Squirrelly, pulling away from the phone.

Imelda replaced the cordless phone on its base and left the room.

"And people think *I'm* a bit flipped out," muttered Squirrelly, who suddenly realized that she had sat up in surprise during the conversation.

She experimented with moving her legs and fell into such a spasm of writhing, twisting, screaming anguish that Imelda, fearing for her mistress, immediately called for an ambulance.

THE PARAMEDICS rushed in, took one look and one of them said, "Back spasm."

The other, sniffing the air and seeing Squirrelly's dilated eyes, added, "High as a kite, too."

They brought in a spine board and tried to strap her to it. But Squirrelly only writhed and screamed more loudly.

The paramedics were trying to figure out what next to do when a resounding bell-like voice punctuated by heavy footfalls that shook the pine flooring announced, "I am Kula the Mongol, possessor of herpes in abundance, and I will slay any Christian who defiles the Bunji Lama with his unworthy hands."

The paramedics looked up, saw a hulking Asian brandishing a silver dagger and immediately backed away.

"We don't want any trouble, friend," one of them said.

"And if you stand away from that woman," a squeaky voice added, "there will be none."

The next person to enter was a little wisp of an Oriental wearing a kimono of scarlet silk. His serious gaze fell upon Squirrelly Chicane, half-strapped to the spine board. With a shriek, he fell upon the board and flung it aside.

"Western medicine!" he said derisively. "It is fortunate that we arrived in time, before they inserted foreign objects down the Bunji Lama's throat or removed her ears."

"They remove the ears of the sick here?" Lobsang said.

"Western doctors are quacks. They believe it is their right to remove any organ or appendage once they pronounce it to be infested with cancer."

"Oh, right," said Remo. "Ear cancer. That's a real killer."

And in the middle of this a dreamy voice called up from the floor, "Who's the Bunji Lamb?"

No one answered that question. Instead, Squirrelly Chicane found herself looking up into a sweet Asian face. It reminded her of the trusting faces she had seen in China years ago, when she had been there on a goodwill tour. To this day, people still criticized her for going and for praising the Chinese authorities after she had returned home. Republicans, mostly. They were so unenlightened.

"Who are you?" she asked the sweet, trustworthy face.

"I am the Master of Sinanju, and I have come to relieve you of your suffering."

"I think my chakras are out of whack, Mr. Sinatra."

Another Oriental face came into view. It looked worried.

"I am Lobsang Drom, of Tibet. You know of the chakras?"

"Yes, of course."

"You are Buddhist?"

"Yes," said the other Oriental.

"Baptist," Squirrelly offered.

"Bap-tist?"

"It is the American word for Buddhist," said the trustworthy-looking Oriental.

"Sounds about right to me," said Squirrelly, going with the flow.

"Can you heal her, Master?"

"Yes, can you heal me, Mr. Sinatra?" asked Squirrelly, who wondered if the old man was some distant cousin of Frank's.

Then the trustworthy Oriental reached behind her head with one hand and began manipulating her spine. Immediately, Squirrelly started feeling very warm in the area of her neck, and a sleepiness suffused her mind. She drifted off, and in the darkness behind her eyelids, she could see her chakras—one set now— falling into line.

Her eyes snapped open suddenly, and she felt firm fingers withdraw from her neck.

"You may sit up now," said the old Oriental, standing up.

Squirrelly gathered her dancer's legs under her. They worked fine. She sat up. Her back responded without protest. There was no pain, no stiffness, no hesitancy.

"Chiropractic?" she asked, assuming a lotus position.

And the trustworthy old Oriental turned his head to spit into the roaring fire.

"Your humors were unbalanced," he said. "There was too much wind in your spine. I have released the bad wind."

Squirrelly blinked. She had never heard of wind in the spine. But it sounded really New Age, so it must be true. That was her personal philosophy in a nutshell: if it sounded right, it was.

Squirrelly saw now there were four strangers in the room, not counting her maid and the two paramedics, who were packing up their spine board and first-aid equipment with sheepish expressions. They quietly slipped away.

Two were the Asians she had seen. The third was also an Asian. But different from the two. He looked like Conan the Hulk. The fourth man was white, very casually dressed, and had the biggest wrists Squirrelly had ever seen in her life.

There was something indefinably interesting about the way he moved. She couldn't take her eyes off him.

And the others couldn't take their eyes off her. Which was perfectly understandable, she decided. After all, wasn't she Squirrelly Chicane, toast of stage, screen, song and many lives?

Squirrelly bestowed upon them her most alluring smile.

"Let me guess, you're a delegation from the People's Republic, sent to convey greetings upon the occasion of my sixtieth birthday."

The faces of the three Asians fell, and the old one spit into the fireplace again.

"Wrong guess," muttered Squirrelly. "Okay, I'll bite. Who are you?"

"I am the Master of Sinanju, destined to be known as Chiun the Great, and I bring with me the Most Holy Lobsang Drom Rinpoche and Kula the Mongol."

"Who's the hunk?"

Everyone scowled at that. Especially the hunk himself.

"A minor servant," said the sweet-faced Chiun.

"Trade you my maid for him."

"No deal," said the hunk with the wrists.

"You don't want to be my boy toy?" Squirrelly asked in a pouty voice.

"I'm a free agent."

"Enough!" cried the Master of Sinanju. "Remo, fetch the trunk of the former Bunji Lama."

And the white guy named Remo stepped from the room, moving, Squirrelly saw with pleasure, like a dancer. Better than Nureyev. With cuter buns, too.

While he was gone, the old Oriental said, in a voice that lost its squeakiness with each word, "O flame-haired one of many lives, we have journeyed far to bring you momentous tidings."

Squirrelly began singing, "Happy birthday to me. Happy birthday to me. I hope the hunk is a Chippendale dancer, because he's built like a tree...."

When no one joined in, she stopped. "Okay, this isn't about my birthday. So, tell a girl."

"An oracle has told us of your dwelling here in the land called Malibu," said Chiun, "and lo, it has spoken the truth. We have found you here."

"The Master of Sinanju speaks truly," said the Mongol, Kula.

"Truly, he has," added the Tibetan, Lobster. Or whatever his name was.

"I'm in the book," said Squirrelly.

"And now the time has come to test the veracity of the oracle's other revelation," said Chiun.

"An oracle has been talking about me? Behind my back?"

"The oracle has named you the next Bunji Lama."

"I never heard of the Bunji Lamb," said Squirrelly, "I did meet the Dehli Lamb at a party once. He was with Richard Gere. Any relation?"

This time it was the Tibetan who spit into the fireplace.

"When the Bunji Lama comes to the natural end of his life," he said, "it is his destiny to be reincarnated into the body of an infant born at the exact moment of his death. By certain secret signs is the next body recognized. In the case of the last Bunji Lama, he prophesied that the body fate had decreed for his next fleshly house would be born far from Tibet, and so he further prophesied the certain signs by which his regents could recognize him."

"This sounds really, really cosmic," said Squirrelly.

The Master of Sinanju proclaimed, "Behold, the white woman Squirrelly Chicane. Has she not red hair?"

"Yes."

"Truly."

"Not even dyed," said Squirrelly, patting her carroty shag.

"It is well to remember that the first prediction of the forty-sixth Bunji Lama was that his next body would possess hair the hue of fire."

"That's me," said Squirrelly. "Oh, my God! Was I the Bunji Lamb in a previous life?"

"The first test has been passed. Now it is time to see if this woman recognizes any relics of her former life."

"Show me a relic! Show me a relic!" Squirrelly said excitely.

At that moment Remo returned with the trunk and before Squirrelly's mesmerized gaze, it was opened to reveal a dead, musty smell and a headless seated mummy. Its head sat in its lap as if that were the natural place for it.

"What's that?" she asked,

"The old Bunji Lama," said Lobsang, prying a bronze ceremonial object from the dead mummy's clenched brown fingers. He brought it over to dangle it before Squirrelly's wide eyes.

"Do you recognize this *dorje?*"

"*Dorje?*"

"Ceremonial thunderbolt," said Lobsang. "It is the symbol of the Bunji Lama's temporal power."

Squirrelly's brow knit in perplexity. "No. Darn it, it doesn't ring a bell."

"She has passed the second test!" Chiun proclaimed.

"I have?"

"It was predicted that the forty-seventh Bunji Lama would recognize none of the trappings of his former body."

"My God. It's true. I don't recognize it at all." And looking at the lichen-eaten face of the old Bunji Lama, she added, "As a matter of fact, I don't recognize me at all."

"Bulldooky," said Remo. "Of course she doesn't recognize it. She never saw it before in her life. What kinda of cockamamy test is that?"

"Silence, white eyes!" said Lobsang.

"There are other tests," said the Master of Sinanju. "Reveal to us your left shoulder."

Squirrelly peeled her pink pajama top off her shoulder, unbuttoning the top buttons so Remo could get a peek at her cleavage. He pretended to look out the window with a bored expression. Squirrelly figured he was sneaking a peek in the reflection of the windowpane. Men were so obvious.

"Behold the mark! It is the sign that has appeared on the shoulder of the Bunji Lama down through the ages."

Squirrelly started. The old Oriental was pointing with a perfectly manicured fingernail at her bare shoulder. She pulled it around, saying, "Mark! What mark?"

And there it was, a dimplelike pit on her shoulder.

"My God! Look at it. It's some kind of birthmark I never noticed before."

"That's your vaccination mark, you dip," said Remo.

"What is this *chiling* word—'vaccination?'" Lobsang demanded.

"It is a rare word meaning the mark of the Bunji Lama—for even in this backward land the fame of the Bunji Lama has spread!" explained the old man.

The Tibetan was hovering close now, squinting at the mark. His long face was unhappy.

"It is the right mark, isn't it?" Squirrelly asked. "Oh, tell me it is. I've been between past lives for so long I've had a serious case of the blahs."

"It is as the texts describe." said Lobsang. "But you are a female with white eyes. No white eyes has ever been a *tulku.*"

"What's a *tulku?*"

"An incarnation."

"Call me a white-eyed *tulku.* Except they're blue, you know."

"There is another test, one not prophesied by the last Bunji Lama, but known to all Worshipful Nameless Ones in the Dark Who See the Light That is Coming," Lobsang said slowly.

"What's that?"

"I must see your navel."

"Sure." And Squirrelly obligingly lifted her pajama top high enough so the lower curve of her breasts was revealed. Remo continued to pretend to be looking out the window.

"It is true!" Lobsang gasped. "Her navel protrudes, just as did all previous Bunji Lamas'!"

"You mean I'm the Bunji Lamb because I'm an outie—"

Chiun lifted a quieting hand. "There remains one final test."

"What is it? What is it? I'll take it, whatever it is. I'm great with tests. Crossword puzzles. Scrabble. You name it."

"There remains the joss," intoned Chiun.

"Yes, the joss," said Kula. "Have you a Buddhist shrine in this place, O Light That Might Be?"

"No."

"Then where do you worship your ancestors?"

"Usually I just call home and talk to my folks."

"If the joss is not found, she is disqualified," Lobsang said sternly.

"But I don't wanna be disqualified," moaned Squirrelly. "I wanna be the Bunji Lamb. I deserve to be the Bunji Lamb. I've been just about everything else. Except the Queen of Sheba. My friend Poopi has dibs on her."

"Does this mean we can go home now?" asked Remo.

"Not until this entire house is searched and the joss found or not found," said Chiun firmly.

"Somebody tell me what a joss is and I'll help you look," Squirrelly said helpfully.

"It is an icon unique in all the world, which with his dying breath the last Bunji Lama described in detail," said Chiun, casting his eyes around the room but avoiding the mantel over the crackling fire.

So it was that Remo Williams, trying to look everywhere but directly at Squirrelly Chicane, spotted the sword-wielding golden statuette without a face.

He blinked. He started to open his mouth, caught himself and slipped up to the fireplace to stand directly in front of the statue, blocking it from view.

"Why don't you guys check the other rooms?" he said casually. "I got this one covered."

## 9

The minute the others left the living room of Squirrelly Chicane's Malibu beach house, Remo turned, grabbed a gold-plated statuette off the mantelpiece and tried to find a place to stash it.

The redwood furniture was spare and modern. Not a single cushion to hide anything under. Under the couch looked inviting, but knowing Chiun, Remo figured that would be the first place he'd look.

That left the fireplace. Remo hated to do it—the statue wasn't his property—but this might be an emergency. Whatever Chiun was up to, trouble was sure to follow.

Remo tossed the statue into the fireplace so it landed behind the burning log.

Except the log wasn't really a log, but some kind of papier-mâché pseudolog. The minute the statue hit it, the thing cracked in half with a mushy sound and a shower of sparks.

The statue lay in the flames and whirling bits of burning paper exposed for anyone to see.

"Damn," said Remo.

He had no choice. He had to hide the damned thing. Getting down on one knee, Remo reached into the flames. His hand went in and out so fast it was a pink blur, driving a wall of air before it and pushing aside the hungry flames. The hairs on the back of his hand weren't so much as singed when he pulled it out again.

The statue was hot, though. Holding it lightly so the hot metal wouldn't sear his fingertips, Remo rushed it over to the Bunji Lama's trunk and stuffed it behind the mummy's squatting form. Then he closed the trunk.

When the Master of Sinanju returned a few minutes later, Remo tried to look innocent.

Chiun, seeing his expression, said, "What have you been up to?"

"Nothing. Just turning the log." Remo pointed at the shattered log and kept his face relaxed.

Then Kula stormed in saying, "I have found it! I have found it! The defaced joss!"

And he held up the golden statue that was familiar to anyone who ever watched an Academy Award ceremony.

"It is the joss that was foretold!" Chiun cried. "Exactly as foretold."

"It is?" said Squirrelly.

"This is your joss?" demanded Lobsang.

"Yes, of course it's mine."

"I found it holding open the door to the well room," said Kula. "Like a worthless object."

"Yeah, I use that one for a doorstop. What's a girl to do when she has so many josses?"

"It does not look like a Buddha," Lobsang said. "What is this joss called?"

"Oscar."

"Os-car? How came you by it?"

"That thing? Oh, I've only had it for a million years."

Just then, everyone noticed the smoke.

"Where is that smoke coming from?" asked Chiun, crinkling his tiny nose.

"It comes from the trunk of the old Bunji Lama," said Kula. "See? It has closed itself. Now it is smoking. The Bunji Lama craves our attention."

"Oh, hell," muttered Remo. "Here it comes."

Kula threw open the trunk. Pungent smoke rolled out. It smelled like a compost pile on fire.

"What is it you wish to reveal, O Light That Was?" asked Lobsang of the wizened form.

But the old Bunji Lama simply sat there, smoking. Then, all at once, his gold brocade robe surged up in fire.

"It is being consumed!" Lobsang cried. "The old Bunji Lama is leaving us. What can it mean?"

"It means," Remo said dryly, "that he caught fire."

As they watched, the mummy blackened, shriveled and collapsed into a pile of sooty bones and ash.

Revealed was a statue of gold, blank of face and holding a sword point down in his joined hands.

"Look," Kula gasped, "it is another faceless joss. Exactly like the first."

"It is a sign," said Chiun. "The Bunji Lama has offered proof that the joss of the new Bunji Lama is the true one by magically producing its mate!"

"Is this truth?" Lobsang asked Squirrelly.

"Sounds good to me," Squirrelly giggled.

And at that, both Lobsang Drom and Kula the Mongol prostrated themselves before Squirrelly Chicane, saying, "We are your servants, O Light That has Come at Last."

With a shriek of glee, Squirrelly Chicane cried, "I'm the Bunji Lamb! I'm the Bunji Lamb! I knew it!

I knew it! I have such awesome karma! This is better than winning at 'Wheel of Fortune'!''

''It's Bunji Lama,'' said Remo unhappily.

Squirrelly was dancing around the room now. ''Wait'll I tell my friends. Wait'll I call my mother! I'm the Bunji Lamb. And I'm gonna be the Bunjiest Lamb that ever was.''

''This is the greatest scam that ever was,'' sobbed Kula, brushing a tear from his eye.

Remo sidled up to the Master of Sinanju and whispered, ''I hate to pop everyone's bubble, but I stashed that Oscar in the trunk.''

''I know,'' said Chiun.

''How'd you know?''

''Because I knew you had recognized the joss where the others did not when I beheld the dazed look upon your pale face.''

''Wait a minute! Are you telling me you took everyone out of the room because you knew I'd stash the statue?''

''Yes.''

''Why didn't you just point it out yourself?''

''Because I have pointed out every other portent. It was someone else's turn.''

''What about the other statue?''

Chiun shrugged. ''Sometimes the gods smile twice in one day.''

''Great. Now I'm a part of one of your con jobs.''

''No one forced you to do what you did.''

''So what do we do now?''

''Celebrate the good fortune of our Buddhist friends who have discovered their long-lost high priestess,'' said Chiun.

"High is right," said Remo, eyeing the spectacle of Squirrelly Chicane as she squatted down, and like an aging beatnik, began beating out a drum solo on Lobsang Drom's bald and uncomplaining head.

"So," SQUIRRELLY WAS saying after settling down onto a divan. "Tell me about the Bunji Lamb. What was I like? Who were my lovers? Did I have a craving for chocolate-covered cherries?"

They were seated in a circle about the room, on the floor, in lotus positions. The maid had served tofu and carrot juice. Squirrelly was digging into a large bowl of double-peach frozen yogurt.

Remo sat away from the others because he didn't like the way Squirrelly was eyeing him. If there was such a felony as lascivious gaze, she'd do the maximum jail term.

"It does not matter what you were, Bunji Rinpoche," said Lobsang. "What matters is what you are to be."

"Huh?"

"You are the Bunji Lama."

"You mean I *was* the Bunji Lamb."

"'Lama,'" said Remo. "Get it right."

Squirrelly frowned at her yogurt. "Llama. Isn't that an animal? I saw a herd of them last time I was in Peru. They smelled worse than wet sheep."

Lobsang Drom intoned, "O Light That Is, you were the Bunji Lama in times past and you are the Bunji Lama anew. You have always been the Bunji Lama. You will always be the Bunji Lama until you have achieved perfect Buddhahood and the cycle of incarnations is no longer necessary for you."

Squirrelly brought the yogurt to her firm mouth and let it slide down her throat before saying, "I'm not following this. How can I be the Bunji Llama in this life if I'm already Squirrelly Chicane?"

"Now that you know who you truly are, you are no longer Squirrelly Chicane," Lobsang explained. "Now you are the Bunji Lama."

"Okay," Squirrelly said slowly. "I'm the Bunji Llama. I accept that. Let's get serious about this. I'm the Bunji Llama. First thing I need to know is what does the Bunji Llama wear?"

Lobsang Drom blinked.

"Wear?"

"Yes. What's my wardrobe? I *do* get a wardrobe, don't I?"

"Yes. I have brought your meditation robes."

Chiun spoke up. "Remo, fetch the meditation robes of the new Bunji Lama."

Remo got up to go.

"Walk slowly, Remo," Squirrelly called after him. "I want to meditate on your buns."

Remo backed out of the room wearing an unhappy expression.

He returned a moment later and surrendered a small ebony chest. Lobsang Drom set it before him and opened it reverently. Out came a silken robe. With silent ceremony he offered it folded to Squirrelly Chicane.

Squirrelly took it, unfolded it, and her aging gamin face went slack.

"Saffron? That's not my color. Do you have anything in burgundy?"

Lobsang flinched.

"Her education has been neglected," Chiun said quickly. "It is obvious that the new Bunji Lama, after being lost for so long, suffers from loss of memory."

Lobsang nodded. "Yes, she suffers from loss of memory."

"I do?"

"She must be reeducated," added Chiun.

"You are a Buddhist?" Lobsang asked Squirrelly.

"Baptist."

"It is the same thing," said Chiun.

"Like hell it is," said Remo.

"I don't think we've been properly introduced," Squirrelly said suddenly, smiling in Remo's direction. "I'm Squirrelly Chicane."

"Remo Buttafuoco," said Remo.

"Any relation?"

"He's my sister."

"Sister?"

"Yeah, that part hasn't come out yet."

Squirrelly looked blank. "You know, I've suspected that for some time."

"Good for you."

Lobsang said, "You know the sutras?"

Squirrelly looked up from her empty yogurt cup. "Sutras?"

"Yes, you have learned these as a child?"

"I have a copy of the *Kama Sutra*." She looked toward Remo and smiled sweetly. "I know it by heart. Practice makes perfect."

"From this day forward," said Lobsang, "you must embrace celibacy."

"Celibacy!"

"You will eat no meat, no eggs, and meditate daily."

"I already do those things."

"Proof that she is truly Buddhist even if she has lost her way," cried Chiun.

"Look, whatever it takes, I'll do it. I'm really, really into being the Bunji Lamb. Or Llama. Whatever."

"You'll be sorry," said Remo.

"Hush," admonished Chiun.

"Why do you say that?" Squirrelly wanted to know.

"Because I've been on one of Chiun's little outings before. Everybody eats dung except him."

"I can see you're really evolved."

"Well, I don't go around thinking I've lived before."

"You have," said Squirrelly. "You just have to be open-minded like me."

"You're open-minded because you've got holes in your head."

"Remo has lived before," Chiun said blandly.

"The hell I have."

"You were once Lu the Disgraced. A Korean and a Master of Sinanju."

"Is this true, White Tiger?" asked Kula. "Were you once a Korean in a past life?"

Everyone looked to Remo with expectant and welcoming eyes. He felt like an alcoholic stepping into his first AA meeting.

"I don't want to talk about it," he said, and abruptly left the house.

REMO WALKED ALONG the beach. His face was a scowl, and there was an uneasiness in the pit of his stomach. Yet his feet left no discernible marks in the soft sand. Leaving no trace of his passing was so ingrained he was no longer conscious of the fact that he was doing it.

It was night now. The surf was murmuring in some ancient tongue, and the water swept up to spread a cold blanket of bitter cream on the sand. It would have erased his footprints had he left any.

Remo had been raised a Catholic. He had also been taught Western physics, which said it was not possible for a human being to outrun a speeding car, climb the sheer side of a building, dodge a bullet and drive a stiff finger into a block of steel—all feats Remo had learned to perform at Chiun's feet.

Just as his illusions about the physical world around him and his place in it had been stripped away by the Master of Sinanju, so had his religious beliefs been challenged.

When Dr. Harold W. Smith had hired Chiun to train Remo, he wanted only a Sinanju-trained white assassin who could operate in American society. What Smith got was a white man who grew to be more and more a part of the long lineage of Sinanju.

Twenty years later Remo stood with one foot in both worlds. He had learned to live with it. He was loyal to his country still. But a part of him was continually tugged toward the bleak fishing village on the West Korea Bay that had given rise to the House of Sinanju, which for centuries before the birth of Christ had served the thrones of the Old World.

Remo shared no blood with them, as far as he knew. But he was connected to all past Masters through powerful bonds of duty and tradition and honor. Only once or twice in a century was a Master of Sinanju created. And he was the first white man. It was an honor. Remo was proud of it.

Years ago, on one of their earliest missions, Chiun had told Remo about a prophecy of Sinanju, that one day a Master of Sinanju would train a white man who had died in the art of the sun source. And that white man—the dead white tiger, the stories called him—would be the avatar of Shiva the Destroyer. The Hindu god of destruction.

Remo had scoffed at that story. It was just another colorful fable told to mask a harsh reality, like sending the babies home to the sea. For a long time he figured it was something Chiun made up to cover his embarrassment over having to take on a non-Korean pupil.

But things had happened to Remo to make him wonder. He had experienced brief blackouts. When he emerged from them, he found he had done things. Sometimes it was as simple as an enemy lying dead at his feet and Remo having no recollection of killing him. Sometimes it was more. During the Gulf War he had lost several days' worth of memory.

That time Chiun had tried to explain that Shiva had possessed Remo, and the time was approaching when he would take total possession of Remo's mortal form.

That day Remo had walked out of the room, too.

On their last assignment, Remo had experienced one of those episodes again. This time he had a dim recollection of it.

Neither he nor Chiun had spoken of it then or after. But it had been an awkward, unspoken thing between them ever since. Remo wanted no part of any other life or consciousness. He just wanted to be Remo.

Chiun, he could tell, was growing more and more nervous about these episodes. Whatever the predictions had been, the reality was much more menacing. Chiun feared losing Remo to the Shiva consciousness. For to lose Remo was to have the Sinanju line end—a line that Chiun was convinced Remo belonged to by blood. Korean blood.

That was impossible, Remo knew.

And then there was Lu the Disgraced, the Sinanju Master who had served ancient Rome and through his weakness allowed the most important client Sinanju had ever had to fall.

Remo had scoffed at that story—until he had met and fell in love with Ivory, a Sri Lankan woman whom he had never met before but whom he had recognized the instant he met her—and somehow remembered. From another life.

Two thousand years ago they had been lovers, Chiun had told him. Remo was Master Lu and she was a priestess of Kali, the mortal enemy of Shiva. In that life, as in this, cruel death had sundered them at their moment of greatest fulfillment. Remo had moved on. And mostly buried the memories. Until now.

It had seemed so real at the time. The memories coming back were Technicolor vivid.

Was he really Shiva? Had he been Lu?

"Who the hell am I?" Remo muttered to himself as he walked along the sand.

Out in the Pacific the incoming waves were topped with thin white combers. He paused to watch them form, crest and collapse on the sand, as eternal as the stars over his head.

The waves formed and collapsed. The stars burned with a cold fire. Man was born and he died. Who could say that his spirit wasn't reborn in other times?

"Ah, the hell with it," Remo said, and started back to the house. One thing was sure. Squirrelly Chicane wasn't the Bunji Lama. That was just another of Chiun's legendary cons.

## 10

Squirrelly Chicane lounged in her pink heart-shaped bed eating chocolate-covered cherries.

"Mom! Hi! It's me, Squirl. I have the most *fabulous* news."

"You met a man."

"Better than that. I met *four* men."

"Isn't that a little much even for you, dear?"

"No. It's not like that, mother. Really. Get your mind out of the gutter. Four men came to visit me today with the most unbelievable news."

"What? What?"

"I'm the Bunji Lamb. Or Llama. Or something like that."

"Squirrelly Chicane, have you been nipping at that Wild Turkey bourbon your father gave you last Christmas?"

"Will you stop? Will you just stop this instant? Now, as I was saying, I'm the forty-seventh reincarnation of the Bunji Lamb. In fact, I'm *all* of them—stretching back to the Wood Dragon Year. Don't even *ask* how many centuries ago that was. And it gets better. The Bunji Lamb is the reincarnation of—rum-pum-pum-pum-pum-pum—Buddha!"

"The fat ugly person with the big belly and the long earlobes?"

Squirrelly looked at her pink nails. "I don't know exactly which Buddha. I guess so. Will you stop interrupting? Oh, I'm so excited I can hardly think straight."

"Squirrelly dear, if you think you're the reincarnation of some heathen deity, you really aren't thinking straight. Stop being so giggly for a moment and think. How can you be all those persons when you've already told people you've been so many other persons?"

"Mother, have you ever considered the possibility that this just might be too cosmic for someone who's never left Virginia except to have a secret hysterectomy?"

"Leave my operation out of this. Even if you accept that rubbish, a body can have just so many lives. It's only common sense. Something you, I am sorry to say, have been shortchanged on."

"For your information, they proved it beyond a shadow of a doubt."

"How, pray tell?"

Squirrelly tucked her legs under her, noticing that she had to pull the left one in by hand. It would probably have hurt except that she was feeling no pain from the brandy in the cherries. She was on her second box.

"You know that Oscar I earned for *Medium Esteem?* The one, dear mother, in which I was playing a certain buttinsky older female relative whom I will not name but who bears an uncanny resemblance to *your* mother?"

"Yes."

"Well, it just so happens it was the spitting image of some Tibetan idol or something that the last Bunji

Lamb, who was me in a male body, predicted that the future me, which is the me you are currently talking to, would own. Wasn't I wonderful? I had the foresight to think of all that. And I was just a mere man."

"Squirrelly, are you on drugs? Shall I call Betty Ford?"

"It's just like you to rain on my reincarnations. You know that brassy know-it-all woman I played in *Letters from Limbo?* Well, that wasn't acting. I was imitating *you.*"

Click.

"That's right," Squirrelly called into the dead phone, "hang up on me. See if I care. You're only my mother for *this* life. I hope you die and come back as a silkworm."

The phone rang again. Squirrelly counted three rings and said tartly, "If you're calling to apologize, you're too late. My feelings are too terribly hurt for apologies to work."

"Squirl, baby-doll," came the voice of her agent. "Why would I call to apologize?"

"Julius! Listen, dear, I'm so glad you called."

"Good. Have I got a script for you."

"Screw the script. I have stumbled upon the role of a lifetime, Julius."

"What's that?"

"I'm the Bunji Lamb."

"Is that like a Punji stick? Because if it is, I'd stay away from it. My cousin Irv, who was in Vietnam, stepped on one once. They had to whack his foot off at the ankle. To this day he doesn't walk. He hops."

"For your information, the Bunji Lamb is the spiritual leader of Tibet."

"Tibet Tibet?"

"Tibet Tibet. That's correct. I have the most incredible offer to go to Tibet and be the Bunji Lamb."

"You mean *play* the Bunji Lamb?"

"No, I said 'be.' Not play. Be. I've evolved beyond mere acting."

"Hold the phone. Are we talking about a movie here?"

"A book. A movie. At worst, a miniseries based on a book. I want you to put the package together for me."

"Who do I call?"

"I don't know. The government of Tibet, I guess. One of their reps is here with me. A dried-up Yul Brynner type named Lobsang."

"Lobsang. Lobsang. The name rings a bell. Is he producing?"

"He's more of a coach. He's showing me the ropes. You know, language, customs, stuff like that. I already know my title in Tibetan. It's *Bunji Bogd*. You should see the scrumptious saffron number he gave me to wear. It clashes something awful with my hair and nails, but I think I can fix that."

"Squirrelly, baby. Sweets. You're a million miles ahead of me. How can I put together a package for you without a director, producer or locations scouted?"

"Find someone. Anyone good. How about Hardy Bricker?"

"Bricker? No one can find him. You know, they're whispering that the government got to him because of that assassination movie of his. Maybe he was right, after all."

"Then try Robert Altman. I don't care. I'm not fussy. I can carry this project. Maybe I'll direct."

"You?"

"Why not? It's about the Bunji Lamb. It's set in Tibet. The Bunji Lamb is the long-lost spiritual leader of Tibet. And I'm the Bunji Lamb. What could be more perfect?"

"This sounds like a high-adventure thing. We may need Spielberg or Lucas. Someone of that caliber. And what about the script?"

"We don't need a script! We'll go. I'll liberate the country, write a book about my experiences, and someone can adapt it. I'm thinking of calling it *Lamb of Light*. How's that for a boffo title?"

"What's this about liberating the country?"

"Oops. Almost forgot," said Squirrelly, fishing for a particularly fat chocolate-covered cherry. She picked it apart with her perfectly-capped teeth as she talked. "It seems there's this itsy-bitsy disagreement between the government of China and the Tibetanese, or whatever they call themselves. I'm sure it's been blown all out of proportion. Goodness knows when I visited China back during the Nixon regime it was a lovely country with a very enlightened leadership. I still know a few low people in high places. Once I get to Tibet and claim the Lion Throne—isn't that a scream? I'm the Bunji Lamb and I'm going to sit on the Lion Throne. Isn't there an old saying about the lion lying down with the lamb? Anyway, once I'm there, I'll just make a few calls and straighten it all out."

There was a long silence on the line, broken only by the measured breathing of both parties.

Finally Julius said, "Squirrelly, sweetheart. What are you smoking?"

"Listen, Julie. You know I'm not one to lose my temper. Just talk to Universal or Amblin or whomever. Work out the money end. Then we'll all go to Tibet together."

"I don't do locations, you know that. I only have to drive past a Thai restaurant and my bowels clench."

"And listen, I'm having a party tonight. I'm calling it a little lost Bunji Lamb coming-out party. Drop by. I'll introduce you to Lobsang. You and he can talk. *Ciao*. Or as we Bunji Lambs say, *kale pheb*. It means 'go softly.' That's Tibetan for *Ciao*."

Click.

Squirrelly Chicane leaned back in bed and stretched her limber dancer's body. It was the night of her sixtieth birthday, and she felt as if her entire life stretched before her.

"I wonder if this would work better as a musical?" she muttered. "Maybe I could convince that Remo hunk to be a chorus boy—or whatever they call them."

## 11

"I hope you're happy with yourself," Remo Williams was saying as he brought in the last of the precious lacquered trunks.

The Master of Sinanju sat on his tatami mat on the polished hardwood floor of Squirrelly Chicane's guest house, facing the television screen. He said nothing. There was nothing to say.

His pupil continued addressing imaginary wrongs. "I hope you really enjoyed treating me like a second-class citizen in my own country. In front of your friends."

This time the Master of Sinanju deigned to answer. "Kula was your friend before he was my friend," he said. "In Mongolia he was your Mongol, not mine."

"Well, he sure acted like one of your friends this time around," said Remo, setting down Chiun's trunk. He began pacing the room, wasting both breath and energy.

"He has sworn allegiance to Boldbator Khan, whom I discovered riding the barren steppes and whom I encouraged to grasp the birthright that was his. Now I have done it again."

"Like hell, you have. Boldbator was one thing. Squirrelly Chicane is another. She's an actress, for Christ's sake."

"What better choice to play the greatest role a person can be asked to play? That of the long-lost Bunji Lama."

"Tibet is practically in revolt. There's a civil war going on over there. You just made it ten times worse."

"The outcome has not yet been ordained."

"Ten times worse," Remo repeated. "And for what? Gold?"

"A roomful of gold," Chiun corrected. "A mere purse of gold, or six purses of gold, would not have been sufficient. But for a roomful of gold, the Master of Sinanju was willing to put aside the few fading moments of the end days of his bitter life and undertake the momentous and exhausting search for the long-lost Bunji Lama."

"Exhausting? It took you a freaking day."

"Less. Technically, fourteen of your hours."

"Nice work if you can get it."

"I got lucky."

"Did you see the look on Lobsang's and poor Kula's faces when they decided Squirrelly was the Bunji Lama?" Remo continued. "They were practically in tears."

"Yes, it was very moving."

"It was a scam!"

"Yes. Kula said that. He is very perceptive. For a horse Mongol."

"How you can accept gold under false pretenses and not feel bad about it is beyond me."

"Many things are beyond you," Chiun said coolly. "But to answer your shouted question—I will feel bad if the outcome of the events I have set into motion decree that I feel bad. Until then, I am content. I have earned a roomful of gold, and the long-suffering Tibetan people will soon have their precious Bunji Lama restored to them.''

''You know they're planning to sneak her into Tibet.''

''The Lion Throne has been too long vacant.''

''And she'll probably get killed. The Chinese have beaten Tibet into the ground.''

''Rumors spread by whites. No one knows what is happening in Lhasa, which is the capital of Tibet.''

''What if Squirrelly gets herself killed?''

''It is very simple. She will be reincarnated once again. And now that I have set her on the proper path, in her next life she will begin as the forty-seventh Bunji Lama, as is her birthright, without the burden of this wasted white interlude.''

''I don't believe that crap.''

''No, you believe other crap. You believe in goodness and justice and a gaudy bolt of cloth called a flag because it is a different pattern and color from the bolts of cloth of other countries. In Vietnam you were willing to throw your life away because fat men in starched uniforms told you it was the correct thing to do. You are willing to die for a slice of your mother's apple pie, and you without even a mother. Are these not the fables of your ignorant youth?''

The Master of Sinanju's pupil looked pained and said nothing.

''You believed in these things,'' the Master went on in a less stern tone. ''But you remember Lu the Disgraced. And you have heard the voice of Shiva emerge from your own throat.''

''Shove it.''

"And this is why you are so angry and troubled. You do not understand these things. You wish to bury them in the dead part of your mind. But you cannot. You are still a child in many ways. It is very sad."

"The hell it is."

"Spoken like a true child. Now be silent. The California news is coming on. Perhaps there will be tidings of interest."

Chiun picked up the remote control that lay in his lap and pressed the On button. The blow-dried head of a local television anchor appeared on the screen. He began speaking in the clear, bell-like tones of those native to the California region of America.

"Topping our news this evening, the Chinese crackdown on Tibet is in its ninth week and the secretary general of the United Nations is calling for Beijing to put an end to martial law and withdraw her troops. Reports of secret executions cannot be confirmed, but refugees continue to carry out of the beleaguered former kingdom horrific tales of murder, torture and other human-rights abuses. From his exile in India, the Dalai Lama has issued a statement that is widely seen as a mild rebuke. And in Beijing a statement attributed to the Panchen Lama has urged the Tibetan people to lay down their arms and cooperate with the people's republic."

"Who's the Panchen Lama?" asked Remo.

"A tool of Beijing. It is his destiny to hand up the Tibetan people into oppression."

"Same old story," muttered Remo. "The UN will fart around until it's too late to help the people on the ground."

"Whites do not care about Asians," sniffed Chiun. "Forceful words will be spoken in ringing voices, but in the end no hands will be lifted."

"No argument there."

"In other news," the newscaster was saying, "the manager for Squirrelly Chicane, award-winning actress, author and advocate of past-life experiences, has declared herself the forty-seventh Bunji Lama and announced that she will go to Tibet and reason with the Chinese military leaders there."

"News travels fast," Remo grunted.

"It is to be hoped that it also travels far," said the Master of Sinanju in a distant voice.

Remo regarded Chiun with a questioning eye, but he pretended not to notice.

## 12

Denholm Fong was doing his morning tai chi exercises when the faxphone began tweedling.

He let the air flow out of his stomach as he extended his right arm, brought his left hand back and planted both feet on the ground. He refused to break his rhythm, even though it was the unlisted faxphone that was emitting sound and paper.

Fong stepped in a circle around the walled-in patio of his Bel Air home that he had purchased for cash, he told his neighbors, from the sale of his first screenplay, *Shanghai Cats*.

It was an excellent cover story. Southern California was filled with writers making handsome livings off spec screenplays that were optioned and never produced. And so, after moving into Bel Air, Denholm Fong made it a point to periodically throw a party celebrating his latest "sale."

That no film was ever made mattered not at all to Fong's neighbors. They accepted it as business as usual. This was Hollywood, where no one was rejected without compensation.

The trouble was, it had begin to chafe Denholm Fong's ego. People really were making crazy money in this strange country of America writing screenplays that producers paid fabulous sums for and that ended up collecting dust in filing cabinets.

Denholm Fong took to writing screenplays for real. Why not? All his neighbors were doing it. And the unlisted faxphone seldom sounded these days. His true business had been quiet. The biannual stipend from Beijing covered living expenses, but not the boredom that vexed Denholm Fong's days and nights.

It had been so long since the unlisted faxphone had rung that Fong had at first no reaction. He waited for the sounds to cease, then he brought his exercises to an end and walked limber and casual into the house.

There was a single sheet of plain paper in the faxphone output box. He picked it up. It was simply a copy of a Reuter's report that had been faxed from a number in Hong Kong so that there was no phone record of communication between Beijing, China and Denholm Fong—a Chinese-American living in Bel Air, California, who had entered the U.S.A. in the aftermath of the Tiananmen Square massacre to claim asylum, dropped out of UCLA after two terms and now listed "screenwriter" on his 1040 Form.

The article was in Cantonese. It was brief. It reported, in the clipped deadpan prose of newspaper copy the world over, that the American actress Squirrelly Chicane had claimed the title of Bunji Lama, the spiritual leader of Tibet who had last died in the early 1930s. She planned to go to Lhasa as soon as Chinese authorities processed her visa.

There was no cover sheet. No instruction, coded or otherwise. The Chinese Intelligence Service was too clever for that.

The fax transmission might have been simply an amusing clipping sent by one cousin to another across the gulf of the Pacific Ocean. Self-explanatory. Good for a laugh. No reply necessary. Trust you are living the good life in America, cousin.

And so Denholm Fong read it over once, neither smiled nor frowned and let it fall casually from his fingers into a waiting wastepaper basket. No surveillance camera, no hidden CIA microphone, no suspicious spy could possibly divine the fact that China's top assassin-in-residence in the United States had been notified of his next victim.

Denholm Fong dropped into the executive chair before his dormant computer and began calling around.

"Squirrelly? It's Denholm. Listen, darling, I heard the wonderful news. What a part! Congratulations. What's that? A party? I'd love to come. Of course I'll bring a friend. *Ciao.*"

Click.

"Cousin Nigel? Hello, It's Denholm. My dear friend Squirrelly Chicane is throwing a party tonight, and I'd like you to accompany me. Would you be good enough to tell a few of the others? I'm trying to finish up my latest script. It's called *Katmandu Cats.* Yes, I'm still mining the cat thing."

Hanging up, Denholm Fong booted up his computer. If he stayed focused, he might be able to finish a working draft of his latest script before Squirrelly's party started. Surely the party would be packed with eager producers who just might give it a read once the hostess had been shoveled into a body bag.

After all, this was Hollywood, where even sudden death didn't get in the way of business. Unless, of course, you happened to be one of the suddenly dead.

IT WAS, the Hollywood community agreed, one of the best parties anyone had thrown in a long, long time.

Even after the terrorists came and tried to slaughter the hostess. Some of the invitees were later heard to say that the terrorists were the best part.

Everyone who was hot that week had been invited. They crammed Squirrelly Chicane's Malibu beach house, percolated in and out of the guest house to indulge in various encounters and vices, then spilled out onto her private beach.

Squirrelly herself held court in her living room with her impressive array of entertainment-industry awards standing at attention on the mantelpiece, the Oscar that had catapulted her to new heights positioned exactly in the center. The air was redolent with a sickly sweet smell coming from a hand-rolled cigarette that was being passed around.

"As soon as the visa problem is cleared up," she was saying, "Tibet, watch out!"

"How does it feel to be a high priestess?" asked a well-known director as he handed off the cigarette.

Squirrelly looked in both directions, grinned and said, "Gotta make sure that sour old Lobsang isn't around when I do this. He always has a yak. Watch."

Squirrelly knocked hot ash off the cigarette and said, "I'm the high priestess, right?"

She took a quick hit, held it in and released aromatic smoke in a cloud of high-pitched giggling, shrieking, "Now I'm the higher priestess! Isn't that a hoot?"

Everyone thought is was a hoot. It was the biggest hoot anyone ever thought of. No one, Squirrelly Chicane was assured, could in the history of the human race, never mind Hollywood, think up a bigger hoot. Pass the joint, please.

THE TERRORISTS got past the private security stationed at the private entrance leading to Squirrelly Chicane's Malibu home by saying, "We're with Sony Pictures."

The first car was allowed to enter.

The second car was not challenged, either.

The valets finished parking both cars at about the same time, and the friends of Denholm Fong began to mix with the crowd, make small talk, sample expensive finger sandwiches and sip assorted intoxicants. They looked relaxed, polished and very southern California. They were all in the film business, they pointedly told anyone who asked and a few who didn't. Most claimed to be Japanese producers or bankers. Japanese money was very important in Hollywood these days. It was enough to impress people who might, but probably would not, know a Japanese from a Chinese at twenty paces.

By the time Denholm Fong pulled up to the gate and identified himself, the party had shifted into second gear. Anyone who wasn't high was drunk or borderline intoxicated.

It would be, Fong saw with a single appraising glance as he stepped from his black Porsche, a piece of cake.

He looked perfectly natural as he strolled onto the beach, smiling and nodding his head to those who waved to him in recognition.

Everyone was here, he thought. Good. There would be no problem. He might even make that long-wished-for connection.

Then he saw the old Korean.

The old Korean wore traditional clothing. Not the trousers of the Korean peasant of the south or the gray work uniform of Fong's North Korean comrades, but the Japanese-style kimono that Koreans almost never wore.

Except for one very special Korean.

It was, in the face of it, utterly impossible. This was a typical ostentatious Hollywood party. It was true that the occasion was rather unusual. And he was expecting Tibetans. He saw no Tibetans. Probably they were wringing their hands in horror at the unspiritual display of opulence.

But the Korean, who looked as if he had first drawn breath in the previous century, was dressed exactly like a Master of Sinanju.

Denholm Fong was a political assassin. He knew his adversaries. He knew also his competition. It was known in Beijing that the House of Sinanju had degenerated to the point that it now worked for the United States.

There could be no doubt. The Reigning Master of Sinanju was present. Fong paused to accept a stuffed crab leg from a silver tray a waiter offered him. He tasted it carefully as he studied the little man who must be the legendary Master of Sinanju.

The little man moved about the crowd like a fussy hen. He wore a disapproving expression on his wrinkled features. His kimono was a riotous thing of shimmering scarlet-and-violet silks.

As Fong watched, the old Korean seemed to be slipping up to each of his own agents. While they blended well in their chic clothes, expensive haircuts and mirrored sunglasses, they nevertheless stood out from the others in one unavoidable respect: they were all ethnic Chinese.

Each time the old man approached one of Fong's agents, the man lost color.

What could he be telling them? Fong wondered.

Denholm waited for the little man to walk away from Nigel before approaching his friend.

"What did that man say to you, Nigel?"

Nigel's voice was very tight as he replied, "The old dragon said that I had come to the wrong party. Cat is not being served."

"A Korean, without a doubt."

"I respectfully request permission to empty my weapon into the old dragon when the time comes."

"The time," Fong said as he caught a flash of saffron out of one corner of his eye, "has come."

Squirrelly Chicane stepped onto the veranda overlooking the beach. She wore the saffron robes of a high lama. On her head, leaning forward drunkenly, perched one of those conical lama hats that resembled a horn of plenty.

"Is everybody having a great time?" she called out, trying to hold the hornlike hat in place.

"Yes!"

Squirrelly hoisted her Oscar high. "Am I the Bunji Lama?"

"Yes!"

"Am I the Bunjiest Lama that ever was?"

"Yes, you are, Squirrelly!" the crowd cried out.

"Good. I want you all to come visit me in Tibet once I settle in and kick out the Chinese army."

Applause greeted the invitation.

"If anyone can kick the Chinese army out of Tibet," someone said, "it's Squirrelly."

"Absolutely. Look at how many Oscars she has."

And over the cacophony of sounds, Denholm Fong raised his voice and said in Mandarin, "Now!"

Out from under silk and poplin jackets came a narrow range of silenced 9 mm pistols.

Fong let Nigel get his Tec-9 out and trained on the old Korean before he reached into his shoulder holster and grasped his Beretta.

He had already decided to draw it only if absolutely necessary. The others could handle the killing. No point in Beijing's top assassin risking his life and blowing his cover just to liquidate an empty-headed over-the-hill actress with delusions of religious grandeur.

Besides, he had his latest script in the car. The chances of a sale were pretty fair once the shooting stopped and his men had escaped in the confusion.

As a precaution, Fong placed his thumb on the safety catch and pushed. The safety wouldn't budge. It felt as if it were welded in place. No matter, he decided. He held the tiny automatic low in both cupped hands and faced the veranda and his target. The first shots from the others would thin out the crowd and start the real party.

Except that no shots came.

A silver dagger did bury itself in Nigel's jugular, though.

Nigel dropped his weapon and tried to grab at the fountain of blood that bubbled out. He spun in place as if trying to synchronize his hands with the blood flow. It was so unexpected, so comical, that Fong almost laughed.

Then Fong became very busy trying to gather up his bowels and stuff them back into the raw hole that had been his abdominal cavity.

This, too, had happened with great suddenness.

Fong had been in the act of turning when he heard a short rip of a sound. His stomach suddenly felt very empty, and something wet and heavy plopped onto his shoes.

He looked down and recognized the slimy grayish-white loops of human intestines. They were still piling up, and his heart gave a single dull thud when Fong realized that they could only be his.

The old Korean who Fong was certain was the Master of Sinanju was already moving on to his next target. There was not a trace of blood on his extended forefinger with its viciously long killing nail. But there was a hell of a lot of it gushing onto the sand under Fong's feet.

Fong folded up like a cheap telescope on the sand and tried to do something about his unraveling intestinal tract. It appeared intact. It was just hanging out of him. Then the bleeding began.

Fong was too professional to delude himself. There was no hope. He looked up to see how the others were faring and watched, helpless, as one by one his men were taken out with such expert skill that most of the other party goers had no idea what was happening.

A lean white man Fong had brushed past and noticed only because his wrists were freakishly thick stepped up to Lee and took hold of his pistol muzzle. It was a stupid thing to do. He might as well have attempted to fend off a stabbing sword by grasping the sharp blade.

Yet before Lee could squeeze the trigger and destroy the man's hand, the weapon was forced upward. The white guy's free hand came up, slapped full on. When it came away, there was red jelly where Lee's face should have been.

The white guy didn't even pause to watch the body fall. He moved on, found another Chinese agent and took hold of his gun arm by the shoulder. When he pulled, the arm came out of the socket like a cooked shoulder of ham, the pistol slipping unfired from dead fingers.

The dismembered arm was flung carelessly into the sea. The rest dropped into the sand to writhe and scream until a descending shoe imploded the screaming man's larynx.

It was that way all up and down the beach. Fong saw it all. The low kicks shattered ankles and kneecaps and brought exposed throats and skulls down to the sand where heels could be brought down with lethal force. That was the white guy's technique. The old Korean simply drifted up on the blind sides of Fong's dwindling agents and inserted one of those fingernails that looked like delicate ivory and were by reputation as sharp and unbreakable as tempered steel. Stealth and skill as one. And Fong's most highly trained men were no more than helpless children before the awful beauty of it.

Only one man, Wing, had the presence of mind to go for the target. He elevated the perforated muzzle of his Tec-9 and squeezed the trigger. The gun quivered. Wing cursed his weapon. It refused to fire. He pounded it with the flat of his hand. And then Fong recalled his own stubborn Beretta. He yanked it from his jacket, trying not to detach his guts, and saw that the safety latch had been mangled so it could not be undone.

Someone had obviously slipped up on him and accomplished this with great skill and care.

"The white guy..." he breathed. A trained U.S. agent would have spotted the shoulder bulge, unobtrusive as it was.

Denholm Fong would have thrown up except that his stomach was already slipping into the pile made by his escaping viscera. And then all life and consciousness was slipping out of his mortal remains.

While the light was going out of his eyes, Fong smelled a disagreeable body odor and sensed a heavy presence kneel beside him in the sand.

A growling voice said, "I am Kula the Mongol. Why are you not dead, Chinese?"

A Mongol! Fong thought, shuddering. They were more fearsome than Klingons.

"I will cut your throat to send you on your way to another life. Perhaps I will have the honor of killing you in that life, too, Chinese."

Denholm Fong never felt the blade that opened his throat and finished his dying. His last thoughts were of failure. Not of the miserable failure of his duty to the motherland, but the unrealized dream that had been his since he had come to America.

He would never see the worthy name of Denholm Fong up on the silver screen.

REMO WILLIAMS WAS making a pile of bodies in the sand.

The cream of Hollywood stood around applauding as if he and Chiun had been some kind of floor show. Maybe, he thought, if they saw the dead pile high enough without moving, they'd figure it out. But he doubted it.

"That was marvelous, Squirrelly," they were saying.

"The special effects were great!"

"That fake blood looks really, really real."

"It's just Karo syrup with a dash of red food coloring," a punky-looking man said. And he dipped a fried shrimp into a thick scarlet pool in the sand.

He bit down, tasted salt and not sugar, and turned green.

Everyone saw him turn green. Not everyone realized what that meant, but enough of them did. One actress in basic black, too-pale skin and cherry red lips dipped a finger in, tasted and kept tasting. One of the producers present was casting a vampire movie, and a girl had to stand out in this town.

"It's real!" a waiter gasped.

"It is?" said Squirrelly.

"Of course it's real," Remo shouted after depositing another body. "Unless you suddenly remember hiring someone to pretend to kill you."

"Why would anybody want to kill me?"

"Take a look at the guys. What do they look like?"

Lifting her long skirts, Squirrelly came down off the veranda on bare feet.

She looked at the bodies. Everyone looked at the bodies. They made faces. Some scratched their heads or other itchy parts of their anatomies.

"What do they look like?" Remo repeated.

"Dead?" Squirrelly guessed.

"Yeah. Squirl's right. They look dead."

"Okay. Given. They look dead," admitted Remo. "What else do they look?"

More head-scratching and face-making followed. No one offered any theories.

Then Squirrelly said, "Producers! They look like producers."

Remo sighed. "Chinese. They look Chinese."

"The Chinese are my friends," Squirrelly said indignantly. "I was a guest in their country. It was a paradise of sexual equality and happy, productive people living so close to the earth it brought tears of shame to my eyes to think that Americans are denied the kind of fulfillment even the poorest Chinese peasant enjoys as his birthright."

"You were given the VIP bullshit tour. Everybody knows that. And now that you've announced to all the world that you're going to liberate Tibet, they're out to snuff you."

"Remo is right," came the voice of the Master of Sinanju, indicating the stacked dead. "This is the true China."

Squirrelly looked blank. "The true China is dead?"

"The true China is treacherous."

"I don't believe it," said Squirrelly.

"Believe it," said Remo. "Now, before you call the police, we gotta get out of here. Our job is done."

"Why would I call the police?" wondered Squirrelly Chicane.

"To report a crime. To have the bodies carted off to the morgue."

"That's not how we do it in the Hollywood community," Squirrelly said. "The business of Hollywood is publicity, and bad publicity is bad business."

"You can't just leave them here."

"Won't the tide be in soon?" inquired the actress who wanted to play a vampire. She had stopped tasting the blood, and with the aid of a compact mirror was using it to freshen her lipstick.

"Yes," said Lobsang, appearing as if from nowhere. "The tide will be in soon. It will return their useless husks to the sea, for they no longer reside therein."

Squirrelly clapped her hands together like a child. "Oh, that is *so* Buddhist. I love it when you talk like that. Teach me to talk like that."

"Look," Remo said, dumping the last body onto the pile, "do what you want. Chiun and I have stuck around too long as it is." He turned to Chiun. "Isn't that right, Little Father?"

"We have paid our respects to the forty-seventh Bunji Lama and done her a service, as well." Chiun bowed. "Let that be a gift to you, Light That has Come. May you reign in wisdom and glory."

"Do not fear, Master of Sinanju," said Kula stoutly. "I will see to it that the Bunji arrives in Lhasa still wearing her pink skin. Farewell."

Squirrelly waved them off. "*Kale pheb!* Go slowly. Or softly. Or whatever. Has anybody seen my roach clip?"

ON THEIR WAY to the rental car, Remo said to Chiun, "What happens when the Chinese government discovers that Squirrelly's still alive and their agents are dead?"

"They will realize that a message has been sent to them. Perhaps they will discover the wisdom to do the correct thing."

"Is this what you meant by the message traveling far?"

"Possibly," said Chiun.

"Do me a big favor. Let's keep this entire episode between you and me. Okay?"

"Agreed. I do not wish to anger my emperor with my sunlighting."

"That's 'moonlighting.'"

"We practice the sun source. We are sunlighters. And by the next sun I will have much gold to count."

"I still say there's going to be blood on that gold."

"Spoken like a true Buttafuoco," said Chiun, standing by the passenger side door and pretending to look at the waves until Remo got around to opening it for him. Once that was done, he would remind his pupil to fetch his trunks.

**13**

Dr. Harold W. Smith arrived for work promptly at 6:00 a.m. He was a very punctual man. The gate guard had a habit of checking his wristwatch as soon as Smith's beat-up station wagon rolled past the gate, and if it was more than thirty seconds off, he reset it. Smith was that punctual.

The lobby guard knew to expect him to walk in at precisely 6:01. If 6:01 came and went without Smith striding into the lobby attired in his unvarying uniform consisting of a gray three-piece suit, the guard knew that Harold Smith wasn't late. He was out sick. That's how punctual Harold W. Smith was.

Smith's personal secretary knew that her employer invariably stepped off the second-floor elevator at exactly 6:02. When she heard the ding of the elevator, she didn't bother to look up. She just said, "No calls, Dr. Smith." That's how tied to his routine was Harold W. Smith, director of Folcroft Sanitarium, a sleepy little private hospital nestled amid the poplars and oaks of Rye, New York.

Once Harold W. Smith closed the door marked Director, the portion of his routine that was known to no one but him began.

He settled into the cracked leather chair before the picture window of two-way glass that gave an excellent view of Long Island Sound. It was wasted on Smith because his back was to it, but it had the advantage of being opaque to prying eyes.

Smith looked at his pathologically neat desk, saw nothing out of place and took that as a sign Folcroft's cover had not been penetrated and pressed a concealed stud under the oaken desk.

A section of the desktop to his immediate left dropped, slid away, and up from the exposed well hummed an ordinary-looking computer terminal. The keyboard unfolded itself, and Smith addressed the keys with his long thin gray fingers.

Everything about Harold Smith was gray. His eyes, shielded by rimless glasses, were gray. As was his thinning hair and his dryish skin. He was the grayest of gray men—colorless, uninteresting, a bureaucrat to the bone.

Smith entered a password known only to him, and the computer screen began scrolling the Bill of Rights, which Harold Smith read silently as a reminder of the awesome responsibility that had sat on his gray shoulders since that long-ago day when a much-admired United States President had plucked him out of the bowels of Langley to offer him the position of director of CURE, the supersecret organization that didn't exist.

His reading done, Smith called up the night's news extracts. Deep in the basement of Folcroft, sealed behind a concrete wall, was a bank of mainframe computers that twenty-four hours a day scanned data banks throughout North America, extracting raw data according to programs Smith himself wrote, seeking threats to U.S. security, whether domestic or foreign.

It had been a light night. Only two events stood out.

Squirrelly Chicane, noted actress, was claiming to be the long-lost Bunji Lama, an obscure Tibetan spiritual leader dead nearly half a century.

Smith frowned. This seemed not to fall under any of the program rubrics he created. Then he read further and saw that Beijing had denounced the announcement as a transparent American provocation.

Smith blinked. It had been a long time since Beijing had used such harsh language to describe a U.S. action. Relations between the two countries these days were relatively settled.

Smith went on to the next extract.

It was the report of the death of an obscure screenwriter named Denholm Fong. Fong's body had washed up on a California beach, disemboweled.

Smith blinked again. This was not right. Was the computer acting up?

He pressed the question-mark key, and the computer responded by highlighting the single common word in both reports.

The word was "Malibu."

"Odd," said Smith in the dry, lemony voice that betrayed his New England upbringing. "Could there be a connection?"

Smith logged off the extract program and ran a background check on Denholm Fong.

Smith had only to glance over the dead man's bank account activity, IRS files and permanent-resident immigration status in order to come to a conclusion.

"A Red Chinese sleeper agent," he muttered. "But who killed him—and why?"

Smith considered that matter for a few silent moments, decided there was insufficient data for a working theory and dumped his findings into a new file he labeled "Bunji" for brevity's sake. He instructed the computer to dump any related discoveries into the Bunji file. Perhaps a pattern would reveal itself.

Smith turned his attention to Folcroft matters. From time to time the terminal would beep and display an incoming fragment of data that programming had culled out of the billions of bytes of raw data being transmitted across the nation. Nothing escaped the Folcroft Five, and nothing that they brought to his attention escaped the tired gray eyes of Harold W. Smith.

It was close to noon when the intercom buzzed and Smith said, "Yes, Mrs. Mikulka?"

"A Mr. Buttafuoco to see you."

Smith blinked. "First name?"

"Remo," said the very recognizable voice of Remo Williams.

"Yes, send him in," said Smith quickly, adjusting his hunter green Dartmouth tie.

"Remo, what brings you here?" asked Smith after Remo had closed the door after him.

"Just thought I'd drop by," Remo said in a subdued voice.

"You do not just drop by. Is something wrong?"

Remo dropped onto the long couch by the door and crossed his legs. He looked everywhere except directly at his employer.

"Nah. I was just in the neighborhood."

"Remo, you are never just in the neighborhood. What is wrong?"

"Nothing," said Remo, absently rotating his thick wrists. Smith recognized the habit as something Remo fell into when restless or agitated.

"Have it your way," Smith said dismissively. "But I am very busy."

Remo came out of his seat and wandered over to the terminal.

"Anything up?" he asked.

"No."

Remo's face fell. "Too bad. I wouldn't mind an assignment right about now. You know, just for something to do."

"I would think that you would enjoy some time off after your last assignment."

"The HELP scare? It wasn't so bad." Remo was looking out the window now. Seen in profile, his face was troubled.

Smith took off his glasses and began cleaning them with a cloth. "According to Master Chiun, you came close to death at the hands of that Sri Lankan woman assassin. Have there been any aftereffects of that poison?"

"No. I feel great. I shrugged that stuff off like a twenty-four hour flu."

"People do not shrug off lethal toxins," Smith pointed out.

"I do."

Smith cleared his throat and said, "Er, Master Chiun said you had one of those...episodes again."

Remo whirled. "He told you about it?"

"Yes. He has told me about most of them."

Remo frowned. His mouth compressed, and he seemed to be looking inward.

"Is there anything you'd like to tell me, Remo?" asked Smith in a voice he tried to keep calm.

Remo shrugged. "What's to tell? I don't remember them."

"Any of them?"

"I remember some of it, yeah. I remember the voice."

"You heard the voice?"

"Sometimes I hear it in my head. Sometimes it comes out of me."

"Is that why you've come here?"

"Smitty, you know the crap Chiun believes in. The legends of Shiva?"

"Chiun has explained it to me."

"It's just superstition, isn't it?"

Smith hesitated. He had seen Remo when one of those spells had overtaken him. The Remo he knew had talents that outclassed the greatest athletes and martial artists ever known. The Remo who had spoken in another voice was utterly alien to anything human and displayed attributes far beyond the amplified skills that could be explained by Sinanju training.

"Define superstition," said Smith.

Remo turned away from the window. "Oh, come off it, Smith. You can't tell me you buy any of it."

"I buy nothing," returned Smith in a crisp voice. "But since my first encounter with the Master of Sinanju, my natural skepticism has taken successive pummelings. I prefer not to dwell on things I cannot adequately explain."

"I'm not talking Sinanju. I'm talking—" Remo waved his arms "—that Squirrelly Chicane bull."

Smith leaned back in his chair. "I do not believe in reincarnation, if that is what you are driving at."

Remo suddenly returned to the desk, set his hands on the desktop and leaned close to Smith's thin face.

"Smitty, this place is full of specialists. Ever hear of a condition that could explain this voice I hear?"

Smith considered. "Yes, there is a condition known as Psychogenic Fugue State. Its chief symptom is a complete personality displacement in which the subject's personality is sublimated for that of another's. In profound cases the subject talks and acts in a manner distinctly different from his usual self. I have sometimes wondered if it applied to your case."

"Case? I don't have a case!"

"You are hearing voices. You admit this."

"I'm making the voice. Or my throat is."

"Would you like to see a psychiatrist, Remo?"

"Yes. No!"

"Well, which is it?"

"I'd like for all this metaphysical junk to just fly away. But I'll settle for somebody explaining it for me."

"Dr. Gerling might be able to shed some light. Would you like to speak with him?"

"Let me think about it. Okay. If I've slipped my track, I'm not sure I'm in a big rush to find out."

"What if I simply explain your situation to him and get back to you on his opinion?"

"Okay. I can live with that."

"Good," said Harold Smith. "Is there anything else?"

A desk drawer began ringing. Smith opened it, lifted out a standard AT&T desk telephone the color of a fire engine and lifted the receiver. There was no dial.

"Yes, Mr. President?" said Harold Smith after clearing his throat.

Remo turned his back and pretended not to be listening, but every word spoken by the President of the United States over the dedicated line to Washington reached his ears.

"Dr. Smith," the President said in his hoarse but mellow down-home voice. "How are you?"

"I am well, Mr. President," said Smith in a voice that communicated his mild impatience with idle talk. Smith let the silence hang between Folcroft and the White House.

"Well, yes. Glad to hear it, Smith. I need your input on something."

"Do you have a matter requiring my people?" Smith asked.

"Yes and no," said the President uncomfortably.

"Which is it?" returned Smith.

Remo made a hand motion that meant speed it up. Smith ignored him.

"I wonder if you've read about—I hesitate to bring this up—Squirrelly Chicane?"

"I have," admitted Smith.

"Well, she's a friend of my wife, who as you may have heard, has appointed herself head of the Presidential Commission on Tibetan Independence, and she's bound and determined to go to Tibet and see this thing through."

"Who—the First Lady or Squirrelly Chicane?"

"Squirrelly. The First Lady appointed her a special envoy of something when this crazy lama thing was announced. Myself, I don't swallow all this New Age stuff—and let me say that neither does the First Lady—but as I said, she and Squirrelly are friends."

Smith furrowed his pale brow. "I am not following this."

"My wife has asked the Chinese state department to expedite Squirrelly Chicane's visa application to enter Tibet."

"Mr. President, don't you realize the implications of that act?"

"Well, we can't stop her. Either of them, actually. And Squirrelly's free to travel where she wants to go."

"Yes, but her presence in Tibet could lead to open revolt."

"Isn't that what they have over there already?"

"Lhasa is in an uproar, but the countryside is relatively passive now. The introduction of a volatile and unpredictable element like Miss Chicane—"

"'Unpredictable' is correct," the President said wryly. "I recognize the seriousness of the situation, but as I said, she's determined to go, and the First Lady is especially interested in the situation over there in Tibet. I know I'm not empowered to order you to accept assignments, Smith. I can only suggest them—"

"A built-in safeguard designed to avoid executive-branch abuse of CURE."

"And I want it clearly understood that I'm not insisting on this," returned the President. He lowered his voice as if to protect against an eavesdropper. It became ingratiating. "But do you think you could see your way clear to sending your people along to kinda chaperone Squirrelly?"

Harold Smith stared into space a moment. His lemony expression did not change a particle.

Remo turned and made throat-cutting gestures and shook his head violently. Smith ignored him. He and he alone had sole authority to accept or decline Presidential tasks.

"No, Mr. President, I do not see this as within the CURE mandate."

"I'm sorry you feel that way," the President said in a disconsolate tone.

"I do not feel that way. That is simply the way it is. Conditions in Tibet, regrettable as they are, have no bearing on U.S. security. But if Miss Chicane goes to Tibet, a rift could develop between the U.S. and China. I can only advise you against allowing her to go. The rest I leave to your judgment."

"If it were up to me—"

"It *is* up to you. You are the President of the United States."

"You don't know my wife, the copresident."

"Mr. President," Smith said sternly, "the American people did not elect a copresident. There is no such constitutional office. There is only a president and a vice-president. Your wife is your wife, not an elected official."

"I share my every decision with her. She's my rock. There are no secrets from her."

Smith went instantly white. His voice cracked on his next word. "Mr. President, you did not tell her about the organization?"

"I take that back. I held that one back. Just in case of a divorce."

"I hesitate to mention this," said Smith, "but last month the red telephone rang, and when I answered, a suspicious woman's voice demanded to know who I was."

The President let out a weary sigh. "Yeah, she told me. I'm sorry, Smith. I really am. She was thinking of redecorating the Lincoln bedroom and found the red phone stashed in the night table. Naturally she picked it up, and—"

"What did you tell her?"

"I fibbed. I told her it was the hot line to Canada or something."

"I trust she believed you."

"Well, not exactly," the President admitted in a sheepish tone. "I think she thinks it's some kind of secret line to an old girlfriend."

"Do not disabuse her of that notion," said Smith.

"Are you crazy?"

"Mr. President, it is better for you to have a public divorce than to have the existence of CURE come out on your watch. You could be impeached for allowing CURE to continue."

"Don't think the notion doesn't haunt me."

"Good day, Mr. President. If you have other matters directly pertaining to national security, do not hesitate to bring them to my attention."

With that, Harold Smith hung up.

Remo came up to the desk. "Good thing you said no."

"Why is that?" said Smith, returning the red phone to the drawer and closing it.

"Because there's no way I'm doing bodyguard duty on that Squirrelly Chicane. Whoever named her has her personality down pat. Every nut idea on the planet is in her personal collection."

"You seem to know her reputation quite well."

"Chiun's been talking about her a lot lately. I think he's developing a crush on her or something."

"I see," said Smith.

The terminal beeped, and Smith said, "Excuse me." He stared at the screen for a moment and muttered, "Odd."

"What's odd?" Remo demanded.

"Another Chinese body has washed ashore in Malibu."

"Must be some immigrant-smuggling scheme gone bad," said Remo.

"You could be right. Except that the first body was of a screenwriter who had been in this country some time. I have reason to believe he was a Chinese sleeper agent."

"What makes you say that?"

"Yearly deposits into his bank account from a Hong Kong bank. Yet the man claims income from the sale of scripts to various domestic film-production companies, and his IRS records do not jibe with my findings."

"Sounds circumstantial."

"Perhaps you might look into it," Smith suggested.

"No, thanks."

Smith looked up from his screen, his gray face tinged with phosphorescent green.

"I understood you were interested in an assignment."

"I am. Point me to a drug dealer or a serial killer, and I'll have them in the boneyard by sundown. Those two are already there. You don't need me."

Smith regarded his enforcement arm for a silent moment. The computer beeped again. Smith glanced at the screen.

"Another Chinese body," he remarked. "This one has been identified. Hmm. It seems he also has connections to Hollywood. A producer of films, although no credits are available."

"I hear ticket sales are down. Maybe someone's trying to thin out the competition a little."

"Unlikely," said Smith. "I sincerely hope that these bodies have nothing to do with Squirrelly Chicane's bizarre announcement that she is the new Bunji Lama."

"Me, too," Remo said hastily. "Well, gotta run."

"I will relay Dr. Gerling's opinion when I have it."

"Great, great," said Remo, shutting the door.

Smith stared at the closed door with a puzzled expression riding his patrician features. Remo was behaving more strangely than usual. He hoped it was nothing serious. Usually Chiun's behavior was the more worrisome. He made a mental note to consult with Dr. Gerling at day's end.

His computer beeped twice in warning, and Smith noticed it was precisely 11:59. Instantly he pressed the hidden stud that sent the CURE terminal slipping back into concealment.

At exactly two seconds past noon, Mrs. Mikulka knocked once and entered carrying a maroon tray.

"It's noon, Dr. Smith. I have your prune-whip yogurt."

"Thank you, Mrs. Mikulka," said Smith, who had trained his secretary to be almost as punctual as he. Two seconds was a tolerable variable. But just barely.

## 14

Squirrelly Chicane missed her heart-shaped pink bed. She missed her tape deck and assorted Kitaro and Yanni tapes. But most of all she missed Remo Buttafuoco.

He had saved her life. The pot had to wear off before she realized what had really happened during her beach party.

And all day long bodies kept washing up on the beach.

She had asked Kula to throw them back, and he always did. He made a great bodyguard, even if he was forever complaining of having a humongous case of herpes. If Squirrelly asked him to do something, he did it. He was like a big faithful puppy dog. Once she caught him on his hands and knees drinking out of the toilet like a mastiff. That was probably why he was called a Mongrol.

Still, she missed Remo. But not as much as she missed sleeping in a real bed. The floor wouldn't have been so bad, but both Kula and Lobsang had insisted upon her sleeping on a shelf above the floor. They called it a *kang,* explaining that Bunji Lamas traditionally slept on a *kang.*

The trouble was, Squirrelly kept rolling off. Her back wasn't up to the ordeal. And every time she complained to Lobsang, he fed her a piping-hot cup of tea loaded with rancid melted butter. The man had absolutely no fear of cholesterol.

"There is a lady on the telephone for you, Buddha-Sent One," Kula announced through the closed door where he stood guard, vowing to lay down his life and his yaks and his herpes before any Chinese assassin could get past him.

"What lady?"

"She says she is the number-one lady."

"The number one . . . you mean the First Lady?"

"That is what I said, Presence. The number-one lady."

"That's the call I've been waiting for! Quick, be a good Mongrol and fetch the phone here."

Kula entered, handed over the cordless receiver and bowed himself out of the room. Just watching his contorted posture made Squirrelly's own back cringe.

"Hello?" she said excitedly.

"Squirrelly, this is the First Lady speaking."

"How'd it go? Did you get my visa?"

"Well, it took a real struggle. The Chinese authorities gave me the biggest runaround. First they said it was impossible to process your application in less than three months. Then they admitted they could, but they couldn't guarantee your safety from what they called counterrevolutionary elements."

Squirrelly frowned. "Funny how they turned on me so fast. We used to be such friends. So, how'd you coax them off the mark?"

"First," said the First Lady, "I threatened to revoke their preferred-trade status, then I pointed out that I headed the Presidential Commission on Tibetan Independence and if you, my official representative, couldn't go, then *I* was going."

"You didn't?" Squirrelly squealed.

"I did."

"And they gave in?"

"Caved in. Like a house of cards."

"I love it! I love it! When do I leave?"

"As soon as you want. Listen, it would be a good idea if you went to India first and got the blessing of the Dalai Lama."

"The cute little munchkin with the glasses? He's adorable."

"Make it very high profile. The higher the better. That way they won't dare mess with you."

"I'll give him a kiss for you."

"I'll be watching your progress on CNN. Gotta run. I have meetings all day long. Good luck."

Squirrelly Chicane hung up the phone and immediately dialed a Virginia number.

"Mother, I'm going! This is so great. And listen to this, I'm going to pay the Delhi Lamb a courtesy call."

"Try not to sleep with him, dear. He's a religious figure."

Squirrelly made her voice chilly. "The thought *never* crossed my mind."

"But it would. The older you get, the more like your brother you seem."

"Just for that, no postcards from Tibet for you." And Squirrelly hung up. She leaned back on her hard *kang,* and wondered if there was some ecclesiastical law against two lamas getting it on. She would have to remember to ask Lobsang. He knew all that secret Buddhist stuff.

**15**

The minister of state security entered Beijing's Great Hall of the People wearing his gray Mao suit and carrying his empty hands at his sides.

The premier of China in his own gray Mao suit sat with his hands folded. The premier nodded, indicating the empty chair to his immediate left. His eyes were heavy of lid, as if sleep beckoned. This seeming inattentiveness had fooled many a rival in the near past.

The minister of state security eased into the seat and waited for the premier to speak. They were alone in the Great Hall of the People. That did not mean that they were either unobserved or that their words would not carry to plotting ears. China was at a crossroads. She looked inward, but increasingly the outer world intruded. These were worrisome times.

"What news?" asked the premier in a diffident voice.

"From those who sleep, no word."

The premier's heavy-lidded eyes grew heavier still.

"Perhaps," he said, "their sleep will be long and restful."

"There is no reason to doubt this, Comrade Premier," said the security minister.

And by these oblique words, bland but carefully chosen, both men understood that their sleeper agents in California, across the Pacific Ocean, were either dead or incapacitated.

The silence between them grew long and heavy.

Presently the premier broke it. "Is the visitor who was expected still to come?"

"The visitor has elected to drop in on a relative she did not know existed before journeying farther."

"In times past, these two did not get along so well," the premier noted. "I wonder if this has changed."

"I have not heard."

The premier frowned. "Darkness piles upon darkness, and no one knows when the sun will rise."

"Perhaps the visitor will elect to remain in the house of her newfound relative and not journey farther."

"Can this be encouraged?"

"Anything is possible," said the security minister.

"This would be a good thing if it can be done correctly," said the premier, closing his heavy lids as if to surrender to sleep.

Seeing this, the minister of state security rose from his seat, knowing that the meeting had concluded. Without another word, he padded from the Great Hall of the People to communicate with his assets in India, who would be instructed to proceed with caution inasmuch as the wife of the United States President had taken a personal interest in the Bunji Lama.

**16**

The FedEx trucks were parked in every available parking spot in the street before the impossibly ugly edifice the Master of Sinanju had dubbed Castle Sinanju when Remo Williams pulled up. Although he had a private blacktop parking lot large enough to accommodate more than a dozen cars, Remo had to park his blue Buick Regal on a side street and walk back.

"Christ," Remo muttered under his breath. "I hope Chiun hasn't gone on another Home Shopping Network binge."

The FedEx trucks sat very low on their springs, he noticed. The couriers were walking pretty low to their centers of gravity, too, as they tried to deliver the small wooden crates without herniating themselves.

Then Remo remembered.

"The gold!"

He beat a courier to the door and opened it for him.

"I don't suppose you're M.O.S. Chiun," the courier said, puffing.

Remo took the boom-box-sized crate from the man with one hand. As if it had entered another atmosphere where gravity exerted less pull, the box seemed to become almost buoyant in Remo's hand.

"Nope, but I'm empowered to sign for him."

The courier wiped his brow with his blue uniform sleeve as Remo signed the voucher.

"What's in this thing anyway—lead diving shoes?" the courier grumbled.

Remo shook his head. "Dwarf star matter."

"Huh?"

"Dwarf star matter. Sometimes pieces of it fall to earth. They're so dense that a chunk the size of a basketball weighs as much as Detroit. In order to transport it they have to break it up into tiny pieces. The one in your box is the size of a shirt button."

"You're kidding me."

"I'd show you, but if it falls out of the crate, we'll need a crane to pick it up," Remo said.

"So how come you're handling that crate like it contained marshmallows?"

"I used to bench press dwarf star matter. It's part of my job training."

The courier passed the story along to his fellow drivers, and they began wondering aloud if Remo wouldn't mind carrying the other boxes in, since he had a knack for it.

Remo did mind, but not as much as he minded standing out on the front steps explaining dwarf star matter to twenty different people, all waving clipboards.

By the time Remo got every crate stacked in the inner hall, the Master of Sinanju had deigned to come down.

"Is this what I hope it is?" he squeaked excitedly. "Has my gold arrived?"

"What did you think those trucks were all about? And don't tell me you didn't notice them."

Chiun stopped at the bottom of the inner stairs, sniffed delicately and said, "You have been to see Smith."

"Says who?"

"Says the after-shave lotion clinging to your person. It is the scent that only he wears."

Damn, thought Remo. Chiun had him. Smith wore a cologne that had been discontinued in 1972, and he had purchased a thirty-year supply closeout for two cents on the dollar. "Okay," Remo said tiredly, "I admit it. I saw Smith."

Chiun narrowed his eyes. "About what?"

"Personal stuff."

"What is so personal that you cannot share it with the one who adopted you?"

"Get off my back, Chiun."

"You did not tell Smith about my sunlighting?"

"Rest assured, the name of Squirrelly Chicane did not pass my lips. Except once."

"What is this? What is this?"

"While I was there, the President called. He asked Smith if we could baby-sit Squirrelly in Tibet."

"And what did Smith say?"

"Don't sweat it. Smith said no."

"No? Why did Smith say no? Did he not think we were worthy of the task? Or did he think you were unworthy of so important a responsibility? Oh, Remo, your ineptitude has caused the house great shame."

"It has not. Smith didn't think the Bunji Lama was a CURE problem."

"No?"

"No. Now where do you want this freaking gold?"

"My gold is not freaking."

"This gold is. It weighs a ton."

"It would not be gold if it did not."

"Touché. So where do I put it?"

"I would prefer to have it placed in the meditation room where I may meditate on its fineness and superior quality."

"Don't kid me. You just wanna see that it's all there."

"That, too."

Remo started stacking the crates and carrying them upstairs, ten at a time, five balanced in each palm. He made it look easy. In fact, the balancing allowed him to bear the weight without breaking his forearms.

When all the crates were stacked in the meditation room, some spilling out into the hall, Remo said, "I'm going to bed. I'm bushed."

Chiun's fingernails came together with a click, then disappeared into his generous kimono sleeves. "You are not going to open them for me?" he asked in a wheedling voice.

"No."

"Since you are tired, I forgive you."

"Thanks," said Remo, turning to go.

"Do not forget to shower. You smell like a white."

"I *am* white."

"It is only your skin that is white. It means no more than that the skin of the new Bunji Lama is white."

Remo paused at the door to his bedroom. "If Squirrelly Chicane really is the Bunji Lama, then I *am* a Korean."

Chiun called back, "Do not fall asleep too soon, for wisdom is upon you. Better that you meditate on the truths you have just enunciated."

Remo slammed the door behind him. The entire building reverberated for a full minute after.

THE MASTER REGARDED the closed door with its discordant vibrations for several moments in silence. His parchment face was a mask in which hazel eyes gleamed with an opaque light.

Padding into the meditation room, he ignored the crates of gold that his shrewd bargaining had earned.

Instead, he picked up the telephone and depressed the 1 button as he had seen his pupil do so often. Strange sounds came from the earpiece as the call was routed to a trailer park in Moore, Oklahoma, to foil tracing. Finally the ringing began.

The voice of Harold W. Smith came on the line. "Yes?"

"Hail, Emperor Smith. Greetings from the House of Sinanju."

"Master Chiun. What can I do for you?"

"Remo tells me he has been to see you."

"He has. He is concerned about these...er... seizures."

Chiun clutched the phone more tightly. "Has there been another?"

"No."

"This is good."

"Remo asked me to consult with one of the psychiatrists here," Smith said.

"That is not like him."

"I know, Master Chiun. But he seems unusually troubled."

"It will pass."

"It is to be hoped. I cannot allow my enforcement arm to be at large if he is suffering from some sort of multiple-personality disorder."

"Fear not, Smith. It is nothing of the sort. Remo is merely going through a phase. It will pass."

"And when it does, will Remo be the Remo we know?"

Chiun compressed his thin, papery lips and said nothing. It was a question he could not answer. Possibly a question without any good answer.

"Remo informs me that the matter of Squirrelly Chicane has been brought to your attention," Chiun said at length.

"I declined the President's request that we bodyguard her. It is not our problem."

"Even if some difficulty befalls her?"

"She is an American citizen exercising her prerogative to travel where she will."

"It occurs to me, O Emperor, that perhaps all Remo needs is a vacation."

"I would prefer that one of you remain on standby. Something may come up."

"Very wise, O Smith. Allow me to suggest that Remo be the one to remain standing by. He does that better than I."

"If you wish to take a vacation, by all means. Go."

"I have some property that I must return to my native village. But I do not wish to squander a vacation doing so, for it will be duty, not pleasure, that compels my journey."

"I fail to understand," said Smith.

Chiun's voice lifted. "Do you not recall in my last contract, the clause numbered seventy-eight?"

"Clause seventy-eight?"

"The clause that allows the Master of Sinanju to take leave when he will. Unpaid leave."

"You mean a sabbatical?"

"If that is the proper word, yes."

"By all means, Master Chiun, take a sabbatical."

"Your understanding knows no bounds."

And the Master hung up. Immediately he began packing. Only one trunk this time. The taxi driver managed it quite successfully, causing no damage and retaining his limbs.

Chiun did not awaken Remo. Nor did he bring his roomful of gold with him. There were things more important than gold. Not many, but a few.

One of the most important things was that Remo not accompany him to Tibet. For he might recognize it, and the consequences of that not even the gods could predict.

**17**

High over the Indian Ocean, Squirrelly Chicane was cramming for her high-profile meeting with the Dalai Lama.

She sat cross-legged on an overstuffed cushion that was in turn placed on an exquisite Oriental rug. She swam in her saffron robes, but Lobsang wouldn't allow her to have it taken in by even the finest of Beverly Hills couturiers. Her maroon lama's miter cast a rhinoceros-horn shadow over the pages of her book, making the words hard to read by the overhead lights.

It was night, so throwing aside one of the window hangings on Kula's private plane wouldn't have helped.

It was a neat plane, Squirrelly thought. Like a flying barge. No wonder Kula called it his skyboat. If Cleopatra had lived in the twentieth century, she would have had one just like it.

They were on the last leg of their flight to Delhi. Or Bombay or wherever it was they were going.

When Lobsang had first explained that they were going to the holy land, Squirrelly had said, "We're going to Israel!"

They had looked at her funny. But then they always looked at her funny. They were still getting used to the idea of a Bunji Lama who was both white and female.

"To Buddhists," Lobsang patiently explained, "India is the holy land."

"I've never been to India," Squirrelly had said. "I don't think."

"It is a wonderful land, not only because it is the cradle of Buddhism, but because it is free. Unlike Tibet."

"After I'm done, Tibet will be free."

"First you must relearn your faith."

"I brought my entire collection of Hermann Hesse and William S. Burroughs books."

The two looked blank. Cute but blank.

Squirrelly showed them her copy of *Dharma Lion* and after Kula has translated the title, Lobsang had smiled happily. They were so easy to please.

So Squirrelly had sat down to read. The funny thing was, her copy of *Zen and the Art of Motorcycle Maintenance* had vanished. She knew she had brought it aboard. They had hardly let her bring anything. Lobsang had turned away most of her luggage, saying that her purpose as the Bunji Lama was to renounce the physical world.

They let her keep her stash of *bhang*. For some reason, they had no problem with that. That was when Squirrelly knew that she was going to really like being a Buddhist.

The more she read, the more it confirmed her sense that she had found the perfect spiritual identity in the perfect body. She was the Bunji Lama and she was still Squirrelly Chicane. It was better than sharing that Siamese soul with Mae West.

She liked everything she read about Buddhism. All people and things were in harmony, because everything that happened was predestined to happen. Therefore, no one ever screwed up in the cosmic sense.

"It's all scripted!" Squirrelly had blurted out in a moment of true epiphany. "It all connects!"

Of course, killing was prohibited. Yet no person or thing ever really died in the absolute Western sense of dying. Instead, a soul moved up or down the karmic ladder according to the life that had been led. So while it was bad to kill, no one should be punished for it. Karma would take care of everything.

Further, there were seven heavens and seven hells, instead of the harsh pass-fail Christian system. When you died, you dropped your body like last year's fashions. And when you wanted to pray, you spun a little gimcrack and it prayed for you.

Wonderfully balanced, unjudgmental and hands-off, it was the perfect belief system, Squirrelly decided.

And Buddhas. There were hundreds of Buddhas. As the Bunji Lama, Squirrelly was the reincarnation of the Buddha to Come, who was a really good Buddha to be because everyone looked forward to his return. As a Buddha, Squirrelly would be continually reborn into the world in order to regenerate it by relieving its suffering.

"This makes perfect sense to me," Squirrelly said, patting the dyed-saffron curls that peeped out from under her miterlike lama's cap.

Then the engine whine began to change pitch, and Kula came back from the pilot's compartment to say, "We have arrived, Bunji."

"Fabulous," said Squirrelly, going to a window.

She looked down and saw nothing. Literally. The earth below was like freshly washed blackboard.

"Where is the city? Where are the lights?"

"They are telling us that there are no lights," Kula said unconcernedly.

"What happened to them?"

"No electricity."

"How thoughtful. Conserving the lights at night when they're not needed."

"They are also forbidding us to land."

"Why?"

"The Hindu fear Beijing's displeasure."

"So what do we do?"

Kula beamed. "We land, of course. For we fear no one's displeasure but Buddha's."

The landing was rough. The airport was without power, too. So there was no radar in the tower, no marker lights on the runways, and the boarding ramps were inoperative.

Squirrelly didn't care. The jet's flat tires could be fixed, and she didn't need a ramp. She took a puff of her roach and closed her eyes. But Kula pulled her back before she could invoke her newfound powers of levitation.

After they had rolled the air stairs up to the plane, Kula threw open the hatch. Squirrelly, trying to keep her maroon lama's hat in place, stepped out onto the top step.

First she noticed the crowds. There were none.

Then she noticed the smell.

"What is that awful smell?" she asked, pinching her nose shut and breathing through her mouth.

"What smell?" asked Kula.

Squirrelly yanked him out onto the step with her.

"*That* smell!"

"That is India."

"It smells like a cesspool," Squirrelly said in a nasal tone.

Kula nodded. "Yes, India."

Lobsang joined them, tasted the air with his long nose, seemed to find it acceptable and said, "We have landed in India."

"Does it all smell like this?" Squirrelly asked, still holding her nose.

"This good?" asked Lobsang.

"This *bad.*"

"Some of it is worse. Come, we cannot tarry. Chinese agents may be lurking about."

"Shouldn't we wait for the reception committee? Usually I get the key to the city when I land in a foreign capital."

"The key to New Delhi," Kula said, hustling her down the steps, "is not to remain here for very long."

There was a car waiting. It looked like some British model that had seen better days. Squirrelly got in the back and rolled up the windows. As the car left the airport, the soupy heat made her open them again.

For the remainder of the ride, she alternately rolled the windows up when the smell got to be too much and down again when the heat started wilting her hat.

New Delhi, even blacked out, was a mess. Traffic was a nightmare. A lumbering red bus almost sideswiped them. Wrenching the wheel, Kula swiped back, running the bus off the road and into a ditch where it rolled over three times before coming to a dusty halt on its side.

It seemed that every other bus they encountered tried to run them off the road.

"What's wrong with these bus drivers?" Squirrelly demanded huffily.

Kula shrugged his broad shoulders. "They live in New Delhi, are devout Buddhists and therefore have nothing to lose by dying suddenly. The odds of a better next life are overwhelming."

Beside her, Lobsang was talking. "Now, the Dalai Lama wears a pleasant face," he was saying. "Do not be deceived, Presence. He will be envious of your karmic station."

"I wonder if he'll remember me," Squirrelly murmured.

"From which life?"

"From this one. I met him at a party once. He was a very nice little man."

"When you met him that time, he failed to recognize you for the Bunji Lama, his ancient rival. Now it will be different. Beware the serpent behind the mask. He will appeal to your more trustworthy instincts. He will preach dangerous ideas."

"Like what?"

"Pacifism." The word was a short cobra's hiss.

In front Kula spit on the floorboard.

Squirrelly wrinkled up her gamin face. "Isn't that what Buddha taught?"

"Lord Buddha," Lobsang said in precise tones, "did not suffer under the iron yoke of communism."

And the brittleness in the close confines of the bus-dodging car made Squirrelly Chicane shiver and wonder what she had gotten herself into.

THE DALAI LAMA STOOD outside his temple in exile, surrounded by his retinue, when they entered the dusty hill town of Dharamsala, north of New Delhi, in the shadow of Mun Peak.

He was just as Squirrelly remembered him—a little man with merry but wise eyes behind aviator sunglasses. His robe was maroon. His retinue all wore saffron hats. Squirrelly remembered Lobsang telling her that the Dalai Lama headed the yellow-hat sect of Tibetan Buddhism. As the Bunji Lama, she was the head of the red-hat sect. Personally she would have preferred burgundy.

Walking with her ceremonial bronze *dorje* clutched in one hand, trying to keep her maroon miter in place, Squirrelly floated up the dirt road to where the Dalai Lama awaited.

The Dalai Lama stood with his hands clasped in prayer, his face a pleasant mask. He neither smiled nor blinked, nor did he otherwise acknowledge Squirrelly's arrival. Not even when Squirrelly stopped just six feet in front of him.

"What do I say?" she whispered to Lobsang.

"Say nothing."

"What's he waiting for?"

"For you to bow."

"So why aren't I bowing?"

"To bow would be to acknowledge inferior status."

"Listen, to get out of this frigging heat, I'd get down on my hands and knees and kiss his little saffron sandals."

"Do not bow!" Lobsang warned. "It is in this moment that your supremacy will be decided."

"Does a curtsy count?"

"Do nothing!"

So Squirrelly didn't curtsy. Neither did the Dalai Lama bow.

Then Lobsang spoke up. "Your Holiness, I present to you the forty-seventh Bunji Lama, presently occupying a body known as Squirrelly Chicane."

The Dalai Lama blinked. Members of his retinue craned their shaved heads forward as if seeing her for the first time.

"Is this the selfsame Squirrelly Chicane who was in *Brass Honeysuckle?*" asked one.

Lobsang looked to Squirrelly, at a loss for words.

"Say yes," Squirrelly murmured.

"The answer is yes," said Lobsang.

The stony faces of the regents of the Dalai Lama broke out into smiles of recognition. "It is Squirrelly Chicane!"

They began crowding around.

"Is Richard Gere well?" one asked.

"He's doing great," Squirrelly said, laughing. "Chants every day."

"What tidings from the lotus land of the West?" asked another.

Through it all the Dalai Lama stood impassive behind his mirror aviator glasses.

"He's not budging," Squirrelly whispered to Lobsang.

"He is stubborn," Lobsang advised.

"Yeah? Well, I know just how to break the ice. Here, hold this," said Squirrelly passing her *dorje* to Lobsang. Snapping her fingers once, she accepted a silk-wrapped package from Kula. Untying the drawstring, she brought to light the gleaming Academy Award she had won for *Medium Esteem*.

"Check this out," she crowed.

"It is the icon of the long-lost Bunji Lama!" the regents gasped.

And to the astonishment of all, except Squirrelly Chicane, the Dalai Lama lifted his prayerful hands to his forehead and bowed not once, but five times low and deep.

"May I have your autograph, enlightened one?" he asked humbly.

After that it went swimmingly, Squirrelly thought. They retired to the Dalai Lama's personal quarters, where the regents shut the doors and they drank tea—thankfully without rancid butter—sitting face-to-face on cushions. The Dalai Lama admired Squirrelly's Oscar while she got a good look at his Nobel Peace Prize.

"Strange are the ways in which the Wheel of Destiny turns," said the Dalai Lama.

"I saw this coming, you know. I'm a Taurus. They have the *best* karma."

"Now that you are recognized as the Bunji Lama, what will you do?"

"Liberate Tibet. That's what I'm here for," said Squirrelly, admiring the Nobel. "How hard is it to earn one of these things, anyway?"

The Dalai Lama hesitated over his bowl of tea. "Why do you ask, Bunji?"

"One of these would look great over my mantel between my Oscar and Golden Globe. By the way, may I call you Delhi?"

"'Dalai.' It means 'ocean.' My title means 'ocean of wisdom.' And yes, you may call me that if it is your desire."

"That reminds me. Let's dish, lama to lama." Squirrelly leaned forward. "When we feel the urge, what do we lamas do?"

"We do nothing. To sublimate the lower urges is our purpose in this life."

"Exactly how long have you been sublimating?" Squirrelly wondered.

"All my lives."

"Okaaay. Tell me, if you couldn't free your people after forty years, how'd you snare this baby?"

"I earned the Nobel by keeping the peace. For my way is the way of nonviolence. Is that not your way, Bunji?"

"I've always been nonviolent. Not that it's been easy. Sometimes I wanna give my little brother such a smack."

"I am pleased to hear this. Aggression is not the answer to the problem of Tibet, for the Chinese are many, and Tibetans few and poor."

"Don't sweat the Chinese. I've handled them before."

"These words gladden my heart. For I am the last Dalai Lama. It has so been prophesied. After me there will be no more, and my people are beside themselves at the prospect. But now that the Bunji has returned, hope will spring anew. Perhaps in two or even three decades, Tibet will breathe the sweet air of freedom once more."

Squirrelly squinted under her fleece-lined lama's cap. "Two or three decades? I figure it'll take two or three weeks."

"Weeks?"

"Sure," Squirrelly said, ticking off her plans on her saffron-nailed fingers. "Two or three weeks to liberate Tibet. Maybe another week or so for a goodwill tour of the major villages. Six months to write the book. And three to film."

"Film?"

Squirrelly flung her arms wide as if to encompass the entire world. "Won't this make a great movie? Internationally famous American actress plucked from cosmic obscurity to liberate a downtrodden people. Talk about high concept!"

"I fail to follow your thinking, Bunji Rinpoche."

"Oh, I love it when people call me that. Listen, you have a really photogenic face. Wanna play yourself?"

"Play?"

"I may end up doing *Lamb of Light* as a musical, though. Like *Evita*. How good are your pipes?"

"But you are the Bunji. It is your destiny to rule Tibet—if the Chinese do not assassinate you first."

"They already tried that," Squirrelly said dismissively. "Now that I have the First Lady on my side, I'm protected. If anything happens to me, she'd have them nuked."

"You would not encourage a nuclear attack on China?"

"Not me. By that time I'll be well into my next life and as long as I didn't come back as a Chinese citizen, I probably wouldn't care."

A knock came at the door. The Dalai Lama perked up.

"Ah, it is dinner. We will eat and talk more. Enter."

Servants entered, bearing fragrant foods on silver trays.

Kula and Lobsang hovered nearby.

Squirrelly tasted the air. "Smells scrumptious. What is all this stuff?"

"That is *tsampa*."

"Looks like Maypo. What about this soup?"

"That is *thukpa*—noodle soup. Very tasty."

"Tibetan pasta? I love it!"

"Do not eat yet."

"Why not? Do we say some kind of Buddhist grace first?"

"We must await the food taster."

"Food taster?"

"It is a precaution in case of poison."

"Who would try to poison you? You're so sweet."

"You," said the Dalai Lama without rancor.

"Hey, give a gal a break. I'm a fellow Buddhist, after all."

The food taster came in, bowed to each of them, and, under the watchful eyes of Lobsang Drom, Kula and the Dalai Lama's retinue, and the horrified eyes of Squirrelly Chicane, lifted each bowl in turn and slurped up generous portions.

"Don't you feed this guy?" Squirrelly asked.

"He is kept in a state of perpetual famishment," the Dalai Lama explained, "so that he will not balk at the task before him."

After he had tasted everything, the food taster sat down and everyone looked expectant.

Squirrelly squinted at him. "What are we waiting for, this poor guy to die?"

"Yes," said Kula.

"Oh. How long does that usually take?"

"If the food has cooled and he still breathes, the food is unpoisoned."

"Oooh, I hate cold food."

"As the Bunji Lama, it is your sacred duty to renounce the temptations of the material world," Lobsang intoned.

"Hot food isn't a temptation, but a necessity," said Squirrelly, dipping a surreptitious finger into her *tsampa*. Maybe she could sneak a taste while everybody was waiting for the food taster to keel over.

Squirrelly had her *tsampa*-smeared finger tucked up under her chin and was about to go for it when the food taster turned a sickly green and keeled left. He began breathing in a labored fashion. This lasted not very long at all. Just until the death rattle.

After the color left his face for the last time, the others grew stony of visage. The retinue of the Dalai Lama glared at Lobsang and Kula, who glowered back. Kula fingered his dagger.

Squirrelly swallowed hard. "The food's poisoned, huh?"

"Yes," said Lobsang. "But whose food? The Bunji's or the Dalai's?"

The glaring and glowering resumed.

"Tell you what," offered Squirrelly, wiping her forefinger on the cushion, "why don't we just throw it all out and start over? I make a mean seven-bean salad."

"I will fetch the cook," said Kula, storming from the room.

The cook was fetched. He was a plump little Tibetan with a face like unbaked cookie dough. He trembled like a human pudding in a steady wind.

"Why did you poison the food, cook?" Kula demanded.

"I did not."

Kula brought his silver dagger up to the cook's throbbing jugular. "You lie! I slit the throats of liars."

"I did not poison the food! It was the Chinese man."

"What Chinese man?"

"He told me that my sister in Lhasa would be violated if I did not look the other way while he put something in the food."

"Whose food? The Bunji's or the Dalai's?"

"The Bunji's."

"You are certain?"

"I would not lie, Mongol," quavered the cook. "For I know you would slit my throat if I did this."

"Good. It is good that you told the truth," said Kula, abruptly yanking the cook's head around to slice his throat open.

"Why did you do that?" Squirrelly cried, turning away.

"I also slit the throats of traitors," said Kula, wiping his blade clean on the dead man's hair.

Squirrelly stared at the dead cook a long time. Then it hit her.

"They tried to kill me," she said in a dull, shocked voice.

"Yes," said Kula.

"We must find the compassion to forgive them," intoned the Dalai Lama.

"They tried to kill me again. Even with the First Lady on my side." Her voice was smoldering now.

"The Chinese are in truth demons," said Lobsang. "Demons without souls."

"Take your anger and transmute it into understanding," intoned the Dalai Lama. "Use your newfound understanding to bring about true harmony. Illuminate the Universe with your light."

Squirrelly Chicane rose from her cushion, her blue eyes stark. Lifting a trembling fist to the ceiling, she said, "This means war!"

"War is not the way of Buddha," the Dalai Lama said anxiously. "It is unworthy of one who is in truth a Living Buddha."

"Well, war is the way of this Buddha!" Squirrelly vowed. "We're going to march in there and kick their yellow butts all the way back to Beijing!"

The Dalai bowed his head in sorrow.

"She is a fighting Buddhist, after all," Kula said in an emotion-choked voice. "It is better than I dared hope for."

**18**

It was the end of the month and time to pay the bills that had piled up on Dr. Harold W. Smith's Spartan desk.

The Folcroft bills were in the low five figures. It was possible to dispose of them with only a cursory glance at the various invoices, bills and utility notices.

That done, he took a deep breath and two Alka-Seltzer washed down by spring water from his office dispenser before looking into the CURE-related bills.

These—principally credit-card bills and other incidentals—were sent to a blind post-office box to which only Smith had the key. It was not an ideal situation, but he could not trust Remo, and certainly not Chiun, to remember to pay their own bills on time.

And regardless of how high these bills were, Harold W. Smith always paid them promptly. It rankled his frugal New England soul to spend taxpayer dollars on what often seemed frivolous items, such as Remo's quarterly car trade-in. But in the end it was a small price to pay to keep Remo and Chiun, if not happy, at least not disposed to complain often.

And he never, ever paid credit-card interest. Not in the days when it was a modest six percent and certainly not now that the credit-card companies had begun charging usurious interest rates.

The bills this month amounted to a surprisingly small sum, Smith was relieved to see. Less than fifty thousand dollars. This was down from the last quarter after Chiun had discovered the Home Shopping Network and splurged, seemingly, on one of every item offered over a two-week period, including two cases of a product inexplicably called Hair in a Can.

Smith took another gulp of Alka-Seltzer and examined the charges line by line.

In the card that was issued to Remo Buttafuoco, he noticed a round-trip airlines ticket for two. He wondered where Remo and Chiun had gone. Then he saw on the very next line a two-day car rental from a Los Angeles franchise of a well-known agency. The next item indicated the car had been serviced in Malibu.

Smith frowned. Malibu. Malibu. Why did Malibu ring a warning bell in his memory?

And then he remembered. The attempt on Squirrelly Chicane three days before in Malibu, and the waves of suspicious dead Chinese bodies that had been washing up on the beach ever since.

"What on earth . . ."

Face slack with concern, Smith went to his computer and checked the Bunji file.

Six bodies now. As he read the latest reports, he realized that the dead men had been killed in ways that were consistent with both Remo and Chiun's methods of operation. The disemboweled man might as easily have been eviscerated by a superhard fingernail as a knife. And those who had been found with crushed larynxes and faces jellied beyond recognition bore Remo's hallmarks. He should have recognized the signs before, Smith realized grimly.

Harold Smith picked up the phone and dialed Remo's contact number.

A sleepy voice answered, "I'm not home. Go away."

"Remo. This is Smith."

"Smitty, what's the good word? Or in your case, the bad one?"

"The word," Smith said stiffly, "is that I know you and Chiun were involved with the Chinese deaths in Malibu."

"Okay," Remo said without skipping a beat. "It's too early in the morning to lie. We were."

"Please explain the situation to me, Remo," Smith said coldly. "This was not an authorized operation."

"You'd better talk to Chiun. It was kinda his operation."

"I would like to hear it from you first."

Remo's voice turned away and lifted. "Hey, Chiun! Smitty's on the phone for you!"

"Remo, I said—"

"Chiun! You up?"

Silence.

Remo's voice came back. "Damn. Hold the phone, Smitty."

Smith gripped the telephone receiver with unshakable tightness as he listened to the faint sounds of doors opening and closing and Remo returning.

"He's gone," said Remo.

"I will hear your explanation first."

"You don't understand, Smitty. Chiun's really gone. Two of his trunks are missing, but the freaking gold's still here."

"Gold. What gold?"

"The freaking gold he got off those Mongols."

"Mongols? What Mongols? Remo, start at the beginning, please."

"How about I just cut to the chase and let's see where that takes us," Remo said unhappily.

"Go ahead."

"You know the story about the Tibetan monk who showed up on Squirrelly Chicane's doorstep and proclaimed her the Bunji Lama?"

"Yes."

"Well, first he showed up on my doorstep. Along with that Mongol, Kula. Remember him from the Gulf War?"

"Go on."

"Well, they asked Chiun to help them find the Bunji Lama."

"Find? You mean—"

"Yeah, Chiun led them straight to Squirrelly. He went through a lot of hocus-pocus to set them up for the scam, but in the end he just turned on 'The Poopi Silverfish Show' and there she was."

"Poopi Silverfish?"

"No, Squirrelly Chicane. She was into one of her past-life rags, and Lobsang just lapped it up."

"Lobsang was the Tibetan monk?"

"You got it."

"Where do you fit into this, Remo?"

"Me? I was just along for the ride. Carrying luggage and collecting abuse. When the Chinese tried to hit Squirrelly, Chiun and I were there and we hit them first. That's about the only good thing that came out of the trip."

"I disagree," Smith said in a cold voice. "It would have been far better had Squirrelly Chicane been assassinated than she go through with her ridiculous scheme to insert herself into the Tibetan situation."

"Don't look now, but I think Chiun's gone and introduced himself into the Tibetan situation, too."

"You may be right, Remo," said Smith in a tight voice. "He called me yesterday and requested a sabbatical."

"He say where he was going?"

"Back to the village of Sinanju, was my understanding."

"That should be easy to check. Just dial 1-800-SINANJU. If he's not there or expected, he's off to Tibet."

"One moment, Remo," said Smith, switching phone lines. He dialed 1-800-SINANJU, and a querulous old voice began speaking in Korean.

"I...er...seek the Master of Sinanju," Smith said in carefully enunciated English.

"His awesome magnificence is not here," the voice said, switching to formal but thick English.

"Is he expected?"

"He is not expected. Do you wish someone dispatched? Or a throne toppled?"

"Thank you, no, I will call later."

"Others give inferior service. Provide your telephone number, and the Master of Sinanju will return your call if you are found worthy of the honor."

"Thank you, no."

Switching lines again, Smith told Remo, "He is not expected in Sinanju. He must be in Tibet."

"Great," Remo groaned. "I don't know who to feel sorry for, the Tibetans or the Chinese."

"Remo," Smith said urgently, "it is imperative that Squirrelly Chicane not upset the balance of power in Tibet."

"Balance? It's a Chinese slave state. Where's the balance?"

"Here is the balance. Remo, Tibet is largely plateau. It is, in effect, the high ground of Asia. From there the Chinese look down upon India, which they consider an enemy. Tibet is a natural impassable barrier to the hostile forces beneath it. Also we know that the Chinese store some of their short-range missiles in the more inaccessible parts of Tibet. They consider the Tibetan question very sensitive and they are determined to hold on to it."

"So I see by the papers."

"Open revolt in Tibet could bring in Mongolia or India, which have religious ties to Tibet. If there is a new Sino-Indian conflict, Pakistan, China's ally and India's bitter enemy, will no doubt open up a second front. Pakistan is a nuclear power. You know what that means?"

"Yeah. Bye-bye, India. Damn."

"Leave for Tibet immediately, Remo."

"What happened to 'Tibet is none of our business'?"

"It wasn't and it isn't. But now that I know that the Master of Sinanju has triggered the chain of events now building toward crisis, it is our responsibility to interdict Squirrelly Chicane."

"What do you mean 'we,' white eyes?" Remo muttered.

**19**

The night before she was to leave India for Tibet, the forty-seventh Bunji Lama could not sleep.

She tossed on her *kang* and dreamed wild dreams. This much the scriptures later recorded. What they failed to record was that chocolate-covered cherries as much as insomnia kept her from sleep.

She sat up, too enervated for rest, and with her perfect teeth—indicating her high state of spiritual evolution—she broke the outer chocolate shell and sucked the sweet nectar that was within.

From time to time she hummed to herself. Often she sang softly.

"I am the Buddha.
The Buddha is me.
I found myself under the bodhi tree.
Don't cry for me, Pasadeeenaaa."

Outside the Dalai Lama's Dharamsala abode, the Tibetan exile community gathered around, spinning their tassled prayer wheels in their hands. Those who understood English translated for the others.

"The new Bunji Lama sings as sweetly as any woman," it was said.

"Move over, Evita," the Bunji was heard to sing.

This was not so easily translated, and became a point of much contention to Buddhist scholars in the next century.

"Bunji! Bunji!" they cried. "Give us your blessings, O Bunji."

Squirrelly Chicane heard the calls, but did not understand the words. She did not need to understand. It was her public calling, her new public, and she could not ignore them.

Swathed in her saffron robes, her peaked lama's cap making her seem taller than her diminutive dancer's stature, she stepped out onto the great balcony where the Dalai Lama held his audiences.

She was blowing kisses to the wild approval of the crowd when Lobsang appeared at her side.

"What are they saying?" she asked.

"They wish only to drink in your wisdom, Buddha Sent," Lobsang said.

"I'll pontificate, you translate," Squirrelly said. Lifting her voice, she said, "Today is the first day of the rest of your life."

Lobsang recast the words into Tibetan and then Hindi.

"Squeeze the day!" Squirrelly added.

The crowd gasped. They began to prostrate themselves, throwing their bodies to the ground and bumping their foreheads on the dirt. It looked wonderfully aerobic.

"They are with you, Bunji," Lobsang said.

"Great! Tell them—oh, tell them life is just a bowl of cherries."

Lobsang translated. The prostrating abruptly ceased. Blinking, dubious eyes lifted toward the Bunji Lama.

"What's wrong?" Squirrelly asked.

"They do not understand cherries."

"What's to understand? A cherry is a cherry."

"They are poor and have never seen a cherry, much less eaten one."

"Then tell them life is a bowl of *tsampa*."

After Lobsang translated this, a sea of foreheads began bumping the ground again.

"You know," Squirrelly said as she basked in the strenuous worship of her new public, "I can see an exercise video coming out of this—*Bumping with the Bunji*."

WHEN THE SUN CAME UP, the gilt palanquin of the Dalai was brought from storage. The Tibetans wept to see it. It had been used to bear the Dalai into exile and now it was to carry the greatest lama of all time back to Lhasa, where she would seize the Lion Throne and cast out the cruel Han Chinese.

They lined the road leading to the mountain pass. All the way to the border they stood side by side like human flowers.

Some were fortunate enough to witness the Bunji emerge from the house of the Dalai Lama. They gaped to see the Dalai prostrate himself six times to the Bunji and the Bunji did not bow back once.

Then, with stately majesty, the Bunji stepped into the palanquin, and the bearers lifted it with not a grunt of complaint.

It was as if the Bunji weighed less than a snapdragon.

The palanquin lurched forward. A ferocious Mongol walked ahead of it, glowering and searching the faces of the crowd for would-be assassins. He carried high the saffron parasol of the Dalai Lama, signifying that a torch had been passed to a new spiritual leader.

The regent of the Bunji strode beside the palanquin. Lobsang Drom walked proud with his head held high, but no one had eyes for him.

All eyes were fixed on the Bunji Lama.

"The Bunji has as sweet a face as any woman's," it was said. All noticed the Bunji's saffron robes. Even the Bunji's nails, long and tapered, were saffron. Truly, people whispered, this was the god-king of the old days returned.

As the palanquin moved closer to the border, the crowds began to follow. They formed a tail, a thousand people long. They were Tibetans and Indians, Khampas and Nepalese.

In their individual languages, they cried out their joy and their hopes.

"*Bunji Lama zindabad!*" cried the Indians in Hindi. "Long live the Bunji Lama."

"*Lama kieno!*" shouted the Tibetans. "Know it, O Lama!"

"We're gonna kick Chinese butt," the Bunji shouted back, and although no one in those days knew what it meant, the cry of the Bunji Lama was taken up by the lips of all worshipers, regardless of nationality. Apart for centuries, they were united by the Light That had Come.

"We're gonna kick Chinese butt!" they chanted over and over, few understanding their own words.

"Your people are with you, Presence," Kula the Mongol boomed out in his thunderous voice.

"This," the Bunji was overheard to say, "is only the first reel."

INTO THE MOUNTAINOUS frontier of what the Chinese authorities called the Tibetan Autonomous Region, a man came running. He wore the dark turban and bushy beard of a Sikh hill man.

Panting, he approached the checkpoint where People's Liberation Army border troops guarded the narrow pass that the Dalai Lama had taken into ignominious exile decades before. Beyond it lay the snowy dome called Mt. Kailas, and at its foot the impossibly blue sky-mirrors of Lakes Manasarowar and Rakas Tal.

For over an hour the nervous PLA soldiers detected a growing mutter to the west, very disturbing to the ears. There were rumors of the Bunji Lama's return, but being Chinese, they knew not what it meant.

"Do not shoot! Do not shoot! I am Han! Like you, I am Han!"

The Han soldiers of Beijing held their fire. The hill man came ripping off his beard and turban to show that he was of their blood and color. A Chinese.

"I am Wangdi Chung," he said, puffing. "And I have failed to poison the Bunji Lama. She comes."

"She?"

"It is a she."

The soldiers of Beijing looked at one another in puzzlement. One woman. What was the difficulty? She would be taken into custody if her papers were not in order. And since the soldiers of Beijing were simple farmers' sons and could not read, the Bunji Lama's papers could not possibly be in order.

"You do not understand, you stupid turtle eggs!" Wangdi Chung cursed. "The Bunji Lama is followed by a thousand adherents."

The soldiers looked at one another again. There were three of them. One, the sergeant, was in charge of the other two. Each man had a Type 57 assault rifle and a side arm. The sergeant had responsibility for their bullets. He went to the steel ammunition box and checked the number of rounds. It was very low. He came back to report this to the agitated Intelligence agent.

"There are enough bullets to kill the Bunji Lama and twenty or twenty-five others if no round goes astray."

"If you kill the Bunji Lama, we will all be torn limb from limb," warned Wangdi Chung.

The soldiers of China laughed. In their years in Tibet, they had not known a Tibetan to do more than curse at an offense.

"They are Buddhists. They will not fight."

"Walking before them is a Mongol warrior as fierce as any I have ever seen."

"One Mongol?"

"One Mongol."

The faces of the Han soldiers said that was different. Very different.

"We do not have enough bullets to stop a Mongol," the sergeant said, looking at his bullets unhappily. "But what can we do? If we abandon our post, we will be executed and our relatives will be sent the bill for the very bullets that execute us."

The soldiers fretted and discussed their conundrum, while down in the hot plains of India, the mutter of human voices grew and swelled and began echoing off the mountains. It took the form of a woman singing:

"I am the Buddha,
The Buddha is me.
Predestination is the place to be!"

"We're gonna kick Chinese butt!" chorused a thousand voices.

After Wangdi Chung translated the English threat into Chinese, the soldiers of Beijing shot him dead and fled into the mountains.

And in this fashion did the historic train of the Bunji Lama enter the mountains that ring Tibet, and Tibet itself.

THE MINISTER of state security debated with himself the best way to communicate failure to the premier of China as he waited for the operator to connect him with the Great Hall of the People.

There was nothing in Mao's *Little Red Book* that fitted the circumstance. Or if there was, he could not find it.

Presently the smoky voice of the premier came on the line. "What is it?"

The security minister hesitated. He must do this clearly yet diplomatically, for the telephone line might have unwelcome ears.

"Speak!"

"When the old gentleman on the border lost his horse, who could know that it was not actually good fortune?" the security minister said, hoping that a Confucian epigram did not offend the premier's ears.

To his surprise, the premier responded with a Confucian epigram of his own. "The head of the cow does not fit the mouth of the horse."

The minister of state security searched his mind for a suitable rejoinder. "When one enters a place, he should follow the customs thereof," he said.

"Ah," said the premier. "I hear thunder out of a clear sky. How many follow the red hat?"

A direct question. He gave a direct answer. "One thousand, two thousand. It is difficult to know how to accommodate so many visitors under my current instructions."

There it was. Out in the open. The minister of state security waited for the reply.

"How many cameras record these events?"

"Cameras?"

"Television cameras."

"None."

"Ah," said the premier. The pause on the line was marked by the premier's slow, labored breathing. It was said that excessive tobacco smoking was the cause. Already the buzzards of the politburo were gathering about the premier, and his life was not yet spent.

"Do you remember the old proverb, 'Kill a monkey to frighten the chickens'?"

"Yes."

"I knew you would," said the premier, who then terminated the conversation.

The minister of state security listened to the buzz of the dead line for a full thirty seconds before he replaced it with a trembling hand.

Here in his office—one of the most powerful in Beijing—he would have to come to a most difficult decision.

It was one thing to arrange for a poisoning on Indian soil and cast suspicion on a rival lama. It was another to engineer the death of the Bunji Lama on

Tibetan soil. If things went badly, blame would attach itself to the state security ministry. And the storm that was gathering promised to move across international borders.

No piece of paper, no whisper of conversation, could lawfully prove that the premier of China had ordered this thing to be done.

Yet it must be done, or the minister of state security would lose the support of the most powerful man in all of China—even if they whispered that he had the life expectancy of an elderly rabbit.

It was a difficult thing, this not knowing what to do.

**20**

The Bunji Lama had a splitting headache as her palanquin was borne through the Gurla Pass and into the mountains. Every two or three hundred feet she called her train to a halt and went behind a rock to regurgitate the contents of her stomach.

"Look how the Bunji shows us that she understands our suffering," the followers of the Bunji Lama whispered. "She has willed herself to share our pain."

It was later so written into the scriptures, but in the early hours of the Bunji Lama's return to Tibet, her sufferings were constant. So were her complaints—although the scriptures made no mention of these things.

"Anybody got any Excedrin extrastrength?" the Bunji called out as she was helped into her palanquin, whose gold-fringed roof protected her from the harsh sun and elements.

"You must overcome all suffering," Lobsang Drom cautioned.

"What's wrong with me? I can't keep down food, and my head feels like some heavy-metal moron mistook it for a bass drum."

"Altitude sickness," explained Kula, pounding his chest. "You are breathing the sacred air of the Himalayas. It is good for you."

"I feel like I'm gonna die!" Squirrelly Chicane moaned, throwing herself onto her silken cushions.

"If you die," warned Lobsang Drom, "you will only have to make this journey again in your next life."

"Don't remind me," Squirrelly said, burying her head under a mountain of pillows. "I gotta do something about this headache."

The palanquin began bumping along mountain trails again, and the procession followed, a thousand voices lifting in prayer and a thousand prayer wheels spinning and spinning.

*"Om mani padme hum,"* they droned.

"Tell them to stop," groaned Squirrelly.

"We cannot. They must pray to ward off the mountain demons and the Chinese."

"Who's the Bunji Lama around here—you or me? Tell them to stop."

"It is impossible," said Lobsang stubbornly.

Squirrelly opened her bloodshot blue eyes and sat up. Her stomach jumped. She hadn't felt this bad since she'd crossed the mystic midlife barrier.

"For a bit player, you act like the director," she said.

"You have much to learn, O Bunji."

The face of the Tibetan looked altogether too smug, Squirrelly thought. She rummaged around in a tiny purse. Maybe there was some aspirin there. She found no aspirin, but there was a half-smoked cigarette, squeezed in a gold roach clip.

"Anybody got a light?" she asked, sticking the butt out of the palanquin.

A helpful Tibetan man trotted up and tried to light it on the run. He was using some kind of tinderbox. It took three minutes, but the cigarette began smoldering fitfully.

Squirrelly smoked her way up into the rarefied air of the roof of the world and tried to concentrate on the task at hand.

She had a first act. That was perfect, except for this altitude-sickness crap. The third act would work itself out. How hard could it be to talk the Chinese into being reasonable? They were Buddhists, too. Closet Buddhists, maybe, but Buddhists to the bone. It was in their blood.

But here she was three hours into what would have to be the second act, and so far all that was happening was a blinding headache and a lot of vomiting.

Audiences wouldn't sit still for watching Squirrelly Chicane actually throwing up in Technicolor. A little suffering went a long way, entertainment-wise.

"Maybe I'll keep the headache and cut all this vomiting."

"You must clear your body of all distractions, Bunji," Lobsang intoned.

That was another thing. She needed a male lead. So far, all she had were character-actor types. If only that yummy Remo had come along. He would have been perfect.

Maybe, Squirrelly thought, if nothing better presented itself, she would expand his part. Write him into the screenplay. Of course, there was no way he was going to be in the book. But audiences would understand if she took certain liberties in order to dramatize events.

But who the hell could play him? Richard Gere? Not intense enough. Steven Seagal? Rumor was he was a rammer. Squirrelly Chicane did not play opposite rammers. Ken Wahl had the right look, but his career had gone so far south the joke was he slept with the penguins. And Fred Ward was losing his hair, for goodness' sake.

It was, she decided as the sickly sweet smoke made her pounding head feel as big as a weather balloon, going to be a huge problem.

THERE WERE TANKS waiting for them at the bottom of the mountain. T-64s with the red star of China on their turrets.

Stony-faced soldiers in olive drab stood blocking the roads, their AK-47s held before them, spike bayonets fixed.

Squirrelly discovered this when Lobsang reached in and shook her awake.

"Bunji. The hour of reckoning has come."

"The what?" Squirrelly said dreamily.

"The climax."

"Oh, I love climaxes," Squirrelly said, turning over and crushing her face against a pillow. "Did I come?"

A strong hand reached in and pulled her out by her hair. She stood in her slippered feet, her maroon lama's cap squashed down on her head.

Squirrelly lifted the lamb's-fleece fringe off her forehead so she could see.

She saw Kula, looking grim.

"Is that any way to treat a lama?" she said.

"We will face the Chinese together."

Squirrelly looked in the direction of the Mongol's sideways glance. She saw three tanks and the soldiers.

"What do I do?" she whispered.

"You will know," said Kula.

An official-looking man in a green uniform advanced, flanked by two soldiers in PLA olive drab.

"I am PSB man. Public Security Bureau," he said. "You are Squirrelly Chicane?"

"I have a visa."

"I will see your visa."

Squirrelly dug it out of her purse.

The PSB man looked at it carefully and said, "I must search your belongings for contraband."

"All I have," said Squirrelly, smiling her best curl-their-toes smile, "are what you see here. My palanquin and a few close personal friends." She waved airily in the direction of her train, whose numbers seemed to reach back to the horizon.

"Do they have entry visa?"

"Permission was given for the Bunji to be accompanied by her retinue," Lobsang pointed out.

"All these?"

"Hey, I'm planning a really big production," Squirrelly said quickly. "I need crew to scout locations, set up liaisons and research local costumes and exteriors. By the way, do you happen to know where we can find some really good Tibetan sound stages?"

The PSB man looked at her with the bland expression of someone who understood little and feared to lose face. "I will examine belongings now," he said.

Squirrelly waved him to her palanquin, where her few belongings were. "Feel free."

Soldiers rushed up and used their spike bayonets to poke among the cushions. Finding nothing, they started spearing them and hurling them away.

"Hey! Be careful! That's my best palanquin."

She was ignored. Behind them the train of the Bunji Lama stood somberly and spun their prayer wheels.

Surreptitiously Squirrelly signaled them to spin faster.

The prayer wheels cranked in agitation, varicolored tassels becoming blurs.

Squirrelly smiled. This was great. Look at that backdrop. The wedgewood sky. The cast of extras. It was the perfect panoramic wide-angle-lens shot. This wouldn't be just another Squirrelly Chicane movie. This was going to be an epic. Maybe the last of the epics. She could already smell the box-office dollars.

Suddenly the PSB official flung her purse to ground. He was holding her roach clip. It squeezed the burned-down butt of her last reefer. Digging farther, he came upon her stash of *bhang*.

"Contraband!" he barked.

"Oh, give me a break," Squirrelly snapped. "It's less than an ounce. Personal use. Savvy?"

The PSB shouted something in Mandarin and waved for the skirmish line of soldiers to advance.

"What did he say?" Squirrelly asked Kula.

Kula gripped his bone-handled knife and hissed, "He has ordered our arrest."

"Arrest?"

"We are to be taken to prison."

"Prison?"

Windburned eyes narrowing, Kula unsheathed his silver dagger.

Squirrelly knocked it from his hand. "Are you crazy?" she spat. "Put that thing away."

"We will not be taken by Chinese," Kula said through tight teeth.

"Don't go Klingon on me. Don't you see this is perfect? The misunderstood and cruelly persecuted Bunji Lama is summarily hauled off to prison. That's our second act!"

**21**

On the outskirts of the frontier town of Zhangmu, just inside Tibet, Remo Williams stood by the side of the Nepalese-Tibetan Friendship Highway waiting for an Isuzu WuShiLing to come by.

So far, all he had seen were the clunky old green Jiefeng trucks. He was starting to think he'd have to settle for a Dongfeng, which, according to the hitchhikers' guidebook he'd picked up in Hong Kong, was not as roomy as a WuShiLing, but definitely faster than a Jiefeng.

Normally Smith's connections could get Remo to almost any spot on earth. But the Chinese had cut off Tibet's few commercial airports, sealed its borders to foreigners, and only necessary commercial truck traffic was passing through ground checkpoints.

Remo had checked in with Smith when he reached the Hong Kong airport.

"There are reports the Bunji Lama has crossed the border of Tibet," Smith had told him, his voice grim, "followed by a train of upward of a thousand pilgrims."

"Any word of Chiun?"

"No," Smith had said.

"Maybe you should call 1-800-GENGHIS."

"I beg your pardon?"

"Boldbator Khan has an 800 number of his own."

"You are joking."

"I called it myself."

Over the miles of intangible phone line, Remo could almost hear Harold Smith mentally debating whether or not to accept Remo's word.

"Can't hurt to call," Remo prompted.

"One moment," said Smith.

He came back a moment later, saying, "The line is busy."

"Must be a run on looting and pillaging," Remo said dryly. "But it was Boldbator who hired Chiun to find the Bunji Lama. Maybe he's trying to chisel another roomful of gold to save her from the Chinese."

"And there is no doubt if Miss Chicane and her entourage have crossed the border, PLA units will be sent to intercept them," Smith said tightly.

"So what do we do?"

Smith was silent a moment. "Change your plans. Do not fly to New Delhi. Go to Nepal. From Katmandu you can enter Tibet and reach any number of points as developments warrant. Contact me when you arrive."

In Katmandu, Remo had called Smith again.

"Squirrelly Chicane has been arrested by the Chinese authorities," Smith reported. "It just came over the wire."

"So much for the First Lady's guarantee."

Smith cleared his throat unhappily. "I believe the charge is drug possession. This could be extremely embarrassing for the First Lady."

"Can't have the First Lady embarrassed," Remo said. "Congress might faint dead away. So what do I do now?"

"Miss Chicane has been taken to Lhasa, the Tibetan capital. Cross the Nepalese border on foot. Once you bypass customs and Public Security Bureau posts, it should be easy to hitchhike to Lhasa along the Friendship Highway."

"Hitchhike? Is that the best you can do?"

"Unfortunately, yes. In Lhasa, make contact there with Bumba Fun."

"Who's he—the local Bozo the clown?"

"Bumba Fun is a member of Chushi Gangdruk. Tibetan resistance."

"The Tibetans have resistance fighters? How come I never heard of them?"

"Because when they are successful," Smith said dryly, "the Chinese occupation suppresses news of their exploits, and when they are not they are tortured and executed in secret. Bumba Fun will be your guide."

"I don't need a guide."

"Do you speak Tibetan?"

"No."

"Can you pass for Tibetan?"

"You know I can't."

"You will need Bumba Fun."

AND SO REMO STOOD on a dusty road on the outskirts of a truck depot just inside Tibet waiting for a modern WuShiLing, or at least a semimodern brown Dongfeng. But definitely not a Jiefeng truck, because the guidebook had warned him they were slow and breakdown prone, and there was hardly any room in the cabin for the driver, never mind a passenger.

After two hours of nothing but Jiefengs, Remo gave up. The next Dongfeng or Jiefeng that came along, he decided, was his. He just hoped the driver had bathed some time in the past six months.

The next truck turned out to be a shiny new Wu-ShiLing, so Remo figured his luck was starting to change.

Following the guidebook's directions, Remo popped his thumbs up, stacking his fists while making butter-churning motions.

The driver brought his truck to a screeching, dusty halt. He had a wise old windburned face with merry eyes. He might have been thirty; he might have been fifty. The harsh mountains aged people mercilessly. He wore a tight-fitting winter hat with hanging earflaps. When he stuck out his tongue in greeting, he reminded Remo of a middle-aged fourth-grader.

"Lhasa?" said Remo.

"Shigatse," said the driver.

"Is that near Lhasa?" asked Remo.

"Yes, yes. Only one, two hundred mile nearby."

"Close enough for government work," said Remo, climbing in.

The driver got the truck in gear and asked, "What your name?"

"Remo."

"Re-mo. Good name. No other name?"

"Buttafuoco," said Remo.

"It is a proud name."

"Back in America you can't hardly go a day without hearing it."

"Journalist?"

"I'm with the *Socialist Workers' Weekly*."

The driver spit.

"But I'm really a CIA agent," Remo added.

The driver gave his chest a pound that made his earflaps dance. "CIA good. Kick Communist behind. Why you go Lhasa? Much trouble there."

"I got a date with the Bunji Lama."

*"Tashi delek."*

"What does that mean?" asked Remo.

The driver laughed. "Good luck. Good luck to you and Bunji Lama. He-he-he-he."

The road was a snake track. Every road in Tibet, it seemed, was a snake track winding in and around towering mountains, scarps and snowcaps and then dropping into valleys that were yellow with mustard and lush green gorges.

Mostly, however, Tibet was a place of mountains. Every time they put a mountain behind them, up ahead loomed three or four new snowcaps. It was like driving through a video-game landscape of repeating horizons, except these were not monotonous but breathtaking in their sheer endlessness.

Remo had never been a big fan of mountains, but he couldn't take his eyes off these.

The driver double-clutched like a madman, taking hairpin turns with a reckless joy. Several times Remo was sure the wheels on his side were spinning over thin air. He kept one hand on the door handle in case they went over and he had to jump free.

The road degenerated to gravel, and in other places was a narrow passage through the remains of a long-ago rockslide. The wreckage of abandoned cars and trucks rusted along the side of the road. The ones that had gone over a too-narrow mountain pass lay smashed among the boulders.

The terrain became barren, windswept, inhospitable.

The air grew thinner. Remo adjusted his respiration rhythms. In Sinanju, breathing was all. Correct breathing, which Chiun had taught him, powered the human machine, turning every cell in the body into a miniature furnace of limitless potential.

Remo slowed the cycles of his breathing, extracting more oxygen with each slowed-down breath. He had dealt with high altitudes before, in Mexico City and elsewhere. But Tibet was the roof of the world. Its mountains were higher than any others. He hoped he could function normally on the lean mixture of Tibet's thin air.

After two hours the throbbing in his oxygen-deprived brain subsided. It was a good sign.

"When do the mountains stop?" Remo asked at one point.

The driver gestured vaguely in the direction of the incredibly blue sky. "Mountains never stop. Go up to sky. Go on forever."

From time to time the driver had to slow to allow a yak herder and two or three black hairy yaks to pass by. Once they flew around a corner and ran into a knot of goats. The goats scrambled up the mountains, jumped off the cliff and dodged every which way.

The driver laughed as if he thought it was the funniest thing on earth.

Looking back, Remo saw, miraculously, no goat roadkill. They had all survived. Even the ones that had jumped had landed on ledges and were now pulling themselves up again.

"How many I get?" the driver wanted to know.

"None."

The driver slapped his steering wheel so hard it should have broken. He grinned. "I best damned driver in Tibet."

"That's what scares me," Remo said glumly.

THEIR LUCK RAN OUT as night fell. Up ahead flashes illuminated the mountains, throwing them into momentary relief. It was as if God were taking flash pictures.

"Maybe Chinese tanks," the Tibetan muttered.

But it wasn't, they saw as they drew into a valley. It was an electrical storm. The sky blazed and sizzled. Thunder came cannonading toward them, bouncing off mountains that acted like natural amplifiers.

Then the rains came, falling in drumming sheets that made the windshield swim and driving impossible for any reasonable person.

In response, the Tibetan driver pressed the accelerator harder.

"Pack it in!" Remo shouted over the engine roar. "Pull over!"

The Tibetan shook his head. "No. River ahead. We can make."

"Are you crazy? Even if you can see the river, it's gotta be choked by all this rain."

Before Remo could stop him, the driver bared his teeth like a wolf and gunned the engine.

The truck roared ahead—and suddenly the color of the water on the windshield turned sloppy brown. The vibrating chassis abruptly settled down.

"We reach river," the driver said, pleased with himself.

The wheels were throwing up muddy water and complaining. Then all of a sudden they stopped.

Remo cracked his window and stuck his head out. His hair was immediately plastered to his head.

He saw that they were floating downstream. The truck was turning a slow circle as the torrent bore them along.

"We're afloat," he told the driver after getting the window cranked up.

"Good. Save gas."

"What if we sink?"

"Can you swim?"

"Yeah."

"Good. I cannot. You must rescue me."

They floated along two or three miles until they struck a rock and the truck reeled and tipped over.

Remo was ready. He got his door open and pulled himself out. Then he reached in and hauled the driver out by his greased hair. The man was already covered with mud.

Remo got him up across his shoulder in a fireman's carry and jumped onto a rock. There were other rocks by which he could make his way to shore.

After letting the driver down, he said, "Nice driving."

"Truck will dry off by winter," the driver said unconcernedly. "We walk rest of way."

"How far?"

"In rain, twice as far," said the driver.

"That's too far," said Remo. But there was nothing else he could do. They started off.

Heads down, eyes squeezed tight against the downpour, they walked more than an hour through slashing rain that quickly made agitated ponds in the arid plateaus. The thunder was constant. Fortunately the lightning was far to the north.

"Won't this rain ever stop?" Remo grumbled.

The driver shrugged. "We have saying—humans say that time passes. Time says that humans pass."

All at once the rain stopped. The lightning and thunder continued. The air had a cleanness to it that Remo, who'd spent most of his life in American cities, rarely tasted.

As he walked, Remo willed his body temperature to rise. Steam began escaping his clothes. After twenty minutes of walking, he was bone-dry.

"Tumo. Good," said the Tibetan approvingly.

"Tumo. What's that?"

"Lamas use it. Make body warm, dry off fast. You smart American."

"Not bad for a white eyes, huh?"

"What you talk? You not white eyes."

"What do you mean?"

"White eyes gray or blue. Your eyes good color. Brown."

"Someone must have steered me wrong," Remo muttered.

Somewhere in the middle of the night, they topped a rise and suddenly they were standing on the brink of an unexpected valley. There was a city down in the valley. Here and there people stood on the roofs of stone houses and the larger buildings.

They were black silhouettes against the intermittent lightning flashes. The electrical storm was coming in.

"Don't those people know enough to get out of the storm?" Remo asked.

"They cannot help themselves. Chinese make them do it."

"Make them do what?"

"Make them catch lightning."

"What do you mean—catch the lightning?"

"Chinese make examples of some Tibetans who displease them. If they catch lightning, they die. If they don't, they live."

The rumble of thunder drew nearer.

"What if they refuse?" Remo asked.

"Entire family killed before their eyes," said the Tibetan sadly. "Man who refuse get bill for bullets used to execute family. It is Chinese custom."

"Maybe it's time to introduce a new custom," said Remo, starting down off the plateau.

## 22

It was written that when the Chinese oppressors confronted the Bunji Lama, the Lamb of Light did not resist them, but allowed herself to be taken by skyboat to the Drapchi Prison in Lhasa.

Not all of her train were taken to Lhasa. Only the Bunji and her immediate retinue. Some say the rest were driven back to the holy land. Others that they were divided into Indians and Tibetans. And as the Indians trudged back to their homeland, the rattle of guns punctuated by grenade explosions and screams smote their horrified ears. After which came a profound silence, and the air filled with the metallic scent of blood.

Being devout Buddhists, they held their anger deep within them and continued their homeward journey.

The truth was never learned. The scriptures recorded only that when the Bunji Lama returned to Lhasa, she arrived on the wings of a Chinese skyboat and no Tibetan who toiled in the fields or in the machine shops knew that the Buddha-Sent One had come at last.

SQUIRRELLY CHICANE took one look at her cell and said, "You have *got* to be kidding!"

She whirled and got up on her tiptoes, hoping to lord over the heads of the soldiers of China.

"If you don't get me better accommodations, the First Lady is going to hear about this. And don't think she won't."

"This best cell in Drapchi Prison."

Squirrelly looked at the cell again. It was a box. Stone walls. Drippings. Sand on the floor. Not even straw. No toilet. No running water.

"Does this look like the kind of place you'd throw a Bunji Lama, the Bunjiest Lama who ever walked the earth?"

The soldiers looked at one another, their glances unreadable. And unceremoniously shoved Squirrelly Chicane into her cell. The iron-barred door was slammed shut, and the key in the lock was turned. It took two grunting guards using all their strength to turn it.

After they had gone, Squirrelly took a deep breath and said, "Yoo-hoo. Kula. Can you hear me?"

"I am in cell."

Lobsang droned, "I am in a cell, as well. It is cold."

"Listen, we gotta escape."

"Escape?" Kula grunted. "Bunji, you insisted that we submit to these Chinese demons."

"And we did. Okay, I've got my second act now. But I don't like the accommodations. What *is* this bucket? Oh, pee-ew. It stinks."

"The Bunji is very fortunate to have a bucket," Lobsang said dolefully. "I will have to go in the sand that is for sleeping."

"Try to hold it in, because we're blowing this Popsicle stand."

"How, Bunji?" asked Kula. "These doors are very stout."

"So? You're a big, strapping Mongrol. You're even stouter. Don't tell me you couldn't bust out if you put your mind to it."

"All things are possible," Kula admitted, "if they are predestined."

Squirrelly summoned up her best little-ol'-me Southern-belle accent. "You can do it, Kula. I know you can. Listen, you get us out of here and you can be my costar. Of course, you won't actually play yourself. Lord knows you're a hunk, but I've seen you act. Strictly wood. Maybe Richard Gere, if he bulks up, can pull it off."

"I do not understand your words, O Buddha Sent. What is it you wish me to do?"

"Get us out of here. Please. The Bunji will bless you a thousand times if you succeed."

Squirrelly listened as the big Mongol began throwing his shoulders against the ironbound door. It shook. In fact, the entire corner of the prison shook. But the door held.

"I have failed you, O Bunji. Forgive me."

"It was meant to be," said Lobsang.

"Don't sweat it," Squirrelly said. "I have a B-plan. When they let me make my call, I'll just dial the First Lady. She'll pull the strings that'll get us out of here."

But when Squirrelly later asked a passing turnkey when she would be allowed to place her phone call, the man only laughed.

"You come back here! I know my constitutional rights. I'm entitled to call my lawyer. I'm an American citizen and an Oscar winner! You hear me?"

**23**

No prayer wheels spun in the hill village of Tingri as Kelsang Darlo stood on the tin roof of his humble stone house in which his family cowered. Kelsang Darlo refused to cower.

Someone had stolen a box of grenades from the hated People's Liberation Army garrison, a former monastery. It was Chushi Gangdruk. Everyone knew it was Chushi Gangdruk. But no one knew who belonged to the Chushi Gangdruk except for those who belonged.

This way, no Tibetan who was not Chushi Gangdruk could give up those who were.

So when the Chinese captain, Ran Guohua, had failed to obtain by torture the whereabouts of his missing grenades from the people of Tingri, he had not given up. He had simply waited for the thunder.

It was spring, the season for thunder and lightning and slashing rain, so Captain Guohua did not wait long.

With his soldiers surrounding him protectively, he had gone house to house, not to search this time, but to pick ten men. Good Tibetans. Men of families who would be missed.

And as the thunder grew louder and more fearsome, he made the ten innocent men climb to the roofs of their own houses to catch the lightning.

It was not the first time that good men of Tingri had been made to catch the lightning. The last time, five had done this and two had died. This time the offense was much greater. Captain Guohua understood that the stolen grenades would be used against his own troops if they were not soon found.

And so ten men were forced to stand exposed to the elements, enduring first the slashing rain. When the rain was over, all ten stood unbowed, their faces wet with a clean fresh rain that masked the shame of their tears of frustration, before the terrible lightning.

And no prayer wheels spun to entreat mercy. The Chinese had smashed them and made the people of Tingri melt down their brass for cannon shells and other violent objects. It was a sacrilege. It had been an unending sacrilege since the Iron Tiger Year so long ago.

If Lord Buddha saw to it that he should drop his body, Kelsang Darlo prayed that his wife and children would be spared further indignities. He tried to understand the soldiers, who were only doing the bidding of the captain, who in turn was only doing the bidding of the leaders in Beijing. But there had been rapes. The young women of Tingri had been offered work, paying work, to be trained as nurses for the PLA. On the first day they were raped.

Later, it was true, they were given nurse training. Those who did not take their own lives became good nurses, but very sad and silent in their duties. It was not like a Tibetan maiden not to be full of life and laughter. But this was the lot of Tibet since the Chinese had come.

A crackling bolt of lightning forked down from the blue-black northern sky. It struck two mountain peaks at once, creating a great spectacle of light.

The thunder came twenty seconds later. It made Kelsang flinch. He feared the thunder more than the lightning.

But he feared the wrath of the green soldiers of China most of all. The lightning struck blindly and without malice. Lightning did not punish. It did not ravish young women. It was only doing what Lord Buddha intended lightning to do.

Kelsang found himself praying for the lightning to strike the Chinese, and the thought made his heart sink in sadness. It was not his way to wish harm on any man. But the hardships the Chinese visited upon his people had shattered his faith.

He found himself praying to other gods—the protectors of the faith, Lhamo, Gonpo and Yama, Lord of Death. Perhaps one of them would take pity on him.

Another bolt appeared. This time to the south, behind the plateau.

Illuminated against the bolt was the figure of a man. Tall—too tall to be a Tibetan or a Chinese. The lightning struck thick and hot, and it lasted long enough to show the man clearly as he came down off the plateau.

He came bareheaded, Kelsang saw, and his clothes were thin and insufficient for the chill Tibetan night. His hands were fists and the wrists were very thick, like lengths of wood.

Kelsang looked down. Two Chinese soldiers, their faces hard under their green helmets, were pointing their assault rifles up at him.

They yelled at Kelsang to keep his head high, so the lightning would know where to strike. Unless he wished to tell the truth now.

There was no truth in Kelsang Darlo, so he lifted his head and looked to the south.

Another thunderbolt came and picked out the thick-wristed shadow. Perhaps he was some hermit come down off the mountains to seek shelter from the storm. A monk, possibly. He would be a very sorry monk when the Chinese caught him, Kelsang thought.

Yet the man was coming undaunted, purposeful and proud. The way his grandfather had walked down the valley in the days when Tibetans were masters of their own land. It was good to see a man walk as if there was no fear in his heart. Tibet had been so long bereft of such men.

Who was this unafraid one? Kelsang wondered.

The next bolt struck to the west. Something exploded, and Kelsang turned. A roof smoldered. And in the pile, a black shape that had been human a moment before gave off smoke and a sweetish charcoal odor that soon came to Kelsang's nose.

Kelsang recognized the roof. It belonged to Paljor Norbu, a simple barley farmer. A good man. Perhaps his next life would be happier, Kelsang thought sadly. He had not been the same since his only daughter, a nurse, had walked off the mountain before the eyes of the entire village.

A wailing coming from under the burning roof reminded Kelsang that there were those who had still to contend with this life.

The next peal of thunder came from very far away. As did the next. East. And then north. Then east again. It seemed that the storm was changing direction. Perhaps, Kelsang thought, only one would catch the lightning this bitter night. Perhaps he would live.

The soldiers of Beijing thought so, too. They began to mutter to themselves. They still had no answers. The captain would punish them if the truth was not uncovered, and if the captain did not, surely the lost grenades themselves would inflict their own punishment at a later, unexpected time.

Then, just as Kelsang began to breathe more easily, he felt the hair at the back of his neck rise and the unmistakable warning tang of ozone filled his nostrils.

The lightning! It had found him. It was coming.

There was no time to think and no possibility of escape. In the millionth of a second it took for his senses to react to the knowledge of impending lightning, Kelsang's brain could only process the certainty of death.

He had no time feel fear or remorse or any emotion. There was only time to die.

A brilliant blue-white light stabbed through Kelsang's closed eyelids as if they were red-tinted glass. The thunderbolt struck with the force of a thousand blows. It seemed to strike his chest like a stone fist that exploded the air from his lungs and knocked him off his feet.

The thunder smote his ears. He was surprised he could hear the thunder. He should be dead. Was he dead? Sometimes men survived lightning. Sometimes it did not kill at once.

Kelsang thought his eyes were open. But all the world was blue-white. Was he dead or just blind? He felt a pain in his lungs, and the quick, sharp intake of his next breath brought pain. He breathed!

Blinking the harsh lightning light from his eyes, Kelsang tried to feel his body.

"Give me your hand, pal," an alien voice said. It was a man's voice, speaking English, a language Kelsang knew imperfectly.

Blindly Kelsang lifted one hand and felt a wrist. Hard, thick, as solid as a yak's horn. The hand grasped his with firm strength, and Kelsang was yanked to his feet.

The blue-white had gone from his eyes, and in the darkness a hard, humorless face looked at him. It was white and strong like a skull sheathed in porcelain flesh. The man wore simple black clothes. His eyes were deep and dark and without human warmth.

Behind him a fork of lightning seared the night sky, throwing the white man wearing black into relief.

The thunder, when it came seconds later, reminded Kelsang of the man's voice—low, threatening, awful in its muted power.

"Who-who are you?" Kelsang stuttered.

"Doesn't matter. Go home. Protect your family."

And the man stepped back into the darkness. Kelsang watched him go. He shifted from man to shadow to something that seemed to be there and then wasn't.

Kelsang did not go inside his home. He tried to follow the strange white man. In the darkness he tripped over the bodies of the PLA soldiers who had forced him to stand on his roof and brave the elements.

At first Kelsang thought that the soldiers had been relieved of their heads and their helmets had been placed on the stumps of their necks to hide the gory wounds.

But when he looked more closely, Kelsang saw that something had come down with great force on the tops of the helmets, driving them down with a dread force that squeezed their soft human heads into the ridiculously small confines of their helmets.

Kelsang looked for the footprints of the man who had done this awesome thing—the same one he now realized who had struck him with preserving force, carrying him out of the path of the lightning bolt.

There were no footprints. The ground was soft and muddy from the rain. But there were no footprints save for his own and those of the dead soldiers.

Still, Kelsang searched the village for the being who had done these miraculous things.

He found more soldiers. Dead. Dead in horrible, impersonal ways. Heads twisted around backward. Arms torn and flung aside.

Yet none had screamed out as death overtook him.

Even as he thought this, Kelsang heard a man scream. Loud and long. He ran toward the sound.

And there he found Captain Ran Guohua on his knees.

The white man stood over him. It was a joyous sight. The captain on his knees, his head bowed, mouth open in anguish. The white man was simply holding the captain by the back of his neck, somehow exerting enough pressure that the captain's legs refused to move and his arms hung limp in his lap.

As he watched, the white man gave the captain a final wrench, and the captain simply gurgled.

A hand snapped down edge-on and sheared the captain's twisted face off as cleanly as if a broad blade had dropped. The implacable one released the captain's dead carcass, and it fell forward into the mess of its detached face.

Gingerly Kelsang approached the white man. "Jigme."

The white man turned his expressionless face. "What's that?"

"I call you Jigme. In my language, it means 'dreadnaught.' You are the dreadnought who cannot be stopped. Where you come from, Dreadnought?"

The white man pointed toward the mountains to the southwest wordlessly. He seemed preoccupied.

"It is said that among those mountains is the abode of Gonpo," Kelsang said in a trembling voice. "Are you Gonpo?"

The man did not answer directly. "I need to get to Lhasa," he said.

"There are horses."

"No cars?"

"We are poor village. Only Chinese have jeeps here."

"Show me the Chinese jeeps," said the white man, who might not be a man after all.

As REMO WILLIAMS followed the Tibetan whose life he had saved to the other side of the village, people began pouring out of their houses. They saw the dead Chinese soldiers scattered about like so many shattered puppets. The sight made them cry out.

The Tibetan called back to them in his native language. Remo understood almost none of it. Just two words. Gonpo and Jigme. He wondered who Gonpo was supposed to be. Probably some Himalayan legend. The abominable snowman or the local Hercules.

The farther he walked, the more of an entourage Remo acquired. People were crying, reaching out to touch him, pleading and begging him in words that were unintelligible but voices that were universal in tone. Remo kept walking. It was a long way to Lhasa. He had no time for this.

"They want to know if you are really Gonpo," the Tibetan said.

"If it makes them feel better, tell them yes."

"Are you Gonpo?"

"Do I look like Gonpo to you?"

"You look like Gonpo wearing the body of a *chiling*."

"Maybe that's what I am."

"I will call you Gonpo Jigme, then. Gonpo Dreadnought."

And the word was passed back to the other.

"Gonpo Jigme. Gonpo Jigme," they began chanting.

There were no Chinese soldiers at the local garrison. Their jeeps sat idle. Remo picked one, hot-wired the ignition and got the engine going. He loaded extra cans of gas in the back and started off.

The locals ran after him. Remo had to drive slowly in order not to run them down.

"Will you come back, Gonpo Jigme?" one called.

"Doubt it."

"Then who will save us from Chinese reprisals, Gonpo Jigme?"

"Pick up the weapons the Chinese dropped and save yourself."

"We cannot kill the Chinese. It is not our way."

"Then hunker down for a long occupation," said Remo, seeing a break in the mass of people and flooring the gas.

The Chinese jeep surged ahead and soon left the running crowd behind.

Eyes bleak, Remo pushed on north into the endless mountains that seemed to be calling to him.

The strangest part was, they started looking familiar. And Remo had never been in Tibet before.

**24**

Lhasa held its breath.

Everywhere it was whispered that the Bunji Lama was coming to Tibet. No one knew when or where. It was said by some that the Bunji Lama has already been spirited into the city itself. No one could confirm this.

All eyes went hopefully to the Potala, the great 999-room fortress-temple that had been the abode of the Dalai Lama in greater times. It was there that the Lion Throne awaited the future ruler of Tibet. The Dalai Lama had not reclaimed it because he possessed the wisdom to avoid falling back into the toils of the Chinese occupiers. The Panchen Lama had not claimed it because he knew that the Chushi Gangdruk would assassinate his treasonous bones if he dared.

Only the Bunji Lama had the courage to take the throne. All Tibet knew this. The people of Lhasa knew this very well. They also knew that if the *Bunji Bogd* dared to claim the rightful throne, the Chinese would not react well.

And so Lhasa held its breath and cast uneasy eyes toward the sprawling whitewashed Potala perched high on Red Mountain.

No one was watching the road when the old man rode into the outskirts of the city. He was very old yet

black of hair, and sat on his pony like a raven in his red
robes, his slitty eyes casting about with a narrow,
smoldering anger as they fell upon the shattered la-
maseries and other evidences of destroyed traditions.

"They have crushed this place," he muttered under
his breath, and there was no one to hear his complaint.

The old man was spotted by a Chinese soldier, who
saw at once that he rode a gray pony with a black
muzzle. Legend had it these were the strongest of Tibetan ponies, and the Chinese soldier fancied the pony
for himself.

And so he unlocked his Type 56 assault rifle and
approached the old man with the weapon pointed at
him.

"Stop, old one."

The old man pulled back on his reins. The pony
stopped and began flicking its tail like a fly whisk.

The soldier demanded the man's name. *"Kayrang
gi mingla karay sa?"*

*"Nga mingla Dorje sa."*

*"Kayrang lungba kanay ray, Dorje?"* Where are
you from, Dorje?

*"Nga Bowo nay yin."* I am from Bowo.

"It is forbidden to enter Lhasa," the soldier
snapped. "I will have to confiscate your pony."

"If I cannot enter Lhasa," said the old man who
called himself Dorje, "I will need my pony to return
home."

"You cannot return home until I first confiscate
your pony."

"It is not my pony," the old man pleaded, "but my
son's pony. He will whip me if I lose him."

"Would you rather be whipped or go to Drapchi Prison?" the soldier countered.

"I would rather do neither," the old man said gently.

"Then you will do both, stubborn one!" ordered the soldier, pushing the barrel of his rifle into the old man's stomach.

"I will do what you say, for I am an old man and defenseless against a strong young soldier such as you."

With an impatient swing of his rifle muzzle, the soldier motioned the old man to enter the city limits. He walked several paces behind the whisking tail of the gray pony, prepared to shoot the old man in the back if he attempted to flee, and trying not to step on the fresh dung the pony was inexplicably beginning to drop in profusion.

It was very strange. Whenever he watched his feet, the way was clear. But as soon as he turned his attention elsewhere, the dung was suddenly soft under his boots.

Perhaps, the soldier thought, this man was one of the old Bon magicians who still roamed the northern solitudes. It was said they could do strange and terrible things. Freeze a man in his tracks. Scorch his sight. Call down shang-shang birds. The soldier noticed that the hair on the old man's head lay close and intensely black. It was not like hair, but resembled dry black snow.

A shiver of supernatural fear ran up the soldier's spine, and thereafter he dared not take his watchful eyes off the man's back. No shang-shang would sink its fangs into his throat, if he had to walk through all the dung in Tibet.

Thus did the Master of Sinanju come into the city of Lhasa, alone and unsuspected.

## 25

Remo fought to keep his eyes on the road. It was not easy. Sometimes there was no road. He was on his third tank of gas, it was coming up on dawn, and he had no idea where he was, other than somewhere on the winding road to Lhasa.

All around him were mountains. Snowcapped, misty, eternal and hauntingly familiar mountains. Back in the world—he was thinking of the U.S.A. the way he had in his Vietnam days—Remo walked confident and unstoppable through almost any situation he encountered.

Here, for the first time since he had come to the sun source, he felt small, insignificant, unimportant.

And he was getting nowhere.

So he kept his eyes on the elusive, twisting road and tried not to think of how tiny he felt in this alien but eerily familiar land.

Most of all he tried not to think of what he had seen back in that Tibetan village.

Remo had not come to Tibet to save it. He had a simple mission. Find Chiun. Find Squirrelly Chicane. Drag them both back to the world, hopefully without causing any international complications.

Tibet wasn't his problem. Not that he didn't want to see it liberated from Chinese occupation. But the country was huge, infested with dug-in PLA troops, and most of all the Tibetans were docile to the point of gutlessness. Their religion forbade violence, so they accepted their conquerors and put their faith in faraway, impotent religious figures. Remo felt sorry for them. But if they didn't want to fight for their freedom, that was their problem, not his.

He could only think of what would happen if the PLA suddenly showed up in the Rockies. The Chinese would not last long against ordinary Americans, even armed with pistols and hunting rifles.

Freedom. You want it, you have to fight for it. But Remo had not come to Tibet to fight for its freedom. That wasn't the mission. That didn't mean he wouldn't inflict a little pain along the way if the Chinese pissed him off, but he wasn't going to make a point of it. That village had been a fluke.

Remo was freewheeling down one of the rare straightaways on a mountain that looked like every other mountain for the past two hundred miles, his engine off, when he heard a sound from his past.

*Thunk.*

Low, hollow—but unmistakable. In Nam it used to trigger his adrenals and cause him to instinctively duck. It was the sound of a round being dropped into a mortar tube.

Remo eased down on the brake. The jeep jerked to a stop. And a hundred yards in front of the jeep's steel bumper, about where he would have been, the round struck. Exactly where the whistle of the falling round told him it would.

Sand and gravel gushed up. Stinging bits struck the windshield and rattled along the hood and frame of the jeep.

Remo gunned the engine, swerved around the smoking crater and made the bottom of the mountain before his attackers could get organized.

In the side mirror he caught a glimpse of tiny figures hunkered down on a ridge. They were too far away to make out, Chinese troops or Tibetan resistance, it was impossible to tell.

If they were Chinese, he was in trouble. They would have radios. But he had a head start.

Remo piloted the jeep through a valley between mountain scarps that was yellow with poppies. It looked exactly like a a scene out of *The Wizard of Oz.* Somewhere up ahead, he heard the lazy ringing of bells, and Remo wondered if he should try to avoid it.

Farther along, the road simply disappeared, and he found himself running along dry pastureland. That made up his mind. The only way to reach Lhasa was to stay on the road to Lhasa. He had to find the road again.

Checking his side mirror for pursuit, he steered toward the pleasant ringing.

The ugly black shapes of yaks began to appear. Tin bells around their necks made the bucolic sound.

Two yak herders in dusty robes were tending the herd. They looked in Remo's direction with hard, care-worn eyes that held absolutely no welcome.

Yet as Remo drew close, they broke out in applause. The clapping was not exactly hearty, but it was steady. Remo pulled up beside them.

"Lhasa?" he asked.

The two yak herders stopped clapping. They looked at Remo, noticed he was not Chinese and seemed bewildered.

"Lhasa?" said Remo again.

They just stared. Then Remo remembered the Tibetan guidebook on the passenger seat. He thumbed through it a moment and read carefully, *"Wo dao Lhasa.* I'm going to Lhasa."

Abruptly the two men turned their backs on him and walked back to their yaks, calling over their shoulders something that sounded like *"Bu keqi!"*

"What'd I say?" Then Remo realized he had been reading from the Chinese section of the guide. They had said the equivalent of "What are you waiting for?"

Frowning, Remo drove on.

Farther along he spotted smoke. And then round black tents. They reminded him of the felt yurts of the Mongol herdsmen, which they called *gers*. These were smaller. They were scattered around the dun-colored pasture like black beehives. Yaks and a few ponies grazed in the open spaces. Remo saw no people. The only sound was the laughter of children playing.

Remo slowed the jeep as he approached. There was no telling what kind of a welcome he'd get. Heads began poking out of the tent flaps, and the children playing in the dirt with great hilarity suddenly scampered from sight.

"Nice welcome," he muttered. "I feel like the local welcoming committee leper."

In the middle of the sprinkling of tents, Remo shut down the engine and tried his luck with Tibetan.

*"Tashi delay!"* he shouted.

The heads sticking out of the tents were followed by thick bodies. The men of the village gathered around him. They stood impassive and stony faced. After a moment they began clapping.

*"Tujaychay,"* he said, by way of thank you. The clapping subsided. The Tibetans began returning to their tents.

"Wait! *Nga Lhasa dru-giy-yin.* I'm going to Lhasa."

*"Kalishu,"* a voice said.

Remo looked it up. He had just been told goodbye.

"Great," he muttered. "Anyone here speak English?"

No response.

*"Inji-gay shing-giy dugay?"* he said, repeating the question in his best Tibetan.

His best Tibetan was obviously not good enough. No one replied.

"I gotta reach Lhasa. I have a meeting with Bumba Fun."

"Bumba Fun!" a female voice cried. "You seek Bumba Fun?" Remo turned in his seat. A young Tibetan woman was pushing out of one of the big round tents. She wore a native costume of many layers—an apron over a long sleeveless dresslike garment the color of charcoal and over that a white blouse. Her hair hung in tight black braids around a pleasantly bronze face.

"You speak English?" Remo asked.

*"Ray.* Yes."

"Then why didn't you say so?"

"Why you not say looking for Bumba Fun?" she countered.

"Good point. How do I get to Lhasa?"

"Drive north to purple shadow at base of mountain."

"Which mountain?"

The girl pointed north. "That mountain. It called Nagbopori. That mean Black Mountain."

"Okay. Got it. After that?"

"Drive up mountain then down mountain. Keep driving up and down mountain until reach Lhasa."

"Same mountain?"

The girl shook her braids. "No. Many mountain. Take you one day if gas last, never if it run out or tires break."

"Okay. Great. Got it. When I get to Lhasa, how do I find Bumba Fun?"

"Turn jeep around, drive up mountain then down mountain until you come back here. Then I take you to Bumba Fun."

Remo blinked.

"Bumba Fun is here?"

"*Ray*. Yes."

"Then why don't I just skip the Lhasa part and you take me to meet him here and now?"

The Tibetan girl frowned. "You not go to Lhasa?"

"I need to see Bumba Fun more."

"You could see Bumba Fun in Lhasa, too."

"How can I see him in Lhasa if he's here?"

"Bumba Fun in Lhasa and here also," the girl said.

"Are we talking about the same Bumba Fun?" Remo wanted to know.

"How many Bumba Funs you know?"

"I don't know any. How many are there?"

The girl scrunched up her face. "Fifty, maybe sixty Bumba Funs."

"How do I know where I find the right one?"

"All Bumba Funs are correct." The woman looked at Remo with about as much puzzlement, Remo figured, as he was looking at her. Finally she said, "You go to Lhasa to see Bumba Fun or you see Bumba Fun here?''

''I'll settle for the local Fun,'' said Remo, getting out of the jeep.

''Come this way,'' invited the girl.

''Why did everyone clap when I drove up?'' Remo asked, just to keep a fascinating conversation going.

''At first they think you Chinese.''

''Tibetans applaud the Chinese?''

The girl shook her braided hair. ''Beijing insist when Chinese come, we clap to make them feel welcome even though in our hearts we want for ravens to pluck out their eyes.''

''Oh.''

''We call it the clapping tax.''

The girl took him to a tent on the outskirts of the village and swept the entrance flap aside.

''I present to you Bumba Fun,'' she said.

Remo stepped in. The interior of the tent was thick with a smoky buttery odor he associated with Lobsang Drom. It was dark. There was light coming down from the smoke hole in the center of the tent roof, and it made a bright circle. Around the edge of the circle was shadow mixed with stale yak-dung smoke hanging still in the air.

The man seated outside the circle of light looked old. He was big, and reminded Remo of a Mongol, except for the turquoise buttons in his earlobes and the bright red yarn interwoven in his thick hair. He looked up with one brown eye like a tiger's-eye agate. The other eye was a blind milky pearl.

''What your name, *chiling?*'' he asked.

''Around here they call me Gonpo Jigme,'' Remo told him.

Behind him the Tibetan girl gasped. Bumba Fun opened his good eye to its widest.

"You have come down off Mt. Kailas to liberate Tibet?" said Bumba Fun.

"Actually I'm just here to—"

A commotion penetrated the tent. Engine sounds. Yelling. Remo couldn't understand a word.

"The Chinese come!" the girl cried. "They will see the jeep and punish us all."

"I'll handle this," Remo said, pushing out of the tent. "They want me, not you people."

The girl got in his way, her bronze face pleadingly stubborn.

"No! No! You must hide. They must not find you here."

"You forget, I'm Gonpo Jigme."

She put her hands on his chest. "That what I mean. If you kill them all, there will be reprisals. More Chinese come. You must hide. Please!"

Remo hesitated. "What about the jeep? It's stolen."

"We will explain away jeep. Now, quickly. Hide."

Remo ducked back into the tent. He sat down and waited.

"So," he said, "you're Bumba Fun."

"And you are white," said Bumba Fun.

"Sue me."

Bumba Fun stared at Remo with his unwinking tiger's-eye orb and said, "The god does not ride you."

"What god?"

"Gonpo. Also called Mahakala."

"Never heard of him."

"He is known as the Protector of the Tent. You do not know this?"

One ear attuned to the harsh sound of an arriving mechanized column, Remo shrugged. "News to me."

"You are not Gonpo Jigme."

Remo had no answer to that. Instead, he said, "And you're probably not the Bumba Fun I'm looking for."

"Perhaps. But I am the Bumba Fun you have found."

Outside there were voices, high-pitched Chinese shouts and the more subdued strained replies in Tibetan.

Remo crept to the tent flap and peered out.

In the center of the tents, a contingent of Chinese soldiers in PLA green were hectoring the assembled nomads. They took it meekly, with heads bowed low. One Tibetan acting as a spokesman was trying to reason with the PLA commander, whose dark eyes looked as if they had been sliced into his doughy face with the edge of a bayonet. Although Remo couldn't understand a word on either side, he caught the gist of the exchange from the way the commander kept pointing to Remo's abandoned jeep.

In the background other soldiers were going tent to tent, routing out the women and children.

"It's only a matter of time before they come here," Remo told Bumba Fun.

"And it is only a matter of time before they begin shooting until they have their thief."

"Look, this is my problem. Why don't I surrender myself and take my chances?"

"It is a good plan," said Bumba Fun, getting up. "But I will try to reason with them first."

Bumba Fun stepped past Remo and emerged into the light.

He spoke up. The Chinese commander whirled at the sound and pointed at Bumba Fun. PLA troops jumped into action, grabbed Fun and pushed him along with kicking boots and slapping hands.

Remo almost jumped out at that point, but decided to let Fun play out his hand. It was his village. He knew what he was doing.

They made Bumba Fun kneel at the commander's feet by striking him on the shoulders with their rifle butts. The old man went down without resistance.

The soldiers surrounded him. All around them the people of the village watched with the drained faces Remo had seen all over Asia.

It was an interrogation, with the commander screaming, Bumba Fun answering meekly, and Remo clenching his teeth and fists, wanting to jump in.

As he watched, his mind counted the soldiers, factored in the number of weapons and the surest and softest targets. He could take them out. Easy. But with all the women and children standing around, there would be friendly casualties.

Then, in the middle of a screaming tirade, the PLA commander pulled out his side arm and shot Bumba Fun in his bad right eye.

AK-47 rifle muzzles followed the body down, and abruptly, at a sharp order from the commander, swung outward in a circle to menace the cowering villagers. Women clutched their children. Children clutched their mothers' skirts. Men stepped in front of their loved ones.

The commander barked out another order that caused rifle safeties to be latched off.

And seeing what was about to happen, Remo came flying out of the tent, his face a tight white mask of fury.

**26**

The Master of Sinanju kept his papery face stiff as he was escorted through the grim stone walls of Drapchi Prison.

It was a substantial place, much larger now than it had been before the Chinese came. Yet its harsh outlines were the same—a low, one-story structure with thin notches cut in the stone instead of windows. It would have been difficult to breach, for the guards were many and heavily armed.

But the guards, for all their stern purpose and clumsy rifles, were charged with keeping prisoners within. That was their first duty. Their second was to hold the prison against resistance fighters determined to liberate Tibetan prisoners.

When the tiny old man with hair like coal dust on an egg was brought to their gate, a Chinese soldier came out and began an argument over who would take possession of his sturdy gray pony, the guard who had arrested him or the keeper of the gate.

The Master of Sinanju listened frozen faced to their foolish argument.

"This pony belongs to me," insisted the soldier who had arrested him.

"And I outrank you," returned the other. "So it is mine."

The outcome was ordained by rank, but the arresting soldier was stubborn. He only gave in after the superior officer showed superior stiffness of neck.

The arresting soldier trudged off to clean his befouled boots, and the superior officer, a captain, took the pony's reins and led it into the gate, which closed after them with a brassy clang.

Chiun rode serenely on the pony's back, having gained entrance to the impregnable Drapchi Prison by the oldest subterfuge known to man. He was pleased that it still worked on the Chinese, even though the Trojans had tattled its secrets to every idle ear until even the whites knew it.

Inside, the Master was made to dismount, which he did silently. The pony was taken away. It had served its purpose, even if it had cost three gold coins to purchase in the border town of Rutog. The captain, obviously interested only in the pony, handed Chiun off to a mere turnkey.

"Come!" the turnkey snapped.

With feigned meekness, Chiun obeyed. He walked through dank corridors, each with doors that had to be unlocked and locked again when they came to them. The Master of Sinanju took careful note of the way. And of the half-starved faces that sometimes peered through brick-sized holes in the cell doors.

The cell that awaited him was bare and windowless. The door was shut. A key turned noisily and was withdrawn.

Chiun waited until the last footfall had faded beyond the last closed door. Then he lifted his voice.

"I seek the *Bunji Bogd*."

Voices came at once. "The Bunji! The Bunji? Is the Bunji here?"

"Silence, Buddhists. Let your Bunji speak!"

"Is the Bunji among us?" a voice asked anxiously.

"Silence! The Master of Sinanju speaks!"

Silence came. A murmur remained. The Master of Sinanju closed his eyes and sharpened his ears. He counted heartbeats, listening to their individual throbs. None beat with the sound that belonged to the Bunji Lama, whom he had plucked from relative obscurity, nor of Kula the Mongol or Lobsang the Tibetan.

They were not here. Not in this wing. He would have to search them out. Here the difficulties might begin.

The cell door was very simple yet exceedingly stout. An aged wood bound in iron. There was no way to reach the tongue of the lock and no way to destroy the lock without the sound raising an alarm, he saw. The hinges were set on the other side, and iron hasps bolted to the wood held door and hinge as one.

The Master of Sinanju extended his balled fists, revealing the long Knives of Eternity that were his carefully maintained, implacably sharp fingernails. Hardened by diet and exercise, they were more supple than horn yet sharper than the keenest blade.

Curling three fingers and a thumb back, he laid the longest of the nails against the topmost iron strap and began to file away the bolt heads. It could be done more quickly than this, but not without making warning sounds.

Slowness ensured silence. The bolt heads began dropping off, revealing smooth, shiny spots against the black iron.

He caught each one in his free hand and tossed it back into the sleeping sandpile, where they landed with tiny mushy sounds.

When the last bolts had been sheared, the Master of Sinanju peeled the iron strap from the wood with his fingers. The metal groaned in slow surrender.

After that it was a simple task to insert a fingernail against each shiny exposed bolt and push it outward. The falling bolts squeaked, then made rude clickings on the stone floor. In short order the door was no longer secured on its hinges. The Master of Sinanju simply pushed it outward, the lock tongue coming out of its socket like an old tooth.

Out in the dark corridor, illuminated only by an unshaded twenty-five-watt light bulb, the Master of Sinanju spoke up. "Who here yearns for freedom?"

"I do," a man hissed.

"And I!" said a second.

"We all yearn for freedom," insisted a third.

"Who will fight for his freedom if released?" Chiun demanded.

Silence.

"Fighting is not our way," the second man said dully.

The Master of Sinanju shook his blackened head. "Buddhists," he said under his breath, and padded for the corridor. He would have to find another way.

## 27

There were exactly thirteen PLA cadres, and two of them died with Remo's hard index fingers plunging in and out of the backs of their skulls before any of the other eleven became aware of the white-and-black blur suddenly in their midst.

The sound of faces falling into the dirt went unheard over the screaming of Tibetans who feared Chinese bullets. Remo planned it that way. The more cadres he took out before they knew he was there, the quicker he could get this over with. And the more lives he could save.

But one of the dead soldiers had his finger tight on his rifle trigger. Going down, a reflex caused it to tighten.

The AK-47 burped bullets and percussive sound. Dust and earth kicked up in nervous gouts.

That was enough to bring every head turning in Remo's direction, including that of the PLA commander with the knife-slit eyes.

Ignoring the swinging muzzles, Remo moved in on him. It was sloppy tactics, but he had succumbed to anger. Twenty years of training, and he was being driven by fury like some rank amateur.

The commander snapped up his Tokarev. Remo weaved past his first wild shot. Remo let him have that shot. It wasn't worth dodging, but his body, reacting automatically to the concussive shock of the bullet coming out of the barrel as it rode a wave of exploding gunpowder, swerved wide of its own accord. Even anger couldn't suppress that aspect of his training.

Toes digging in with every step, Remo swept back in line. One fist came up. He popped his first two fingers.

They entered the commander's skull via his wide-with-shock eyeballs, and when Remo snapped his hand back, there were two black grottos under the dead man's suborbital ridge that issued thick black cranial blood.

Rounds began snapping about Remo. Twisting, he started to dance. It looked like a dance—a wild jerky dance the human body makes when hammered by bullets from all directions.

The Tibetan girl cried out in anguish. She thought the bullets were knocking Remo, not dead but mortally wounded, around in a mad circle.

The Chinese thought so, too. They were shooting directly at Remo as he flung his arms and legs about with wild abandon, certain their bullets were breaking off chips of human bone from his unprotected limbs.

Their eyes didn't see that the bullets were passing harmlessly through the web Remo was creating with his blurry limbs. They couldn't read bullets in flight. And not having eyes trained to track a bullet the way Remo's eyes could, they didn't see Remo's fingers and toes as they lashed back.

Stuttering rifles cartwheeled out of clutching hands. Kneecaps exploded under the impact of hard toes that were capable of denting steel I-beams. The flat of a white hand swept toward two soldiers who stood shoulder to shoulder, concentrating their fire, and when it passed through their necks, the soldiers simply stopped firing.

They stood rigid for a moment. Then their arms dropped. Their rifles fell from nerveless fingers, and their knees buckled.

Only as they began tipping over did their perfectly severed heads tumble off the spurting stumps of their necks.

It happened in less than the span of a minute. In that time the frightened Tibetan nomads who had turned their faces from the slaughter of the white man they knew as Gonpo Jigme were drinking in the stupefying spectacle of Gonpo Jigme destroying a dozen of Beijing's most ruthless soldiers.

"The god rides him!" the Tibetan girl shouted in English. *"Lha gyalo!"* she added in Tibetan.

Remo allowed three PLA soldiers to track him with their rifles, absolutely without fear for himself. He knew that a rifle was only a longer, slightly more modern version of the medieval contraption called a pistol. Rifles held no terrors for him.

The minute the tracking muzzles followed Remo to a place where no one else stood exposed to the line of fire, Remo stopped, reversed and pivoted on one foot.

His other foot, lifting high, relieved the pair of their weapons with such sudden irresistible force that their arms came out of their sockets with meaty sucking sounds mixed with the snapping of tendons.

Remo crushed their skulls the instant they were down on the ground, howling in their pain and confusion.

That left three. They had exhausted their ammo clips and were yanking the empties out.

It was too easy to take them out then. But Remo did it anyway. He stepped up and said, "Let me show you how to play pong."

Remo's hands were suddenly up and on either side of one soldier's head. They came together as if he were clapping once sharply.

*Pong!*

The man fell with his head suddenly more vertical than horizontal.

Remo caught a second man the same way.

*Pong!*

That PLA man's head erupted like a volcano when the pressure separated the fused bone plates at the top of his skull and a blood-and-brains gruel squirted skyward.

Remo broke the last man's heart with the heel of his palm. It struck the protecting rib cage, and the splintering ribs compressed the heart muscle until it burst like a red balloon.

When the last of the dead lay in the dirt, boots jittering, throats gurgling and brains dying, Remo surveyed the scene.

No Tibetans had died. It was a bonus. He had figured on some unavoidable friendly casualties. The erupting of the first PLA cadre's assault rifle had worked in his favor, not against it.

Remo knelt before the slumped form of Bumba Fun. He touched the old man's neck, found the carotid artery. It was flat. The man was dead. There was no bringing him back.

Behind him the familiar voice of the Tibetan girl whose name he still didn't know reached Remo's ringing ears.

"You are truly Gonpo Jigme," she breathed.

Remo turned. "He told them he stole the jeep, didn't he?"

"Yes."

"Why?"

Hands flat on her apron, the girl looked puzzled. "It was his job. He is Bumba Fun."

"I needed to talk to him," Remo said angrily.

"You may speak with the Bumba Fun in Lhasa."

"How do I know he'll be the right one?"

"Bumba Fun is Chushi Gangdruk *depung*. That mean general. All Chushi Gangdruk generals call themselves Bumba Fun to fool stupid Chinese. They capture Chushi Gangdruk *depung*, and do tortures. And he always tell them his general is called Bumba Fun. Chinese go kill first Bumba Fun they find, think they have killed Chushi Gangdruk leader. This way Bumba Fun never die. Bumba Fun immortal. Chushi Gangdruk fight on."

The girl looked toward the slumped corpse of Bumba Fun. Her chin began trembling. Tears started in her eyes. She fought them back. In the end she won. No tears came.

"He didn't have to die," Remo said bitterly. "I could have handled it."

The girl lifted her chin proudly. "It was his duty to die. He was Bumba Fun."

Remo looked around. The nomads were staring at him with strange expressions on their windburned faces. They were edging closer, as if afraid to approach without permission but too fascinated not to try. They ignored the fallen Chinese weapons.

"The Chinese are going to miss this unit," he said. "You'd better pack up your tents and move on."

The girl shook her head stubbornly. "If we pack up tents, Chinese will not know who to punish. Punish others. We stay. If punishment come, we will be prepared."

"Are you crazy?" Remo exploded. "You'll all be slaughtered."

"And we will come back in another life to resist the Chinese, to die again and again if our karma decrees it necessary."

"What good will that do?"

She lifted her chin defiantly. "Perhaps if enough Tibetan die, the world will begin to care about Tibetans."

Remo had no answer to that. "Look, I need a guide to Lhasa. How about you come along?"

"I cannot. Must stay."

"And die when the PLA catch up to you?"

"It is my duty. You see, that man was my father. I must take his place now."

"Have it your way," said Remo. He went over to the jeeps and trucks and disabled them with quick strokes that unerringly found fatigue spots in metal and vulnerable points elsewhere. He gathered up the rifles, snapping barrels like bread sticks with his bare hands.

When he was done, there wasn't a usable Chinese weapon or vehicle in the camp.

Remo climbed back into his jeep and started the engine. He remembered something.

"What did you mean when you said, 'The god rides him'?" he asked the Tibetan girl.

"You are Gonpo Jigme. Do you not know what is meant?"

"No," Remo admitted.

The girl lowered her eyelashes demurely. "Then the god no longer rides you. When Gonpo Jigme returns, you will know."

Remo sent the jeep around in a circle, pointed it toward the mountain that stood between him and Lhasa. He sat, engine idling, and looked at the girl for a long moment.

"Hey, kid. I don't know your real name."

"Bumba Fun," said the Tibetan girl, waving him away.

Remo put the camp behind him, his face hard. He drove arrow straight toward the purple shadow at the base of the mountain the girl had called Nagbopori. It seemed to call him. But the faster he drove, the farther away it seemed to get. It was like a big granite mirage, always receding.

Remo finally reached it by nightfall. By then the purple shadow had turned black, and he barreled into it. It proved to be a needle-thin cut through one side of the mountain.

From somewhere above, he heard the huffing of a helicopter gunship and pulled into the lee of the declivity until the gunship had passed overhead.

Not long after, he heard the *whuff* and *thoom* of air-to-ground rockets thudding into the earth not many miles to the south.

"Damn!" he breathed.

Remo pulled over and went up a cliff side like a spider.

Reaching the flat top, he could spot flashes of light in the general direction of the nomads' camp. The night seemed to quake with each impact. When it finally stopped, there was only the faraway whirring of the main rotor.

When the gunship returned, it was a fat silhouette against a low smoldering fire on the pastureland.

"You bastards," he said in a too-soft voice. "They were only herdsmen."

Remo picked up a rock and stepped into view. He waved his arms.

The gunship pilot spotted him. Curious, he sent the ungainly craft sweeping in Remo's direction.

Remo dropped his arms and pitched the rock with a deceptively casual throw. The rock left his fingers moving at nearly seventy-five miles per hour.

It struck the gunship pilot in the face doing one-fifty, after punching a perfectly round hole in the Plexiglas windscreen.

The gunship shuddered as the hands and feet at the controls clutched up in death. It began to whirl in place like a confused Christmas ornament on a string.

The surviving crew scrambled to haul the dead pilot off his seat and regain control of the ship.

They had about as much luck doing that as they had in surviving the fiery impact that followed, when the spinning tail rotor struck a rocky escarpment and the big craft disintegrated in a boiling ball of flame.

Which was to say, none.

Remo climbed back down to his jeep and bored through the endless Tibetan night, wondering who Gonpo Jigme was supposed to be. He knew one thing for certain. He was no more Gonpo Jigme than Squirrelly Chicane was the Bunji Lama.

**28**

For a day the forty-seventh Bunji Lama, incarnation of the Buddha to Come, endured the want and privation of Drapchi Prison stoically. She meditated in her cell. She sought higher consciousness. But none was forthcoming. Despite the pain she was forced to endure, she never gave up hope.

"LOOK," Squirrelly Chicane was hollering through her cell door, "if you won't let me make my call, give me back my stash."

Her voice reverberated down the dank corridor. If ears heard her plaintive plea, no voice responded.

"How about that roach? It's almost used-up anyway."

Silence followed her echoes.

"I'll settle for one of those hallucinogenic toads that you have to lick," Squirrelly said hopefully.

When the last echoes died away, so did all hope. Squirrelly sat herself down on the pile of sand that was her bed, moaning, "I can't believe this. I came all this way and I'm reduced to begging for a lick of a toad."

Clapping hands to her saffron shag, she added, "Won't this headache ever go away!"

"Embrace the pain," Lobsang Drom droned. "Transcend the pain."

"You try transcending this pounder!"

"Her Holiness must set an example for the other prisoners," Lobsang reminded her. "By suffering, you work to relieve the sorrows of the world."

"My Bunji butt! I want out of this hellhole. The storyline is dead in the water. I can see the audience going out for popcorn right now. And not coming back. The critics will murder me."

"The Bunji Lama is above all earthly criticism," Lobsang intoned.

"Tell that to Siskel and Ebert! I can just hear the fat one now. 'Squirrelly Chicane should have stuck with the kind of films her audience is used to seeing her in. Blah blah blah.' Like he knows his buns from a bagel!"

Suddenly the lock began to rasp and grate.

"Who's there?" Squirrelly hissed. "Am I being let out?"

"It is I, O Bunji," said a squeaky voice.

"I who?"

"The Master of Sinanju has come to liberate you," the squeaky voice said.

Squirrelly lifted up on her supple toes and tried to look out the tiny cell-door window. She saw nothing but dank corridor.

"I don't see anyone," she complained.

"Who are you talking to, Bunji?" asked Kula worriedly.

"It's that little guy. Sinatra."

"The Master of Sinanju has come to liberate us!" Kula exclaimed.

The key in the lock continued to grate.

"Forget it," Squirrelly said. "It took two of them to lock it, and they left the key in because it'll probably take six of them to unlock it."

The lock squealed with a metallic complaint.

And to Squirrelly Chicane's utter astonishment, the cell door creaked open.

Standing there was the wispy Korean. He wore black. The top of his formerly bald head was black, as well.

"Did you grow hair?" Squirrelly asked.

"It is a disguise," said Chiun dismissively. "Come. We must free the others."

The keys had not been left in the other locks. Chiun knew that the sound of the stubborn locks might have carried. Delay could be dangerous. First he went to Kula's door and examined the hinge pins. They were as thick as rifle barrels. Strong. But also large. Sometimes a large obstacle was more easily defeated.

Kneeling, he struck the lower pins with the edge of his hand. A short, sharp blow. The hinges came apart like a log split by an ax. The top pin surrendered in like fashion.

Impatient, Kula pushed the door outward and set it aside.

The other door hinges were no less resistant to the skills of the Master of Sinanju.

After Lobsang Drom had emerged, Squirrelly Chicane threw her maroon lama's cap into the air.

"This is great! This is great. This is the reel I've been waiting for!" Squirrelly bent and kissed Chiun on the top of his head, saying, "I wish you were tall, dark and handsome, but hey, by the time they cast the part, maybe you will be."

"What is this woman railing about?" the Master of Sinanju asked Kula. The big Mongol shrugged, a resigned who-can-fathom-the-mind-of-a-white-lama shrug.

Squirrelly noticed a strange taste on her lips. She wiped them, and there was a smear of black on her saffron sleeve. "What is this stuff?"

Chiun ignored her. "There is no time to dawdle. We must get past the Chinese guards."

"Just get me to a telephone. I'll have the Marines here in no time."

THERE WAS only one telephone in all of Drapchi Prison. It was a desk model in the office of Colonel Fang Lin of the ministry of state security, in charge of Drapchi Prison.

Right now he was using it to talk to Beijing.

He was having a hard time getting through to Beijing. More specifically, getting through to the minister of state security. It had been on the minister's orders that he had thrown the internationally recognized Squirrelly Chicane into a cell and denied her any contact with America. Now he wanted further instructions.

If only the minister of state security would take his call.

He had been trying all night. He had left messages. None had been returned. Colonel Fang was beginning to get the message: Squirrelly Chicane was a tiger he would have to ride without further instruction. His original orders were simple. Imprison the would-be Bunji Lama until further notice. No food. No water. No contact with the outside world.

The orders were fixed. He could not deviate from them without bringing great reprimands down on his own head.

No food, no water, no contact. In time, if those orders were not countermanded, Squirrelly Chicane would perish of starvation. Blame would be attached to Colonel Fang for not exercising initiative and common sense and preserving her life.

As Colonel Fang hung up the still-ringing telephone receiver, he shook a slim cigarette out of his last box of Pandas. The supply plane was late again. No doubt there would be no contact with Beijing until the Bunji Lama had expired.

As he smoked, Colonel Fang tried to fathom the Byzantine reasons for the security minister not returning his messages. He could only guess at them, but he had been with the PLA for twenty years. He understood how things worked, even if the why was often elusive.

The security minister had received his orders from the premier of China himself. They were stark orders. The security minister had related them to Colonel Fang, and then possibly went on an unexpected vacation. Or arranged for trouble with his office telephone. Phone outages were common in Beijing.

The Bunji Lama would die in Drapchi Prison, and Colonel Fang would receive the blame because if she did not die in Drapchi Prison, the premier would blame the minister of state security, who would in turn blame Colonel Fang for not carrying out his orders to the letter.

It was a typically communist way of dealing with unpleasant duties. And Colonel Fang had grown to hate it.

He smoked furiously, one eye half-closed in sly rumination. On his desk stood the gilt statuette confiscated from the American lama in the hope it was made of true gold. It was not. Still, Colonel Fang had decided to keep it. He had always dreamed of winning an Oscar.

Now who among his underlings could he inveigle to take the blame for the inevitable international storm?

AT THE FIRST SET of control doors, there was a PLA guard standing at attention, chin high, eyes all but concealed by his low green helmet.

The Master of Sinanju waved to those who followed to remain behind and then he padded toward the lone sentry.

The sentry heard nothing of his approach, of course. How could he? He was a dull-witted Chinese, and a steel helmet covered his unhearing ears.

So when the rifle left his clenched hands, skinning his trigger finger, the guard was quite surprised to look down and see an ancient Korean standing not two feet in front of him and below his normal line of sight, holding the rifle.

Snarling a pungent curse, the guard reached down to recapture his precious assault rifle. The rifle suddenly dropped from the old Korean's grasp to clatter on the stone floor. He bent at the waist.

This brought his helmeted head within the reach of those long-nailed fingers. One nail swept up and traced a quick circle, using the rim of the steel helmet as a guide. The guard never felt the sting of the nail that scored through skin and skull bone.

With a sound like a champagne cork popping, the top of the guard's head jumped straight up, helmet and all.

These sounds were strange in the guard's ears. A quick rasp against skull bone and the noise of a cork popping. The top of his head felt odd.

Something was wrong. He reached up to touch his helmet and felt something warm and throbbing like a great organ.

Then he saw his helmet drop into the line of his vision to join his rifle on the floor. The inside of the helmet was like the inner portion of a halved coconut. Except instead of white coconut meat, he saw raw red bone.

And he knew.

The stabbing fingernail that burst his pounding heart was a mercy.

Chiun took the iron key from the belt of the quivering Chinese guard and unlocked the control door. Then he beckoned the others to follow.

Squirrelly took one look and shut her eyes. Kula paused to claim the assault rifle. Lobsang sniffed, "It is wrong to kill."

"It is wronger to die at the hands of oppressors," retorted the Master of Sinanju.

Three times they encountered guards. Each time the Bunji Lama and her entourage were made to stay back until they heard an ugly sound as of a great cork popping. They learned not to look as they stepped over each fallen PLA soldier.

COLONEL FANG HEARD a hollow popping sound and sat up in his hard wooden chair. His precious cigarette was almost exhausted, so he snuffed it out on the bare desktop and went to the door.

Through the frosted glass in the door, he saw a short shadow. It looked Tibetan. No Tibetan should have been walking unescorted through Drapchi Prison.

He reached into his belt holster for his Tokarev pistol, unlatched the safety and debated with himself whether or not to shoot through the valuable glass. It had been exceedingly difficult to requisition a door with a frosted-glass panel from Beijing, so he decided against it.

Instead, he flung open the door.

There was no one standing there when the door stood open.

The shadow had been there a second before. He was sure of it. Startled, Colonel Fang shut the door. The shadow had returned. He flung open the door a second time. No shadow. No little figure. It was baffling.

He pushed his square head out of the door. The act cost him his life. Without warning, long-nailed fingers grasped his collar with irresistible force, pulling him down.

Colonel Fang felt something sharp run across his forehead, cutting a thin swath through the hair at the back of his skull. He heard a very distinct pop.

After that the strangeness became stranger still.

There was a bald spot in the back of Colonel Fang's head. He knew it intimately, having watched its progress over the past two years of his life through a facing arrangement of mirrors.

Like some discarded coconut husk, the unmistakable bald spot landed at Colonel Fang's booted feet, along with his scalp. It was, he thought with a nervous mental laugh, as if the top of his head had come off.

The thought stayed with Colonel Fang long enough for him to faint. He never came out of that faint because when his face smacked the floor, his brains slopped out of his exposed skull like so much scrambled eggs.

"YUCK!" Squirrelly said, stepping over the fallen colonel. "Couldn't you have done this in a more PG-13 way?"

"There is your telephone," said the Master of Sinanju, gesturing toward the dull black desk instrument.

"Great. Hang on."

Scooping up the receiver, Squirrelly dialed the country code for the U.S.A., then the Washington, D.C., area code and finally the private number of the First Lady.

The phone rang. And rang. And rang.

"She's not answering! What's the matter with her?"

"Perhaps she is asleep," Chiun suggested.

"She can't sleep! She's the First Lady. The First Lady never sleeps!"

"She is sleeping now," said Kula.

Squirrelly hung up the phone and placed the back of her hand to her forehead. "Let me think. Let me think. Who do I call? Not Julius. He'll want to dicker for a percentage. Not my mother. I wouldn't give her the satisfaction. I know, I'll call Warren."

The rotary dial whizzed, and the line rang only once.

"Hello," a bored voice drawled.

Squirrelly grinned in relief. "Warren! I knew you'd be awake."

"Squirrelly."

"The very same. And guess what? I'm in Tibet."

"I read that. How is it?"

"Not so hot. To be perfectly frank, Warren, I'm under arrest. But don't worry. I just escaped."

"Everyone should escape once in a while. Escape their insanity. Escape the taboos of an unenlightened age."

"I need your help, Warren."

"Name it."

"Call Schwarzenegger."

"Schwarz—"

"And Stallone. Try Seagal, Van Damme and any other hunky muscle type you can think of. Tell them to come running. I need to be rescued. Big-time. A real Technicolor Hollywood rescue."

"I thought you said you just escaped."

"I said," Squirrelly said, her voice going steely, "I just escaped *prison.* I didn't escape the *country.* Will you *listen* for once? I need a big splashy rescue. Tell them we're going to liberate Tibet from the evil Chinese."

"I thought they liked you, Squirl."

"We're having creative differences, okay?"

"Sooo. . . you need help? My big sister who has all the answers?"

"Yes, Warren, I need help. Liberating Tibet is no two-week shoot. You should see the size of this place. And the mountains. It's positively crawling with mountains."

The drawl at the other end of the line grew oily and ingratiating. "If I make these calls, what're you gonna do for me?"

"Okay. Okay. I can see where this is going, Warren. You wanna be low lama? You got it. You wanna be Tibetan ambassador to Tahiti? I can arrange that."

"What do the Tibetan girls look like?"

"Short, round and not your type."

"Okay, then I want you."

"Cut it out, Warren."

"You, or I hang up."

"You wouldn't do that to your own sister."

"I've run out of erotic experiences. It's you or I slash my wrists."

"Warren, be my guest. Slash your wrists. Enjoy." And Squirrelly slammed the phone down. "I hope you come back as a sexless worm in your next incarnation, Warren!" she added for good measure.

When she turned, the others were staring at her with round, dubious eyes.

"Don't look at me like that!" she fumed. "You can't pick your relatives, you know."

Kula beamed. "Such wisdom from one who has been Bunji Lama for only three days. Truly the Chinese have no chance against us."

"And we will have no chance if we do not leave this place before alarms are raised," warned Chiun in a stern tone. "Come."

On the way out Squirrelly grabbed her Oscar off the desk.

**29**

The word was flashed from Lhasa to Beijing by military radio: "The Bunji Lama has escaped."

It reached the ears of the premier of China by coded telegram.

In his office in the Great Hall of the People, where the air hung thick and stale with tobacco smoke, the premier smoked furiously as he read the telegram slowly. And then again. Once it had been committed to memory, he used the burning end of his cigarette to set the sensitive telegram alight.

He placed it in the porcelain ashtray in one corner of his desk and watched the edges brown and darken to black as the leaping orange flames danced and consumed the sheet. When it was a delicate ball of unreadable paper, he crushed it to ashes with tobacco-stained fingers so callused they felt none of the dissipating heat.

Only then did he call the minister of state security.

The line rang and rang. Finally an operator came on to report that the line was not currently in working order.

"By whose order?" asked the premier in a hoarse voice.

The operator obviously recognized the voice of the highest authority in the People's Republic of China.

His voice squeaked as he replied, "By order of the minister of state security."

"Get me the minister of public security."

When the correct voice came on the line, the premier issued gruff orders. "Have the minister of state security brought before me without delay."

"In irons?" the minister of public security asked hopefully.

"No. But have irons ready."

The minister of state security arrived within fifteen minutes. He was ushered in looking ashen and wiping his high brow.

"Sit."

The security minister sat. With a casual wave of two fingers that vised a smoking cigarette, the premier waved the security guards to shut the door. He did not have to stipulate that it should be shut as they left. It was understood that this was to be a very private conversation.

"The Bunji has escaped Drapchi Prison," the premier said without preamble.

The minister of state security showed quickwittedness. He jumped to his feet and announced, "I will have those responsible shot for dereliction of duty."

"*You* are responsible."

"But I have been in Beijing all along and out of touch with Lhasa."

"And now you will go to Lhasa and resolve this unpleasant matter."

The security minister, relief in his voice, started for the door. "At once, Comrade Premier."

"Sit. I have not yet told you how you will accomplish this."

The security minister sat down hard. He waited.

"You will not go alone," the premier said in a voice so low it was almost a purr.

The security minister nodded.

"Paper cannot wrap up a fire," the premier said, lapsing into Confucian epigrams. "This cannot remain secret for long."

"The populace has already begun to talk openly of the Bunji's return. They grow restive."

"There is a Western saying," the premier said. "I do not recall how it goes. It is something along the lines of using a flame to fight a conflagration."

"Fighting fire with fire, is what they say."

The premier wrinkled up his bulldog face. "They say it without grace. When you go to Lhasa you will take with you a flame with which to battle this conflagration. Do you know what I mean by this flame?"

"No," the security minister admitted.

The premier eyed his cigarette tip and blew upon it. It flared up red and hot. "It is a small flame," he purred, "and it has not been smoldering long. Therefore, when it flares up it may be an unexpected thing. Perhaps this tiny flame may come to quench the larger conflagration with its purifying heat."

The security minister considered. "The Tashi?"

The premier of China nodded solemnly. "The Tashi."

"Is it not too soon to introduce the Tashi into Tibet?"

"Let us hope," the premier said in a very low voice, "that it is not too late."

Eyes strange, the minister of state security rose to go.

"One last item," the premier said softly.

The security minister turned, face quizzical. "Yes, Comrade Premier?"

"The unworking telephone was a clever subterfuge. I will have to remember it when the vultures of the politburo sink low enough to be picked off in flight."

IN A PALATIAL HOME not many miles west of Beijing, the Tashi sat meditating on a platform that raised him so far above the polished cherrywood floor that he could look down upon even the tallest of his manservants.

His feet were tucked under his saffron-robed body, out of sight. His eyes, very bright yet very wise, were resting upon the pages of a very old book. It was one of his few pleasures, reading these old books.

Television had been banished from the house of the Tashi as a possibly corrupting influence. It was the only thing the Chinese leadership had denied the Tashi. He did not resent this, although television excited his curiosity wonderfully, from the stories he was told by his servants.

So the Tashi turned the pages with short fingers that had never known toil, not even here in the workers' paradise in which he now resided and bided his time, for the hour of his glory was soon to come, the Chinese continually assured him.

It had been a long time already. Perhaps the Chinese, not being followers of Buddha, looked upon time differently than he did. But he tried to be patient because he was the Tashi and it was his responsibility to await the correct astrological conjunction that would presage the fulfillment of his destiny.

The double doors pushed inward, and a servant entered, stopped and prostrated himself in the correct fashion, dropping on his stomach and touching his head to the sumptuous rug.

"Speak," said the Tashi in a voice as sweet as honey.

"The hour has come, O Tashi."

"What is this?" asked the Tashi, closing the heavy book on his silken lap.

"A *fei-chi* awaits to bear you to holy Lhasa, O Tashi."

The Tashi blinked bright brown eyes at the grating Chinese word, meaning "thing that flies," that spoiled the cadences of his servant's perfectly enunciated Tibetan.

"I am ready," said the Tashi, laying the book aside and coming to his full height. With resolute chin and stern expression, he waited for his strong servant to come to lift him down from the high platform on which he stood.

**30**

No mortal eye witnessed the escape of the Bunji Lama and her protectors from Drapchi Prison, but the scriptures duly recorded that this miraculous feat was accomplished with great stealth in utter darkness. And while many oppressors died, they died quietly, oblivious to the doom that stole upon them, which was a blessing and unquestionably the result of the Lamb of Light's infinite mercy.

"MAYBE WE SHOULD SHOOT a few of these guys," Squirrelly Chicane muttered as she slipped out of the gate to Drapchi Prison in the impossibly silver Tibetan moonlight. The Milky Way overhead appeared close enough to touch.

"Why?" demanded Kula, who walked with an AK-47 assault rifle in each hand as if they were toy pistols.

"Because this isn't very dramatic," Squirrelly said.

"Dramatic?"

"We're just stepping over bodies," said Squirrelly, stepping over a PLA body. "Look at these guys. Not a mark on them. It won't translate to film. It's too unrealistic."

Kula waved Squirrelly to wait. Up ahead the Master of Sinanju was at work. "You asked the Master of

Sinanju to separate no more Chinese from their skulls."

"But I didn't say for him to let the rising action go flat."

"You speak in riddles, Bunji."

"Call me Buddha Sent. I like that better. It's more cosmic. And a little gunfire will keep the audience from going to sleep in their seats."

"You are going to give an audience?" Kula asked, puzzled.

"No. I want to *have* an audience. All this creeping around reminds me of *Hudson Hawk*. We need a *North by Northwest* scene."

"I understand," said Kula. Seeing the Master of Sinanju beckon in the darkness—and only because the old Korean chose to be seen—he urged the Bunji Lama ahead.

In the darkness Kula told Chiun, "The Bunji has a vision. She says we are to go north by northwest."

"This is not a good plan," said Chiun.

"But she is the Bunji."

"Call me Buddha Sent."

"Northwest of here is only mountains, and beyond them lies Chamdo and those who live there," said Chiun.

Kula made a face. "Khampas," he grunted.

"What are Khampas?" Squirrelly asked.

"Hill fighters," said Chiun. "Bandits."

"Sissies," said Kula. "They wear red yarn in their hair and think they are like Mongols," he added for Squirrelly's benefit.

Squirrelly said, "Actually they sound kinda neat."

"It is the destiny of the Bunji Lama to claim the Lion Throne," Chiun interrupted. "Nothing must hinder this."

"Yes. Yes. The Lion Throne. Point me to it!"

"There," said Chiun, pointing toward Red Mountain.

In the darkness it was a sprawling white shape in the moonlight with many windows, but only one lit.

"What is it?"

Lobsang said, "Do you not recognize the Potala Palace, Bunji? The seat of your temporal power."

Squirrelly made an unhappy face. "No—should I?"

"It was said by your last body that you would not recognize the trappings of that previous life," Chiun reminded her.

Squirrelly squinted at the titanic shape. "Is that a trapping? Looks kinda big for a trapping."

"We will go to the Potala Palace," said Chiun.

There were soldiers abroad in the night. PLA regulars. PSB watchers. Plain-clothed Chinese. Tibetan collaborators.

They moved through the alleys of Lhasa, unseen. The people of the city slept fitfully. From time to time a jeep whirled past, showing haste but no urgency.

"The alarm has not yet been sounded," Chiun observed.

"Maybe we should sound it," Squirrelly said hopefully.

"What is this?" Chiun demanded.

"Look, we just busted out of prison with all the excitement of a cookout. Unless you're into splatter films. Which I'm not and wouldn't be caught dead in. Now we're moving toward the third act already, and the second act has been strictly wham-bam thank-you ma'am.''

Chiun and Kula looked at her in the darkness.

"Don't you see?" Squirrelly said desperately. "Once I plant my tush on the Lion Throne, it's all over but the withdrawal. We can have a really pow *Miss Saigon* kind of finish.''

The others looked blank.

"Look, I still haven't made up my mind if this is a movie or a musical, so bear with me. Okay?"

"Okay," said Kula, nodding uncertainly.

"If I grab the throne without a fight, it'll fall as flat as *Ishtar.* There's not enough struggle.''

"The Tibetans have struggled for forty years. Is that not struggle enough?" wondered Kula.

"That's their struggle. I'm talking about *my* struggle. That's what this is about. My struggle. The Bunji Lama stands for strugglehood. Let them mount their own production if they want to glorify their personal frigging struggles.''

A helicopter rattled overhead, and they fell silent until it had passed. Kula pointed his rifle muzzles upward and tracked it like a human antiaircraft gun. He did not fire. A warning fingernail prodding the small of his back clarified the decision for him.

Squirrelly continued. "But if the Chinese get wind that we're loose, what will they do?"

"Seek us."

"Exactly," Squirrelly said, clapping her hands. She was getting through to them. Obviously they weren't up on their film lore. "They seek us," she said. "We run. We hide and, after a good rousing struggle, we defeat them and I claim the Lion Throne. Me, Squirrelly Chicane, the sixty and sexellent Bunji Lama.''

"How will we defeat them? We are outnumbered."

Squirrelly leaned closer and dropped her voice conspiratorially. "I don't know. But when we get to that part, do me a huge favor?"

"Yes," said Kula.

"No," said Chiun.

"Let me do the rescuing. I have to save myself. That's absolutely mandatory. The heroine can't be saved by supporting characters in the climax. It just doesn't work. Look at *The Rocketeer*. They went to all that trouble to build up the hero, and in the end Howard Hughes pulls his fat out of the fire for him. Word of mouth got around, and people stayed away in droves."

"I have another solution," said Chiun.

"What?" asked Squirrelly.

"You will take a nap."

"Nap?"

And the Master of Sinanju reached up with two long-nailed fingers and claimed the Bunji Lama's consciousness with a careful tweak of a nerve the gods had placed in her neck for just this hour.

Kula caught the collapsing Squirrelly Chicane and laid her across his broad shoulder. "It is good that you did that, Master. For the strain had caused her to descend into unintelligible babbling."

"Her babbling was perfectly understandable," said Chiun, starting off. "That is why I found it necessary to grant her the gift of sleep."

"You understand her words?"

"Yes."

"Explain them to me, then."

"No," said Chiun, who only wanted to get the Bunji Lama to the safety of the Potala before the alarm was sounded in truth.

After that their true difficulties would begin.

## 31

Remo knew he had made a mistake in bringing down the PLA helicopter gunship when he spotted a thin brown serpent of dust against the mountainous horizon.

The Nepal-Lhasa Highway was an undulating ribbon before him. He was trapped on it. There were no off ramps in Tibet. And here on one of the innumerable mountain passes there was only narrow road and vertical rock.

The serpent of dust could only be an approaching convoy; whether of commercial trucks or military vehicles hardly mattered. Foreigners were barred from Tibet. Chances were good Remo would be turned over to the PSB.

He downshifted. Maybe, Remo thought, he could reach the bottom of the mountain and hide the jeep somewhere in the rocks below before the mechanized column spotted him.

The trouble was, his jeep was also leaving a trail of thin dust that was sure to be spotted in the dying light of the day.

Remo sped toward a pass between two mountains, intent on his driving. The Sinanju skills, second nature to him, were extended even to driving a gas-guzzling jeep. Through the vibrating steering wheel, he was aware of every pebble the tires rolled over, felt every suspension-punishing chuckhole and sensed where the shoulder of the road was too treacherous to support the weight of his vehicle.

The pass was a motorist's nightmare. Curving around the peak, it would narrow without warning, until Remo felt as if he were driving on air.

It was while negotiating one of these tricky curves that the PLA jeep coming in the other direction appeared. There was no room for two vehicles on the narrow road. And there was no time to pass, even if there had been a way to do so without one jeep crashing into the mountainside or plummeting off the yawning cliff.

They were on a collision course moving at nearly fifty miles per hour with no margin for error.

The driver of the jeep wore shock on his bone white face. He would be no help. Remo decided that since he was on his last tank of gas with Lhasa nowhere in sight, he had nothing to lose by driving off the side of the mountain.

The two jeeps closed. Remo held the road until the last possible second, then cut the wheel hard to the right.

The jeep went over the cliff.

Remo was already out of his seat and in midair. He was not going down the mountainside. He executed a back flip that looked as if it were being shown in slow motion and when he landed in the passenger seat next to the wide-eyed jeep driver, he barely made the springs bounce.

The driver, his eyes following the rear of the jeep Remo had just left, became aware of his passenger when a white hand as hard as bone took the wheel.

The driver cursed in Chinese and tried to turn the wheel. It wouldn't budge. The steering wheel might as well have been fixed.

The driver next tried to stomp the brake. Instead, something kicked his brake foot and stomped on the foot that was over the gas. The jeep accelerated.

It was mad. The road was too narrow and circuitous to negotiate at high speed. Especially with two people fighting for control of the steering wheel. Not that it was much of a fight.

The jeep rocked and bounced as if on a shaky track. Every time the nose seemed about to careen over the edge, miraculously it righted itself. And most maddening of all to the Chinese driver was the fact that the alien man controlled the steering wheel with only one hand!

The wild ride came to a halt with breath-stealing suddenness.

Without warning, the foot on the driver's foot that kept the gas pedal pressed to the floorboard came off and tapped the brake.

The jeep jarred to a stop as if it had struck an invisible wall. The driver did not. He kept going, through the windshield, over the hood and beyond.

The driver found himself scrambling for something to hold on to as his body reached the utmost forward impetus and gravity took hold of his stomach and clawed him earthward.

Having no choice, his body obeyed the call of gravity.

His stomach seemed to have stayed behind. Or that was his predominate thought as his helmeted head encountered a wall of stone, and no thought troubled his jellied brain after that.

Remo backed up, turned the jeep around and got back in the direction he had been traveling originally. He lost a little time but he had a fresh tank of gas. With any luck he might slip past the approaching mechanized column.

When it came into view, down on the plain, he changed his mind.

It was a tank column. Three dull green Soviet-style T-62 tanks were muttering along in a line, their domed turrets swiveling this way and that as if to threaten any lurking snipers.

In the lead tank a green-uniformed figure jockeyed the turret-mounted machine gun around and sent short bursts into anything that caught his attention. A trio of grazing yaks—the lifeblood of the Tibetan people—shuddered and bellowed and fell over, half-chewed tufts of grass spilling from their agonized jaws.

Moving on, the machine gunner noticed a twenty-foot seated Buddha carved into the side of a mountain. It looked very old. And to have carved it out of the granite face of a mountain at this oxygen-starved altitude had to have been the toil of years.

The machine gunner elevated his weapon and concentrated his face. The Buddha's face, element worn but placid, disintegrated in spurts of rock dust.

When his ammo belt ran out, the machine gunner calmly lifted a walkie-talkie to his face and began speaking.

The jeep had obviously been a scout, Remo realized. Maybe they were looking for him. Maybe not. But they were going to find him.

And they were going to regret it for the rest of their lives—a very short time.

CAPTAIN DOUFU ITUI of the Fourth Field Army was trying to raise the scout helicopter gunship that had been sent out on a punishment raid. There was no word of it. Or from it.

It was not uncommon for helicopters to falter in these unforgiving mountains with their rarefied air that made even the land-roving tanks gasp for oxygen. No doubt the craft had gone down. Probably an accident.

If not, it was the twice-accursed Chushi Gangdruk. Captain Doufu hoped in his heart that it would be the work of the Chushi Gangdruk. He had not been allowed to train his tank cannon on a Tibetan monastery since Beijing had allowed foreigners into Tibet. He was getting bored with shooting mcre yaks and Buddhas.

And while it was true that there was a temporary ccssation of the influx of foreigners into Tibet during the present uprising, still pictures had been taken of the surviving monasteries. To use them for target practice was frowned on by Beijing.

Nevertheless, it was conceivable one or two could be systematically reduced to rubble and an avalanche contrived or blame placed on the resistance.

Captain Doufu rode in the lead T-62 tank. It was risky, for there were mines buried in the roads from time to time. But previous tank commanders had learned to ride in the rear or middle tanks, and the Chushi Gangdruk had adjusted their tactics accordingly.

Captain Doufu had adjusted his tactics, too. The Chushi Gangdruk hardly ever blew up the lead tank these days.

He rode up in the dome-shaped turret, with the hatch popped open because even here a man needed all the oxygen he could muster. He carried, as did his men, a yellow oxygen pillow slung under one arm, with a clear plastic hose for nostril insertion in case he needed an extra burst of oxygen.

Captain Doufu was surveying the endless inhospitable mountains with his field glasses when the T-62 abruptly halted. He had not given the order to halt, so he yanked the glasses off his eyes and turned his head to vent his anger on the stupid driver.

The driver was looking back at him. He was pointing up toward the road ahead.

A man stood in the middle of the road, in front of the scout jeep he had sent on ahead. But the man was not the assigned driver. He was a white man with great round eyes and thin black clothes that made Captain Doufu shiver to think of being so unprotected here on the roof of the world.

"Advance," ordered Captain Doufu.

The T-62 lunged forward.

The man continued walking casually toward him. He showed no nervousness or agitation, unless one considered the way he rotated his thick wrists agitation. To Captain Doufu's dark, appraising eyes, it appeared that the man was warming them up.

But for what reason? He was plainly unarmed.

The tank crawled ahead, the two others following. They clanked along, remorseless and implacable.

The approaching foreigner continued on an undeviating path, so the driver naturally shifted away, intending to draw up on the man's right side.

The man instead shifted leftward, putting himself in the path of the short tank column.

The driver shifted leftward.

The man got in the way again.

Captain Doufu did a slow burn. Well he knew that in the decadent West the pictures of the lone Chinese counterrevolutionary whose name he could never remember had become famous for stopping a tank column by offering his fragile bones as a barrier.

"What do I do, Captain?" the tank driver asked.

"Drive on. He will step aside."

The tank crawled ahead slowly, its treads crunching loose gravel with an obdurate remorselessness that promised broken bones and crushed internal organs to any being foolish enough to stand up to them.

Except the man remained where he stood, thick wrists rotating like engine pistons warming up.

"Captain—" the driver said nervously.

"Drive on! He will leap aside!"

The tank continued crawling.

The 114 mm Smoothbore cannon barrel passed over the man's unflinching head, creating a long shadow that caused the foreigner's eyes to become like the sockets in a faintly smiling skull. The captain felt a chill of supernatural fear ripple along his stiff spinal column.

"What manner of foreigner is this?" he said gratingly.

The nose of the tank inched toward him, tracks ready to gnash and bite.

Abruptly the man dropped from sight.

"Captain!" the driver screamed.

*"Drive on!"*

The tank passed over the spot where the man had dropped from sight and progressed another four yards.

The clanking of the tracks changed their sound. The sound was unfamiliar to Captain Doufu, but it was a sound like surrender.

He looked over the side. All seemed well. He looked to the rear. And he saw, like two molting snakeskins, the unwound tracks of his very own tank lying flat in the dirt where the tracks of the next tank in line began to pass over them.

The meeting of track and tread was horrible. A grinding, snapping cacophony. The second tank threw a track and began to shift madly as the driver fought for control of his steel steed.

"Column halt!" Captain Doufu cried. But it was too late.

The third tank had not kept a proper interval, and it rammed the second tank. The colliding machines made a clang like the bell of fate resounding over this conquered land.

And suddenly something grasped Captain Doufu's ankles in a grip that made him drop his field glasses and shriek for his life as his ankles were crushed by what felt like squeezing machines.

He was yanked down, where he found himself face-to-face with the foreigner who held his own ankles in hands that looked human but possessed the awful constrictive power of iron clamps.

A hand released one ankle, and the relief was pure pleasure—until the releasing hand took Captain Doufu by his short black hair and rammed his head down into the hatch set in the belly of the tank. The hatch by which the foreigner had somehow penetrated the impregnable T-62 tank, after maiming its tracks.

The top of Captain Doufu's head encountered the hard ground under the tank. The ground won. Captain Doufu was no more.

REMO MOVED through the tank, taking out the driver by the simple expedient of reaching into the driver's compartment and yanking out the vertebrae that supported his neck with the ease of pulling a tree root.

That depopulated the first tank. Remo crawled down the belly hatch, moved low and got to the tangle that was the other two tanks. He eased up on the gas tank, popped a hole with his finger and struck two rocks together close to the trickle of escaping fuel. One spark flew. It was enough.

Remo was a dozen yards away and ahead of the explosion and accelerating across the pasture when the tanks went up.

The ball of fire rose like an angry fist toward the darkening cobalt of the sky. The light made the low thunderhead clouds glow resentfully red as if they were the source of the booming afterexplosions that seemed to fill the universe.

"That's for all the Bumba Funs who won't get to see a free Tibet," Remo muttered, reclaiming his jeep and driving around the steel tangles in which bodies writhed and blackened in the throes of the all-consuming fire of Gonpo Jigme's cold vengeance.

Whoever he was.

**32**

Old Thondup Phintso walked the maze that was the Potala Palace, turning the great cylindrical prayer wheels that squeaked and squealed with each pained revolution.

Save for those in his personal quarters, the vast brass yak-butter lamps had guttered into silence, to be lit only when tourists came.

And save for Thondup Phintso, former abbot of the Potala Palace, now sunk to the status of a lowly tour guide, no one lived in the Potala anymore. Not since the Chinese had come with their loudspeakers and their propaganda and their wheeled vehicles that desecrated the land. Did they not understand that wheels wounded the earth and angered the gods? That the gods would one day exact a just revenge? Or did they simply not care?

The Potala had been stripped of its gold Buddhas, the rare tapestries, everything that could be melted down or used to decorate the homes of communists who had renounced materialism in word only. The Dalai Lama's quarters had been left intact, the calendar still marking the dark day on which he fled into exile. It awaited him. One day he would return. Until that day Thondup Phintso suffered the lot of museum guide, a title without meaning, a lot without joy.

He missed the eerie chanting of the monks that had gone on all the day and much of the night. He missed the amber glow of the great brass urns of yak butter and the pure white flame of sacrifice that had filled every room with a holy lambency.

Only the riotously painted walls remained of the days of enlightenment. Only the smell of yak butter and human sweat remained to fill his nostrils with remembrances.

Thondup walked the halls, spinning the prayer wheels, hoping the gods heard his entreaties. Each squeaking seemed to say, "Banish the Chinese. Banish the Chinese. Return the Dalai."

But the years had come and gone, and the Dalai remained in India. A good place. A holy place. But not his place. Hope was fading in the aging heart of Thondup Phintso, last abbot of the Potala.

There were days when he would have been prepared to accept the guidance of the Panchen Lama, who, although a vassal of Beijing, was still of the faith. But the Panchen Lama had died of suspicious causes in Beijing. A heart attack was the stated cause. But his relatives and even advisers had all died of heart attacks within days of this calamity.

Clearly Beijing had given up on that Panchen Lama. Now it was said that there was a new Panchen Lama. It would be many years until the new Panchen could be invested. More years, Thondup Phintso realized, than he had left in this life.

So he spun his prayer wheels and hoped for a miracle.

THE POUNDING on the great wooden entrance doors went almost unheard deep within the Potala. Yet it carried over the squeaking of the prayer wheels. The Chinese. Only the Chinese would pound on the hallowed doors like that. Only the Chinese would come in the middle of the night, with their uncouth accents and their impious demands.

Gliding like a maroon wraith, Thondup Phintso passed toward the entrance and threw open the great red doors.

He gasped at what his eyes drank in.

It was a Mongol, wearing the peaked cap of his race. Over his shoulders was slung a body, sheathed in saffron. And standing at his side, a Korean, very old, with young commanding eyes of hazel.

"Step aside, Priest," said the Mongol, gruffly pushing past. "Make way for the Master of Sinanju."

Thondup Phintso recoiled. The Master of Sinanju! No Master of Sinanju had trod the dust of Tibet in generations.

"What do you wish here? We are closed."

"Sanctuary, Priest," said the Master of Sinanju.

"The Chinese seek you?"

"Not now. But soon."

Thondup Phintso touched prayerful hands to his forehead. "Sanctuary is yours," he murmured.

The Mongol spanked the backside of the figure slung over his broad shoulders and said, "Where can this one sleep?"

Curious, Thondup Phintso craned his shaved head the better to see the insensate one's features. He caught a glimpse of shaggy hair dyed the hue of saffron and a face drained of healthful color. He blinked.

"A white eyes?"

"Restore your own eyes to your skull, Priest, and take us to the deepest, most secure room in this hovel," the Master of Sinanju ordered.

"This is the Potala, and the safest place is the Dalai's own quarters. But it is forbidden for any but the Dalai to take residence there."

The Mongol growled, "This is the Bunji Lama, pyedog!"

"The Bunji!"

"Quickly!"

Hastily Thondup Phintso threw the great doors closed and, taking up a yak-butter tallow, led the way. The Bunji Lama! The Bunji Lama was here. There had been rumors, but Thondup Phintso paid the prattling of women and the idle ones no heed. The Bunji! He could not refuse the Bunji anything.

Not even, he thought to himself, if the Bunji did belong to the rival red-hat sect.

## 33

The basalt black of the Tibetan night was shading to cobalt, and the snowcapped massifs of some un-named mountain range were turning pink and orange with the rising sun when Remo Williams breasted the top of a rise. He stopped.

Below, in a green valley, lay the concrete sprawl of a small Tibetan city. It filled the valley. There was no way around it unless he backtracked or took to the mountains on foot.

It was not Lhasa. Lhasa, from what Remo had read of it, was a kind of Lamont Cranston Shangri-la. There was nothing of historical Tibet in the gray ur-ban sprawl with its sheet-metal roofs and drab con-crete uniformity below the mountains. Only the Chinese could have built such a cheerless place in the heart of the breathtaking Tibetan landscape.

Remo was debating what to do when something whistled over his head. His Sinanju-trained senses, fixing the trajectory by its sound, told him he was not in danger. He didn't duck. He looked up.

It was an arrow. A polished thing with a raven-feather tail. The tip was not an arrowhead, but a per-forated box. It whistled in flight.

Remo backtracked its flight with searching eyes.

A lone man stood on a cliff, looking down at him. Not Chinese. He looked vaguely Mongolian in his charcoal native costume. He wore an ornate teak box around his neck. And he lifted a hardwood bow high, as if in signal.

Remo had seen too many cowboy movies not to expect what happened next. Stale human odors were also coming to his nostrils.

On the hills surrounding him, a dozen or so similar figures came to their feet. They brandished bows, knives and old-fashioned rifles inlaid with silver and turquoise with fork rests made from antelope horns. They seemed to be waving to him, as if in warning.

The click was soft but distinct as the jeep's right front tire ran over a soft spot in the road.

Remo knew the sound, understood what it meant and threw himself forward and onto the engine hood. There was no time to brake. Not if he wanted to survive the next three seconds.

There came a *whump*. The jeep bucked wildly, then slammed back to earth, flattening the three tires the erupting land mine hadn't shredded.

The engine block had protected him from flying shrapnel. A cloud of acrid smoke and road dust mushroomed up, enveloping the jeep, now lurching toward the edge of the mountain pass.

Remo sprang from the hood, landed, rolled and came to his feet in a graceful series of motions as the jeep careened off the side of the mountain. It bounced off a succession of boulders before it stopped. The gas tank exploded with a whoosh that singed the air.

As the jeep crackled, tires melting, far below, Remo looked up. The Tibetans who had obviously planted the mine looked up and shrugged, as if to say, "We tried to warn you."

Remo lifted his voice. He had nothing to lose. He was surrounded. "Chushi Gangdruk?"

"Who you seek, *chiling?*"

"Bumba Fun." Couldn't hurt to ask, Remo figured.

"Which Bumba Fun?"

"I'll take potluck."

The Tibetan looked vacant.

"Tell him Gonpo Jigme is looking for him."

All around him, Tibetan faces broke apart in startlement. "You are Gonpo Jigme?"

"Yeah."

"We have heard you had come down from Mt. Kailas. Come, come."

Remo started up the sheer rock face. It was the easiest and quickest way for him to reach the man. But the hardy Tibetans, no strangers to scaling mountains, were amazed by the ease with which Remo scaled sheer rock. He seemed to literally float up the rock face.

Remo reached the man, who immediately prostrated himself on the ground. "I am Bumba Fun, O Protector of the Tent."

"Call me Gonpo," said Remo. "All my friends do."

The man got up. "We beg forgiveness for destroying your jeep, Gonpo. We recognized your white face too late to stop you except with our warning arrows."

"I'm headed for Lhasa," Remo said. "I need to get there fast."

"You go to cast out the Chinese enemies of the faith?"

"I go to find the Bunji Lama and pull her chestnuts out of the fire," said Remo.

"There are rumors the Bunji is in Lhasa, to be sure. We will take you through the city, but you must wear Khampa clothes."

"Khampa clothes?"

Bumba Fun struck his chest proudly. "We are Khampa. Fighters. Very fierce. Has Gonpo Jigme not heard of us?"

"Gonpo Jigme hears many things, retains very few," Remo said dryly. He had to hurry this along. No telling how much trouble there was in Lhasa if Squirrelly and Chiun were at large up there.

The other Khampas gathered around Remo and almost broke into knife fights over who would be privileged to donate articles of clothing to Gonpo Jigme. Remo settled it by saying, "Everybody donate one item."

So they started to fight over who would donate which item and which were of greater or lesser value.

In the end Remo was wearing mismatched yak boots with upturned toes, sheepskin pants with the fleece turned inside out and a wool *chuba*. Someone gave him a silver-fox turban. Nothing exactly fit and everything smelled. Remo slapped his body here and there to kill the fleas. Then he was ready.

"You take this," said Bumba Fun, removing the box on a cord around his neck.

"Don't need it."

"Charm box. Ward off Chinese bullets."

"Gonpo Jigme doesn't need charms to ward off bullets," Remo told him. "Now, let's go."

They had to walk. The jeep was burning nicely now. It had been running low on gas anyway.

"How far to Lhasa?" Remo asked as they started down into the valley.

"Less than a day's march," Bumba Fun told him.

"Good. Maybe I can hitch a ride."

"Any true Tibetan would be honored to give Gonpo Jigme a ride to Lhasa, but there is not enough room in the truck for all of us."

"I just need you guys to get me through this city."

"It is called Shigatse, and why does Gonpo Jigme speak English?"

Remo thought fast. "Because Gonpo Jigme took a vow not to speak Tibetan until Tibet was free again."

Bumba Fun translated this for his fellow Khampas. Grunts and nods of approval followed. Mentally Remo wiped his brow.

As they neared the city, music blared out. Remo had seen the loudspeakers posted throughout the town. And the music, martial and strident, was the Chinese national anthem, "The East Is Red."

Remo's face darkened in a frown. "Great. Now the whole neighborhood is going to wake up."

"It is a great day," agreed Bumba Fun.

Remo was wondering how they'd get through the city quietly when Bumba Fun gave a signal to his men. They pulled the box-headed arrows from quivers, nocked them and let fly.

The whistling startled crows, set dogs to barking and was guaranteed to alert any PLA or PSB cadres who happened to have retained their hearing.

"What are you doing?" Remo demanded.

"Announcing to the oppressors your arrival, O Protector of the Tent."

"Are you crazy?"

"The Chinese will run once they realize it is you, Gonpo."

"The Chinese will shoot us where we stand," Remo said flatly.

The Khampa shrugged. "If we are fated to die in your company, so be it."

"You screw this up, and I guarantee you'll come back as a yak in the next life," Remo warned.

The Khampa brightened. "Yaks are good. Give meat, milk and do hard work."

"A three-legged yak with no horns. And fleas."

The Khampa bowed his head. "Command us, O Gonpo, and it will be done as you wish."

"I gotta get through town without the Chinese getting suspicious."

"It will be done."

"Then I'm going to need to get to Lhasa as fast as possible."

"This can be done."

"And no screwups."

"What is a screwup?"

"A three-legged yak without horns."

"No such yaks will trouble your journey, O Gonpo. Await us here."

Remo got down behind a rock and waited. He hated waiting, but even dressed as a Khampa, he had an obviously American face, spoke no Tibetan and would stick out like a sore thumb.

He didn't have to wait long. There was an explosion. It was followed by a coil of black smoke. A siren wailed. The rattle of small-arms fire came and went.

"Damn. They screwed up."

A truck barreling back from town, overloaded with Khampas, made Remo think otherwise. He stepped out into the road and noticed that more Khampas were coming back than had gone in the first place.

"Where'd you pick these guys up?" Remo asked, jumping into the passenger seat, which had been reserved in his honor.

"Chushi Gangdruk everywhere," Bumba Fun said. "Chinese never know what hit them."

"They're all dead?"

"Most. Some may still be dying. It will not be long."

The truck turned around and barreled into town.

The city wasn't any more appealing up close than it was from above. Gray, uniform buildings clicked by. So did Tibetan faces. They were lining the road to wave to him. Most showed him their tongues. Occasionally Remo stuck out his tongue in return.

Along the way they picked up more trucks and the odd jeep, overloaded with boisterous Tibetans.

After they passed out of town, Shigatse resumed exploding. Remo looked back. Fires were starting.

"Why are they burning down their own city?"

"It was built by Chinese. Now that Tibet is free, they want to live in a city built by Tibetans."

"Tibet isn't free yet."

"It is just a matter of another day or two now that Gonpo Jigme rides with the Khampas and the Bunji Lama has come to claim the Lion Throne."

"I had my hopes set on blowing into Lhasa quietly."

"We will blow into Lhasa as quietly as we are blowing out of this city," Bumba Fun assured him. And someone let fly with one of the whistling arrows that seemed to serve no other purpose than to substitute for fireworks.

Remo settled down for the ride. At least he was starting to feel as if he was making progress.

The mountains still seemed to be calling him, though. That part bothered him. How could mountains call him? And why?

**34**

Old Thondup Phintso could not sleep. He tossed on his bedding of old yak skins, dressed in the maroon robe he rarely doffed, wondering what it could all mean.

The Bunji Lama was a *mig gar*—a white eyes. With saffron hair. That at least was a good augury. But a white eyes?

It was said that the Panchen Lama had been discovered in far-off America and while the new Panchen was not white, it was the farthest from Tibet that a *tulku* had been found.

He could not sleep, ruminating on these things, and when the dawn came and the hated blare of the loudspeakers began issuing the tinny discord of "The East Is Red," Thondup Phintso threw off the yak skins and walked barefoot and agitated through the dripping coolness of the Potala.

He came to the quarters of the Bunji Lama. The heavy wood door, carried on the backs of serfs from faraway Bhutan centuries ago, was closed. He put his ear to the moist wood and heard no sound.

Carefully he pushed the door inward. The hinges did not squeak, as he knew they would not.

A shaft of rosy light slanted across the sumptuous quarters. He saw the *kang* and its bedding all disheveled and hesitated, his heart high in his throat.

Then he saw the Bunji.

The Bunji Lama squatted over the chamber pot, saffron skirts hiked over his thighs. His urine tinkled in a golden rill into the waiting brass pot. The Dalai's personal pot.

Thondup Phintso narrowed his eyes. Something was amiss.

The Bunji looked up, blue eyes flashing in annoyance. And from the Bunji's mouth issued a shrill exclamation. "Jesus H. Christ! Can't a Buddha have any privacy around here?"

And eyes widening in shock, Thondup Phintso hastily withdrew. Pulling his robes about him, he ran, feet smacking the stone flooring like solitary applause, for the great wooden doors.

It was sacrilege. The Bunji was not only white, but a woman. Such a creature could never be allowed to claim the Lion Throne.

As much as he detested the thought, Thondup Phintso would bring this sacrilege to the attention of the Public Security Bureau.

If terrible events resulted, he comforted himself with the knowledge that they, like all things, had been ordained from the beginning of time.

THE EASTERN REACHES of Tibet unrolled in a long yellow-green carpet under the flashing wings of the Soviet-built CAAC turboprop plane.

Sitting in the copilot's seat, the minister of state security watched the unending pastureland roll by. It made him uneasy. All that barrenness. To go down in it was to face days, if not weeks, of cruel trekking to civilization, assuming one survived.

Ahead the horizon was a haze of mountain ranges. As forbidding as the eastern reaches were, the mountains would be infinitely worse. He dreaded the landing at Lhasa's Gonggar Airport so much that he could not bear to look at the mountains from a distance. To land at Gonggar, the pilot would have to ride a knifeblade channel between towering peaks in thin air that would test the turboprop engines.

Back in the passenger area, the Tashi squatted in the middle of the aisle, dwarfed by his retinue. He looked tiny, more like a creature out of superstitious mythology than a human being, as he spun the solid-gold prayer wheel that the minister of state security had presented to him as a reward for making the difficult flight to Lhasa. An altogether too pitiful figure on which to place the future of China's claim to Tibet.

In ten, twenty years, after the proper training and indoctrination, yes. It was conceivable. But rulers— even puppet rulers—were not selected and installed overnight. The advent of the Bunji Lama had changed all that. The minister of state security only hoped the Tashi was equal to the Bunji.

But not as much as he hoped that they would survive the landing at Gonggar.

THE BUNJI LAMA, it was recorded, assumed the Lion Throne without fanfare, notice or pomp, as befitted one who came to the sacred Potala in the dead of night on the selfless task of freeing Tibet from sorrow and slavery.

This was done in the early hours of the last morning of the second month of the Iron Dog Year, with no eyes but those of the all-seeing gods to witness the auspicious moment.

SQUIRRELLY CHICANE WAS still sleepy. Her brain felt like it had been soaked in ether. It was not a half-bad feeling, actually. She rather liked it. At least it was better than the pounder the high altitude had given her.

Looking around, she wondered where she was. The walls were painted with Buddhas, bodhisattvas and other mythic creatures. The ceiling was arched and high. The furniture was exquisite, especially the ornate gilt chair off in one corner. There were Chinese dragons or dogs or something decorating it.

Since there wasn't any place more inviting, she went over and sat down.

"Comfy," she said approvingly. Right then and there she decided that her awakening scene would be filmed on location. If the budget allowed. If not, it could probably be recreated on a soundstage in Burbank.

She wondered where she was. Her foggy brain failed to summon up the memory of how she had gotten to this place—wherever she was. Dimly she heard music—brassy, discordant, martial music. It seemed very loud, yet far away.

Squirrelly made a mental note to have the music replaced with a John Williams score—unless she ended up doing a musical. In which case she might take a fling at writing the music herself. After all, who was going to tell her no. She was the Bunji Lama now.

Footsteps came toward the closed wooden door. She arranged her robes about her crossed legs in case it was that dried-up Tibetan Peeping Tom, who had barged in while she was on the john.

"Bunji! Bunji!" It was Kula. The big Mongol barged in as if his mohair pants were on inside out.

He took one look and stopped, the alarm going out of his eyes.

Then he got down on hands and knees and began bumping his forehead on the floor. "This is a very great scam," he sobbed in English.

"What is?" Squirrelly said.

"You have assumed the Lion Throne."

"I have? I mean, I have! Where?"

"Your precious bottom sits upon it, Bunji."

Squirrelly leapt up. "This is the Lion Throne! Really? You're kidding me. You've got to be. Tell me you're kidding."

"I kid thee not, Bunji. The hour Tibet has awaited has come."

Squirrelly dropped back onto the golden seat. "Wow! The Lion Throne. I'm sitting on the Lion Throne. What a moment. I can just feel myself vibrating at a higher cosmic frequency. What should I give as my first decree? Oh, I hate these unscripted moments."

"Protectoress, cause the Chinese who are pounding at the Potala gates to shrivel up into sheep dung."

"What Chinese?"

"We have been betrayed, Bunji."

"We have?"

"The stinking abbot who gave us sanctuary has betrayed us to the hated Han."

"It's karma," cried Squirrelly, leaping to her feet.

Kula got up, too. "What have we done to reap such bad karma?"

"No. No. It's *good* karma. This is perfect! This is great."

"What is?"

Squirrelly spread her hands wide as if to conjure up the scene. "It's the end of the second act. No, wait, the beginning of the third act. The Bunji Lama awakens as if from a dream, instinctively taking her throne. And at her moment of perfect triumph, she is betrayed by one of her subjects. A notorious Peeping Tom, I'll have you know. In bursts her faithful Mongol servant—that's you—with the bad news."

"But you said it was good karma," Kula countered.

Squirrelly began pacing the floor. "It's bad in real life but great cinema. Don't interrupt your Bunji. Now where was I? Oh, yeah. Now she knows she has to take the yak by the horns and win the day." Squirrelly popped her hands together. "The audience will eat this up like popcorn!"

Kula glanced toward the door. "Why are you saying all this, Bunji, when our very lives are in danger?"

"It's a plot point. We have to slip them into the script from time to time."

Kula looked blank.

Squirrelly paced the floor. "Okay, now I gotta turn the tables. But how? How?"

From beyond the door came a great crashing.

Squirrelly stopped in midpace. "What was that?"

"The gates have fallen to the enemies of the faith," said Kula.

"Perfect!" Squirrelly crowed.

"They will flood in like ants," Kula added.

"Fantastic! We're outnumbered a hundred to one. The audience will be on the edges of their seats. Perfect! I love it! I love it! I just love being the Bunji Lama!"

At that moment the Master of Sinanju flew in. "We must flee!" he said.

"Flee? Not on your life. I'm in costume, I have my Lion Throne, and I'm keeping it!"

"The Chinese will overrun us. We cannot fight them all."

"The way is blocked," said Lobsang from the door. "The Bunji must make her stand here."

"She will die," Chiun said firmly.

"If she dies," Lobsang intoned calmly, "it is the will of the gods. The people will hear of this and rise up."

"The Bunji is under the protection of the House of Sinanju. Her death would bring shame upon my house. I will not have it."

Kula stepped up to Lobsang and laid the edge of a dagger against his throat. "We will do as the Master of Sinanju bids."

Squirrelly stamped a bare foot. "Don't I get some say here?"

"You are the Bunji," said Kula, bowing his head in Squirrelly's direction. "Of course we will obey your merest whim."

"Fine. My whim is that we—"

The Master of Sinanju slipped up and touched the back of Squirrelly Chicane's neck. Her mouth kept moving, but no words issued forth. She tried coughing. It only made her throat raw. Not a syllable came out.

My voice! Squirrelly thought with mounting panic. I've lost my voice!

Then she was unceremoniously thrown over Kula's hamlike shoulders and began bouncing with his every rolling step.

"This way!" hissed Chiun.

"This way leads to a cul-de-sac," Lobsang said unhappily. "We will be trapped."

"You may go another way, Priest," Kula said, his voice contemptuous.

At the end of a corridor there was a big brass Buddha, too heavy to be carried away by the Chinese who'd stripped the Potala. The Buddha sat on a wooden dais with his open palms cupped upward. In his palms rested a lotus flower.

Chiun seized it, wrenched it right, then left and finally all the way around. The Buddha began to sink into the floor of its own weight, dais and all, accompanied by a soft gritty hissing.

As the smiling head began dropping, Chiun motioned for the others to mount on the dais. Kula clambered aboard, one hand clapping a struggling Squirrelly Chicane to his shoulder. Lobsang followed, his thin face baffled. They rode the dais down into a cool yawning space as if it were a great freight elevator.

Down below it was very dark. Lobsang lit a yak-butter candle, and its mellow light showed a dripping passage leading toward a clot of crepuscular shadow.

"Follow the passage to its end and await me there," Chiun instructed. "I must restore the Buddha in order to baffle the Chinese. Make haste!"

They complied, moving down the passage enveloped in a halo of malodorous light.

The Master of Sinanju examined the Buddha. It now sat on a pile of soft sand. The turning of the lotus had released catches that supported the idol. Its weight had caused the sand pile to spread outward and the Buddha to slip below the level of the floor. It was a secret a previous Master had learned and duly recorded in the histories of the house. He had not shown how to restore the Buddha, however.

Distantly there were shouts and the heavy fall of rushing feet. Searching PLA cadres. If they discovered the sunken Buddha, all would be lost.

Chiun, understanding that restoring the Buddha would be the work of hours, and not having hours, decided that it would be more efficacious to eradicate all evidence of the secret passage.

The passageway was constructed of mortarless blocks, in the fashion of architecture in Tibet. He retreated to the junction where the passage turned and looked for a keystone. It sat in its niche, fixed and immobile.

The Master of Sinanju laid the flat palm of his hand against it, feeling the ancient stone for cracked or weak points. When the sensitive flesh of his palms told his mind that such a place existed, he made fists of his bony hands.

He struck the spot with one fist, pulled back and struck with the other. Strike. Return. Strike. Return. The stone retreated into its niche with each shock. Finally, it reached the point of no retreat, and the blows of his fists, hard and resolute, began to chip away at the block's innate integrity.

The fists of the Master left no mark on the stone. Then abruptly, without warning, the stone broke apart.

The surrounding blocks began to groan.

Chiun flew down the passage, pipe-stem feet churning, fists pumping, head back.

There had been sufficient time for the others to have reached the egress of the passage, Chiun knew. If the gods were with him, there would be time for him to join them before disaster struck.

The rumble began far back and chased the Master of Sinanju down the passage.

He thanked the gods Remo had not come with them. For surely his clod-footed pupil would now be two or three paces behind, his thick head in imminent danger of being crushed by the falling blocks that now came down in a merciless rain.

## 35

By early morning the caravan that had formed behind the truck carrying Remo Williams to Lhasa was half a mile long.

It was the perfect target for Chinese helicopter gunships or short-range artillery.

They rode through a sleepy hill town unchecked, picking up more trucks and leaving in their wake burning buildings.

"Once word travels, the Chinese are going to be all over us like hair on a yak," Remo said unhappily as he scanned the bright blue morning skies.

Bumba Fun grunted unconcernedly. "They fear Gonpo Jigme. They fear the Dreadnought. They will give back before us. You will see."

"Don't count on it."

A line of gunships appeared on the western horizon. They were moving north.

"Here they come," Remo warned.

But they didn't come. They kept traveling north. Then Remo realized they were headed toward Lhasa.

"Something's up."

"Yes. The Chinese are too frightened to strike at Gonpo the Dreadnought."

"Is there a radio in this thing?" Remo asked, reaching for the dash knobs. He got a radio station. A excitable voice came from the speaker, speaking Tibetan or Chinese. Remo couldn't tell.

"What's he saying?" Remo wanted to know.

"It is Radio Lhasa," said Bumba Fun. "They have declared martial law."

"And..."

"That is all they say. All Tibetans have been ordered indoors. Perhaps word of Gonpo Jigme's nearness has reached them, and they cower in fear of your coming."

"Maybe the Bunji Lama's stirred the place up," Remo countered.

"Oh, yes, the Chinese announcer mentioned the Bunji Lama also."

"What'd he say?"

"The Bunji has been taken to Drapchi Prison."

"That's probably good," Remo decided.

"But he has escaped."

"That's not good."

"Why is that not good, Gonpo?"

"You don't know the Bunji Lama like I know the Bunji Lama."

"I do not know the Bunji Lama at all," Bumba Fun admitted.

Another flight of helicopters appeared and made a beeline for the daunting mountains surrounding Lhasa.

"They must think we're the Chinese cavalry coming to the rescue," Remo said, watching the gunships rattle over a ridge.

Bumba Fun grinned. "We will blow into Lhasa like the end of the world."

"That's what I'm afraid of," said Remo, wondering how he was going to get out of Tibet alive, alone or not, with the entire country being mobilized.

SQUIRRELLY CHICANE WAS royally pissed.

She couldn't vent her holy pissedness. That was the part that pissed her off the most. It was bad enough to be packed around like a side of beef, but not having a say in the matter was just too much.

Beating on Kula's broad back only hurt her fists. Besides, Squirrelly didn't want to break her Oscar.

She was being saved. In all the movies she had ever done, being saved by males annoyed her most. She was over forty before she had been allowed to save her own cinematic behind.

Now, invested as the pontiff of Tibet, for Buddha's sake, and here she was reduced to being saved again. It was a major step backward, image- and career-wise. If only she could speak. She'd give them all a piece of her Bunji mind.

After what seemed like forever they emerged from the dank passage into a cool cavern of some sort. Fresh air blew in steadily. Squirrelly had only a moment to drink in the invigorating air when there came a low rumble from the passage.

And the Master of Sinanju flashed out of the maw, saying, "Make haste! The ceiling may fall at this end."

What is that sound? Squirrelly wondered as she was carried away from the spot. An earthquake?

From the mouth of the passage came another rumble, and the ground under their running feet shook. Out of the stone passage came a breath of fetid air mixed with dust and grit. It met with the incoming fresh air, mixed—and the fetid air won out.

The passage had collapsed. Squirrelly didn't know how. But it meant that the Chinese wouldn't be chasing them.

Nice plot twist, but where could the story go from here? A breakneck chase would have been better.

Otherwise, the ceiling held. The danger was over.

Kula set her on her feet, and she made a point of inflicting the blue lasers of her best on-screen glare at each of them in turn. Kula looked abashed. Lobsang actually flinched. But the Master of Sinanju pointedly ignored her.

Squirrelly hated that. But she was more interested in taking stock of her surroundings. This cavern was amazing. Every corner was a set unto itself. There were stone statuaries cut into the cave walls and great brass tubs of yak butter in which lit wicks floated and burned with a buttery yellow light.

A bank of prayer wheels stood like vertical press rollers, and Squirrelly gave them a spin, mentally praying for her voice to come back. It didn't happen. She wondered if praying to herself had been a mistake.

Carefully they crept toward the fresh air. The clear light of early morning filtered in a little from the near mouth of the cave.

At the entrance—the cavern was some kind of temple cut into the side of a great hill—they stood looking across at the Potala. Its multistoried white levels, like some Hare Khrishna's idea of a condominium, were busy with green-uniformed soldiers. They swarmed along the many-leveled roofs with its golden lions. Smoke and dust boiled out of a cluster of windows.

"A jeep comes," hissed Kula, pointing to the road below.

Instantly everyone squatted down to get out of sight. Except Squirrelly. A hand reached up and yanked her flat.

The jeep passed without incident.

Squirrelly lay on her stomach and tried to make sounds come out of her mouth. She pointed to her mouth angrily. More jeeps whirled by. Tanks clanked, taking up defensive positions. Canvas-backed trucks laden with hard-faced PLA cadres rolled back and forth.

Lobsang hissed, "There are too many Chinese even for a Master of Sinanju and one Mongol."

Squirrelly glowered at them. What was she— chopped yak liver?

From his crouching position, Chiun searched the busy street with his eyes. "Escape will be difficult," he admitted, his hazel eyes narrowing to slits.

"Then we will make our stand here," vowed Kula. "Prepared to die if need be in the service of the Buddha-Sent One."

Die? thought Squirrelly. I can't die. I'm the heroine.

She tried to communicate that, but the three were too busy arguing among themselves to pay her attention. Typical supporting actors.

"Any fool can die," Chiun was saying. "We must seek out a place of true refuge in order to plan our strategy."

His eyes went to a ring of snowcapped peaks that seemed so close but could not be reached on foot without incurring great risk.

Kula followed the Master of Sinanju's gaze. "Yes, the mountains would be a good place."

"But how to reach them," said Lobsang.

Kula checked his AK-47 and said, "I will find us a worthy steed." Without another word, he clambered down the mountainside.

THE NEXT HOUR was one of the most boring yet nervous in Squirrelly Chicane's sixty years on earth. It was worse than waiting for the director to set up a shot.

They withdrew to the cool shadows of the temple cavern and waited. The sounds of motorized infantry, helicopters and the unintelligible shoutings of Chinese commanders came and went. More than once the loudspeakers distributed throughout Lhasa blared shouts and exhortations.

"They are calling upon us to surrender," Chiun said.

"We will never surrender," Lobsang said, stiff-voiced.

Squirrelly said nothing. She spun the prayer wheels furiously, imploring the Buddhas of the Past, Present and Future to give her back her voice. They must have been on another cosmic line, because all she managed were some hoarse gasps.

The *whup-whup-whup* of the helicopter at first sounded like any other. Then it drew alarmingly close. Then its earsplitting racket filled the cavern.

Squirrelly's blue eyes went to the cave mouth. A helicopter bubble hovered just outside like the clear, all-seeing eye of a great dragonfly. Kicked-up dust obscured everything.

Lobsang had possession of one of Kula's AK-47s. He snapped it to his shoulder and aimed toward the pilot.

A hand swept out and relieved the Tibetan of the weapon, and the voice of the Master of Sinanju squeaked, "It is Kula. He has brought us the steed by which we will make our escape."

Squirrelly looked past the helicopter windshield. Sure enough, there sat the big, lovable Mongol. Kula was grinning and pointing upward. Then the helicopter lifted from sight.

After that it was just a matter of climbing to the hilltop to join him under the whirling rotor blades.

"We will escape from right under the noses of the Chinese enemies of the faith," he boasted.

"You can fly this unholy machine safely?" Lobsang asked doubtfully.

"If we die, it was meant to be," laughed Kula.

"If we die," said Chiun, gathering up his skirts to step aboard, "I will hold you personally accountable throughout all your lives to come."

They lifted off and went rattling toward the snowcaps surrounding Lhasa Valley so smoothly that right on the spot Squirrelly decided the scene was too good not to use. She'd just have to rewrite it so *she* commandeered the helicopter. Why not? It was *her* movie. If anyone questioned it, she'd invoke the old dramatic-license chestnut.

**36**

There were fires burning to the south as the CAAC turboprop bearing the minister of state security fought the terrific downdrafts above Gonggar Airport, eighty miles to the south of Lhasa.

Tibet was in revolt. The radio reports verified it. Chushi Gangdruk guerrillas were committing depredations in towns and cities strung all along the Friendship Highway.

There was no doubt that this was the doing of the meddlesome Bunji Lama. The minister of state security prayed to whatever gods still smiled upon China in these unsuperstitious days that the Tashi, chanting mantras in his seat and spinning his golden prayer wheel, would be recognized as a greater power than the white-eyes lama from the other side of the world. If not, the minister of state security was prepared to take measures not sanctioned by Beijing.

He would not lose Tibet. To lose Tibet would be to lose face... if not his head.

The turboprop dropped with sickening suddenness, and the minister forgot all about the Bunji Lama, Tibet and possible loss of face or head.

As he held the paper sack to his pale lips, all he cared about was holding in his breakfast.

WHEN THEY CAME within sight of the town of Gong-gar, Remo Williams told his Khampas, "I want this place left the way we found it."

Bumba Fun shrank behind the driver's seat of the truck as if deflated. "No burning?"

"No nothing. We're making good time."

"But why, O Gonpo?"

"You burn the town, and you'll wreck the airport. I'm going to need the airport to get the Bunji the hell out of Tibet."

"That is a strange reason," Bumba Fun muttered.

"It'll be good practice for when we reach Lhasa."

"But we would not burn Lhasa. It is sacred to Tibet. We would burn only Chinese and their profane buildings."

"We've had enough burning. When we hit Lhasa, I want it done quietly."

"We will hit Lhasa as quietly as Khampas are able," promised Bumba Fun.

"Do better," said Remo. "After I haul the Bunji Lama's butt out of town, it's your show."

Perking up, Bumba Fun bore down on the accelerator like a Khampa possessed.


THE PLA HELICOPTER settled onto the mountain summit, kicking up a cloud of stinging flakes. The skids sank a foot into pristine snow cover.

"We are safe here," grunted Kula as he shut down the rotors.

The Master of Sinanju stepped out onto the frozen snowcap. The air was thin and very bitter to inhale. But it smelled of freedom, and so it was good.

He surveyed the valley below.

Lhasa's fantastical roofs shone in the harsh light of day. But other than the tiny figures in green, no people were about in the streets. Martial law had clamped down upon the ancient city cupped in the eternal mountains. And because the people of Lhasa accepted whatever befell them as preordained from the beginning of time, and the Chinese were many and possessed deadly weapons in plenty, there was no resistance. Mostly it was the latter.

Someone would have to rouse the people to the Bunji's presence in their midst. Only then would they come out of their homes and their hovels and retake the streets.

Only a Master of Sinanju was fit for such a dangerous task, thought Chiun. So be it. When darkness came and the Chinese slept exhausted in their barracks, he would venture down into the city to awaken the people of Tibet from their long nightmare of sleep.

Until then the Master of Sinanju could only wait and hope that no People's Liberation Army helicopter ventured over this particular peak.

AN F-70-CT HELICOPTER stood waiting at the end of the Gonggar Airport runway when the turboprop whined to a safe stop.

The minister of state security spit the last bitter taste of bile and his morning rice into the paper sack and rushed to the exit door. He waved toward the helicopter pilot, then made a circling motion over his head. The pilot engaged the main rotor. The droopy blades began to revolve to the accompaniment of a rising whine.

As he went back to prepare the Tashi for the short hop to Lhasa, the minister of state security thought to himself that the worst was over. He had made Gonggar without injury. And the helicopter was a variation of the Sikorsky Blackhawk specially equipped for high-altitude flying. The pilot would be the best the PLA had to offer.

It was just a matter of introducing the presence of the Tashi into the volatile situation in Lhasa now.

He stood at the foot of the stairs as the Tashi was helped down by his personal servants. The Tashi looked serene. His movements were graceful, delicate, almost sweet. He spun the gold prayer wheel in his left hand with a studied intent.

"The hour of your ascendancy draws near," the minister of state security told his charge when the Tashi's sandals at last stood on Tibetan soil for the first time.

Closing his small eyes, the Tashi merely nodded.

"In honor of this momentous event, I am pleased to present to you a gift worthy of your station," the security minister said, snapping his fingers once.

Out of the aircraft, a cadre came, bearing a prayer wheel almost as tall as himself.

The Tashi's attendants gasped at the sight of it. Turning, the Tashi himself went wide of eye.

It stood over four feet tall, the mahogany shaft as thick around as a shepherd's staff. Surmounting it was a prayer wheel the size and shape of a snare drum. It was made of rare woods, inlaid with silver, gold, jade and semiprecious stones.

The Tashi took it. Planting the staff onto the tarmac, he shook it until the wheel hummed, its red and blue and green stones making streaks of varicolored light.

"It is an auspicious augury," the Tashi said, smiling.

Together they glided toward the waiting helicopter. The Tashi allowed one of his attendants to bear the prayer wheel that had been looted from the Potala in the early weeks of the annexation of Tibet, more than a generation ago. It was too heavy for his small-boned form to carry.

When they were over Gonggar, the minister of state security noticed a line of military trucks and vehicles speeding toward the airport town. PLA reinforcements, obviously.

He took comfort in the fact that by the time they reached Lhasa, the stubborn difficulty of the Bunji Lama would be resolved.

TWO T-72 HEAVY BATTLE tanks stood guard on the street called Yanhe Donglu at the south approach to Lhasa proper. They sat stern to stern, 125 mm Smoothbore cannon pointed menacingly in the direction of Gonggar.

There was enough space between them for a yak to pass—if the yak wasn't pregnant.

"Slow down," Remo told Bumba Fun when they came to the tanks.

"Do you not mean stop?"

"Slow down first. Then stop."

The truck drew to a halt not ten yards from the yawning Smoothbore muzzles.

"What do we do, Gonpo Jigme?" Bumba Fun asked uncertainly. "Those tanks block our path."

"Give me a minute," said Remo, stepping out.

"To do what?"

"Break the tanks," said Remo.

PLA TANK COMMANDER Yun Ting narrowed his eyes at the lone Khampa who stepped out of the lead truck of the unauthorized convoy. He watched the man approach, apparently unarmed. The way the Khampa walked was too casual to suggest a threat. Still, Yun

Ting, seated up in the turret hatch, tripped the lever that controlled the turret's revolutions. The turret jerked left, the better to fix the Khampa with the terrifying maw of its cannon. It was a very intimidating action, designed to promote compliance.

The trouble was the Khampa with the silver-fox turban looked not at all intimidated. Not even when Yun's counterpart in the other tank adjusted his Smoothbore so that the Khampa was fixed in an annihilating cross fire.

The Khampa walked right up to the point where the cannon barrels were within easy reach. Ignoring Yun's shouted demand that he identify himself, the Khampa reached up with casual hands and cupped the lower rims of both barrels in his palms, like some brainless peasant ready to milk the teats of a giant goat.

He used his fingers to feel the hard steel, and Yun noticed they were too white to belong to a true Khampa.

The sound came like a thunderclap. For the rest of his days, Yun thought the sound came first. But he also clearly remembered, in the military prison where they threw him for dereliction of duty, seeing the hands withdraw and snap back in unison. The edges of the twin palms struck the hard rim of the Smoothbore together. And at once the long barrels cracked and split for the entire length.

The thunderous crack that jerked Yun Ting up in his hard seat came then. Not before. His shocked nerves only remembered it the other way.

The twin Smoothbores each fell to the hard asphalt in two sections, perfectly halved.

It was impossible. Unbelievable. And most of all, the insolent Khampa who had destroyed the peoples' property simply stood there in the middle of the road blowing on his fingers and polishing his white knuckles on the breast of his native costume.

His eyes, staring at Yun Ting, were insolent and mocking. They as much as said "I dare you to shoot me now."

It was a dare PLA Tank Commander Yun Ting elected not to take. He called for retreat. There was a machine gun mounted on his turret, it was true, but in his quailing heart, Yun knew it would be of no value against a being who could split the finest steel forged in China with what looked like a casual kung fu chop of each hand.

The T-72s belched noise and smelly exhaust as they jockeyed around, pointed their noseless turrets north and retreated into the city.

To the shamed ears of Yun Ting came the exultant shouts of the Khampas who now had a clear path into the city.

"Gonpo!" they cried. "Gonpo Jigme! *Lha gyalo! De tamche pham!*"

He did not know who or what Gonpo Jigme was. The rest was perfectly understandable Tibetan. "The Gods are victorious," the Khampas were saying. "The demons are defeated."

Yun Ting did not like being referred to as a demon, but he could not argue with the rest of it. Not when he was in full retreat before a single unarmed being who, for all he knew, was one of the long-banished gods of ancient Tibet returned.

**37**

The last mountain peak shot away from under the PLA helicopter's skids, and the Lhasa Valley opened up like a great jewel box. Its grandeur, its roofs and the winding River Lhasa, dominated by the gargantuan Potala Palace, was almost enough to take the minister of state security's breath away had he not been busy with radio contact with the main PLA garrison in the city below.

The situation was strange. The Bunji Lama remained at large, although the city was being scoured to locate this personage. All Tibetans had been ordered to remain indoors. But the Bunji could not be found.

"There may be no need to find the Bunji," the minister of state security informed the ground. "For once the people of Lhasa know that the Tashi is in their midst, the influence of the Bunji clique will have been crushed."

As they were clearing him to land at the Dragon King Pool behind the Potala, the minister spotted the PLA helicopter resting atop a peak on the other side of the valley. He took a pair of field glasses from a door pocket and brought them to his eyes.

After a moment he spoke into his throat mike. "I have found the Bunji," he said without excitement.

There was no need for excitement. The Bunji and her clique of reactionaries were obviously stranded on the mountaintop. There would be no escape for them.

They had reached endgame.

THE MASTER of Sinanju watched Lhasa from his windy vantage point on the mountaintop, his hands tucked in the warm tunnel of his joined kimono sleeves, his parchment features troubled.

Below, the foolish dragonflies of the People's Liberation Army crisscrossed the city, flying low. They searched in vain, he knew.

Still, he considered, they were not the only ones afflicted with excessive vanity. He glanced toward the resting helicopter where the Bunji Lama sat fuming. It was good that he had taken her voice, for in the long hours that lay between this calm hour and darkness her shrill complaints and lamentations would surely have been unendurable. The Bunji grew impatient with every passing minute, and only the Master of Sinanju understood that to wrest control of Lhasa from the Han Chinese was a task possibly without a satisfactory end.

Abruptly a solitary helicopter breasted the mountains to the south. It dropped toward the city below. Just when it seemed that it would alight without causing difficulties, it rose again and climbed toward them.

Like male dragonflies scenting a female, the crisscrossing helicopters whirled up from their rooftop patrols and climbed after the solitary PLA ship.

Every helicopter bore on an unerring course toward their mountaintop position.

As he turned to warn the others, the Master of Sinanju understood that the odds of their taking the day had grown infinitely worse.

"BEHOLD THE CRIMINAL skyboats of the Chinese!"
Bumba Fun shouted, pointing toward the northern
horizon. "See how they flee the approach of Gonpo
Jigme! They fear the dreadnought that has come down
from Mt. Kailas to expel them from our holy land."

"I never heard of Mt. Kailas," said Remo, watching the helicopters strain toward the rarefied air of the
mountains. Up ahead a security checkpoint was being
abandoned as PLA cadres piled into jeeps and headed
north.

"Lhasa is ours!" Bumba Fun exulted.

"Don't count your yaks until you have them by the
horns," Remo warned, thinking that this was too easy.
They were barreling up Dousen Galu, past the Working People's Cultural Palace, and no one had tried to
stop them since he had maimed those two tanks.

Whatever was going on, he had a hunch that Chiun
was somehow involved.

Along the way Bumba Fun and his Khampas called
upon the citizens of Lhasa to turn out in support of
their own liberation. Dull bronze faces appeared at
windows like beaten gongs. But that was all. No one
ventured out of doors. And when they began encoun-
tering pockets of PLA resistance, they were on their
own.

"Buddhists," muttered Remo.

No SOONER HAD the Master of Sinanju broken the dire
news to the Bunji Lama and the others than the air
was full of flying machines. They zipped back and
forth in the thin air, rotors buzzing. There was no escape from them, except downward.

"We cannot remain here," Chiun said tightly.

"We will fight," said Kula. Lifting both AK-47s in his big hands, he peppered any helicopter that dared stray too close.

One, mortally wounded, spiraled down to blossom into a fiery flower far below. Another fired back, shattering the cockpit of their own helicopter. Kula directed his fire toward that ship. The twin streams of lead chewed off the tail rotor. It, too, fell from the sky, a wounded thing of complaining metal.

The Master of Sinanju allowed Kula his sport. When both clips ran empty, the big Mongol dropped his rifles in disgust and drew his silver dagger as if to reach out and snare a passing helicopter for gutting.

In the end they started down off the mountain, plowing through waist-high snow that concealed treacherous boulders.

Cadres in PLA green began rappeling down from their helicopters to places of ambush below the snow line. They crouched in waiting, weapons ready, hard eyes cruel.

Cadres below, helicopters above. And across the pastureland that separated Lhasa proper from the mountain on which they stood came column after column of tanks and jeeps and trucks.

Holding his black skirts before him like a plow, Chiun blazed a trail through the snow sufficient for the Bunji Lama, Kula and Lobsang Drom to follow safely. He grew grim of visage. It was possible to steal past the lurking cadres, possible also for one of his consummate skill to reach the relative safety of Lhasa and be spirited out of Tibet by guile and cunning. But to lead his charges to safety was another matter. Some would die. Perhaps all. All except for the Master of Sinanju himself, of course. He would refuse to die.

Surrender was the only reasonable option. Surrender, and then perhaps the advantage could be regained and the tables turned.

He turned to break the harsh truth to those who had put their trust in him.

Squirrelly Chicane couldn't believe her ears.

Surrender? she shouted. Except no words came out.

"I will never surrender to the Han," vowed Kula.

Attaboy! Squirrelly thought.

"I will surrender if it is ordained that I surrender," added Lobsang in a doleful voice.

You're a big help, Squirrelly thought.

"We must surrender if we are to leave this mountain alive," Chiun insisted.

Never! Squirrelly screamed mentally. This was awful. The whole storyline is falling apart. I've got to get them back on track. They need inspiration. If only I could say something or sing a song. That's it! A song! I need an uplifting song. Their spirits will soar, and all this defeatist talk will end up on the cutting-room floor, where it belongs.

Squirrelly bustled up to the Master of Sinanju and tried to get his attention. She pointed to her mouth, made faces, did everything she could think of except kick him in the shin.

"The Bunji wishes to speak," Kula pointed out.

"She should be heard," Lobsang agreed.

So, reluctantly Chiun reached up to release her vocal cords.

"You may speak," he said.

"It's about time you did that!" Squirrelly complained. "I have a plan."

"The Bunji has a plan," Kula said excitedly.

"Tell us this plan," Chiun said suspiciously.

"Just watch." And without another word, Squirrelly clambered up on a snowy crag within full view of the cadres below, the helicopters above and the tanks and military vehicles assembling at the base of the mountain and burst into song:

"I am the Buddha;
The Buddha is me.
I got my start
Beneath the bodhi tree.
I am the Bunji;
The Bunji is me.
Here I come,
To set Tibet freeeee!"

Squirrelly Chicane's voice lifted to heights never before reached on stage, screen or in real life. Her top note soared, held and soared even higher to unearthly realms of sound.

Every living thing on the mountain from man to snow leopard froze. They looked up toward the source of the arresting note.

And when she felt all the full and undivided attention of her audience, Squirrelly Chicane launched into the chorus.

Unfortunately no one heard a single note of the rest of her performance. They were too busy running from the rumble of sound that started way up above the snow line, grew to a roar and started cascading down the mountain, pushing before it tons of snow, ice and hard, punishing rocks.

Avalanche!

The word exploded in a hundred minds at once.

The Master of Sinanju leapt from his spot and yanked Squirrelly Chicane off the crag. She came unwillingly, but she came.

"Seek shelter!" he cried to the others.

Tons of snow and rocks roared down in a fury of sliding ice and tumbling rock. There was no time to do anything except crouch under substantial stone and pray to whatever gods could hear above the deafening roar of the mountaintop that raced down, gathering speed and substance and destruction.

When it ended, the clear, cold air rang with the sound of no sound.

A bald yellow head streaked with black popped up from the snow. The Master of Sinanju peered about narrowly. He reached down. He pulled Squirrelly Chicane up by her saffron-tinted hair.

"I did it! I did it! Didn't I do it?" she said happily.

Kula and Lobsang emerged next, shaking the snow off like bears coming out of long hibernation.

Below, the base of the mountain had been filled in. A handful of tanks had survived the onslaught. They were racing away.

Above, the helicopters had scattered like so many frightened crows.

"I did it! I did it! I conquered the wicked Chinese!" Squirrelly exulted.

"We are not free yet," intoned Chiun, looking up at the helicopters, already regathering like brazen vultures over a not-quite-dead living thing.

After a few minutes all but one stood off at some distance. The remaining helicopter, Chiun saw, was the one that had led the pack and brought this calamity about.

From a belly-mounted loudspeaker came an authoritative voice, speaking perfect Mandarin. "I offer safe passage to Gonggar Airport. Will you accept this generous offer?''

"Never!" Squirrelly shrieked, shaking her fist at the helicopter. "Isn't that right, men?"

When there was no answer, she said again, "I said, 'Isn't that right, men?'''

They regarded her with doubtful eyes.

"Don't you see! This is the climax. The Bunji Lama calls down a mountaintop onto the bad guys with her magnificent Bunji voice. This will really play! I'd like to see Spielberg top this! Why, I'll bet they're dancing in the streets right now, rejoicing that the bad guys finally got their comeuppance."

All eyes went to Lhasa. There was no question that many who heard the sound of the avalanche had seen the forces of the People's Liberation Army crushed into oblivion.

"They should be pouring into the streets any time now," Squirrelly said breathlessly.

But Lhasa remained quiet.

"What's with them? Don't they understand they've been liberated?"

When it became clear that the answer was no, Squirrelly cupped her hands before her mouth and tried to shout the joyous news across the Lhasa Valley.

The top of the mountain gave a brief warning rumble.

A quick hand touched her throat, and Squirrelly found herself squeaking like an excited mouse, and then nothing came out of her mouth at all.

You're all just jealous because a woman saved you! she tried to shout. They were talking among themselves as if she were a mere extra.

"I have come to set the Bunji Lama on the Lion Throne," the Master of Sinanju said slowly. "This I have done."

"It is true," Kula admitted readily.

"The Bunji Lama is now ruler of Tibet—by all rights."

Forget the exposition, you morons! Squirrelly screamed mentally. My public awaits!

"Perhaps," continued Chiun, "it has been ordained from the start of time that this Bunji Lama is not in truth the Bunji who is destined to liberate Tibet."

Everyone looked at Squirrelly as if she had blown her lines, big-time.

"It is possible," Kula admitted. "After all, she is a white eyes. And female."

"If it is to be, it is to be," said Lobsang. "For who among us can arrest the mighty Wheel of the Inexorable?"

Chiun said, "It is decided, then. We have done all we could. We must flee in order to await a truer hour and a more fortuitous time."

Like hell we are! Squirrelly screamed mentally.

But they had made up their minds. Squirrelly found herself gathered up in Kula's big treacherous arms, and down they went again.

It just couldn't get any worse if she were being forced to play opposite animals or, God forbid, a child actor.

**38**

At the base of the mountain, the followers of the Bunji Lama took possession of an abandoned jeep. They discovered the driver as they drove off. He had been hiding under the chassis, and they left him lying on his stomach with his tongue and the contents of his stomach extruded from his dead, open mouth.

Kula drove. They were not followed into the city, not even by the PLA helicopter that had promised them safe passage. Curiously, it rattled in the direction of Gonggar Airport.

And in Lhasa the rattle of automatic-weapons fire came now and again. Here and there the black smoke lifted to the blue sky.

"The Chinese are fighting," Kula muttered.

"But who are they fighting?" Chiun wondered aloud.

"They are fighting Tibetans," Lobsang said proudly. "The people of Lhasa, knowing that the Bunji is among them, are in open revolt."

"Tibetans do not fight," Kula said contemptuously.

But as they approached the city, the sounds of combat escalated.

The fighting seemed centered around the Public Security Bureau headquarters. Kula swung around it, taking Jiefong Beilu south to XingFu Donglu and cutting up and down empty streets whose windows framed frightened Tibetan faces until the road back to Gonggar came within sight.

Turning a corner, they avoided a head-on collision with a military truck by a margin so narrow that both vehicles exchanged paint samples.

"Khampa drivers!" Kula grumbled. "They are the worst."

"Khampas are fighters," Lobsang said.

"Khampas are bandits and sissies," Kula growled. But something in his rearview mirror brought him up in his seat. The truck was pulling a screeching U-turn and careering after them at high speed.

Kula pressed the accelerator, saying, "I will show them!"

The jeep sped ahead. The truck came roaring after it. Neck and neck they raced toward Gonggar. Every time the truck pulled alongside, Kula wrung more horsepower out of the jeep.

In the end the jeep seemed the clear winner until an annoyed voice lifted over the gunning engine sounds.

"Hey! Pull over! It's me!"

Chiun perked up in his seat. "Remo?"

"Who do you think?" Remo Williams shouted from behind the wheel.

Kula, eyes wide, said, "But you are dressed as a Khampa, White Tiger."

"It's a freaking disguise!" Remo shouted. "Now, pull over."

Kula started braking. A sandaled foot helped his foot stomp on the gas pedal, and a long-fingered hand took the wheel and inexorably steered the jeep to the shoulder of the road.

Remo jumped out of the truck, his silver-fox turban askew.

Chiun leapt out to meet him. "What are you doing in Tibet?" the Master of Sinanju demanded angrily.

"I've been trying to find you for hours," Remo complained. "You've really done it this time, you know. There's a huge international stink brewing."

"I am on sabbatical," Chiun snapped. "No shadow of what I do should properly fall upon America."

"Tell that to Beijing. Smith is having fits. The President is on his back because the First Lady is on his back. Look, we gotta get all of you out of Tibet fast."

"Who is this?" Kula asked of Remo, pointing to Bumba Fun.

Bumba Fun struck his chest, saying, "I am Bumba Fun, the strong right arm of Gonpo Jigme."

"Who is Gonpo Jigme?" asked Kula.

"I am," said Remo.

Chiun inserted himself in front of Remo. "You are Gonpo Jigme?"

"Yeah."

"But you sound like Remo."

"I am Remo."

"You just said that you are Gonpo Jigme."

"I am Gonpo Jigme. Look, this is starting to sound like one of those Bumba Fun conversations I keep having everywhere I go. Let's just get out of here, okay?"

Squirrelly Chicane presented herself to Remo at that moment. She made frantic motions at herself, at Chiun and at her unworking voice.

Remo restored her voice with a touch of a neck nerve.

"What's the idea of blowing in here and stealing my show?" Squirrelly demanded.

"Huh?"

"This is my movie, you—you scene-stealer! And you're way too late if you're here to costar. It's the third act already."

"What's she babbling about?" Remo asked Chiun.

"No one knows," said Chiun. "But we must get you out of Tibet with utmost dispatch."

"Get *me* out of Tibet! I came half way around the world to get *you* out of Tibet."

"I'm going nowhere!" Squirrelly protested. "I'm the Bunji Lamb and in Tibet the word of the Bunji Lamb is absolute law. Now, here's my plan. First, we—"

Remo and Chiun both stifled any further protest with warning gestures of their voice-deadening fingers, and they all climbed back into their respective vehicles and roared off in the direction of Gonggar Airport.

Chiun had joined Remo in the truck. Remo was driving, and Bumba Fun was hunkered down in the truck's bed.

Behind them, Lhasa quaked with explosions.

"I told those Khampas not to make a mess," Remo complained. "The minute they blew into town they couldn't wait to tear into the Chinese."

"When did you become a Khampa?" Chiun sniffed.

"I'm an honorary Khampa." Remo leaned over and whispered, "They think I'm this Gonpo Jigme character."

"And who do you think you are?" Chiun asked.

Remo threw his silver-fox turban out the window and slapped an itchy spot on the back of his head.

"A guy in serious need of a bath," said Remo. Then, noticing that the Master of Sinanju's bald head was streaked with black, he asked. "What's that on your head? It looks like you've been playing in a coal bin."

"It is a part of my disguise."

"Disguise?"

"You are in disguise. Am I not entitled to the same?"

"Well, whatever it is, it's coming off," Remo pointed out.

Checking himself in a side mirror, Chiun plucked from one sleeve a small aerosol can. He used this to liberally apply a black powdery substance to his streaked scalp.

Remo caught a glimpse of the label before the can disappeared back up the sleeve. It read Hair In A Can.

Remo rolled his eyes. Getting out of Tibet couldn't come soon enough for him.

THERE WAS a reception committee waiting for them when they wheeled into Gonggar Airport. Not soldiers, although there were a few of those present but they quickly retreated into the background.

Ordinary Tibetans lined the approach road and formed a semicircle on the tarmac. Prayer wheels, both plain and ornate, spun anxiously. All eyes followed them as they pulled up near a waiting turbo-prop aircraft.

"I don't like the looks of this," Remo said as he searched the crowd with his eyes.

"They will not interfere," said Chiun, but his eyes were concerned as he stepped from the truck.

"Don't be silly," Squirrelly said. "It's my adoring public." She began blowing kisses. "Yoo-hoo. It's me—the Bunji Lama."

The ranks of Tibetans regarded her without emotion.

"What's the matter with them? I've been gone sixty years. You'd think they'd be thrilled to see me."

A middle-aged Chinese in military uniform stepped from the crowd. "I am the one who offered you safe passage," he announced.

"And you will be the one to pay dearly if such passage is not granted," warned Chiun in the man's own language.

"As minister of state security for all of China, I have summoned the people of this area to see you off."

"They are welcome to behold the unhappy sight," said Chiun thinly.

"It is important that the people of Tibet see that the Bunji clique does not care for them and is willing to return to the soft comforts of the West," the security minister purred.

"We go because we chose to depart," said Chiun stiffly.

"But the people of Tibet will not be left without spiritual leadership," the security minister continued smoothly, his words directed to the crowd. "For one has come to this land to offer guidance during these confusing times."

With that the Chinese minister of state security gestured to the east. "For the Tashi has returned to Tibet!" he said loudly.

"The Tashi!" Lobsang hissed.

The Tibetans took up the name, repeating it over and over in hushed reverent tones that gathered in volume to a chant.

"What's the Tashi?" wondered Remo, who had not been able to follow the conversation but noticed the word repeated over and over.

"The Tashi Lama," said Chiun tightly.

"There's another llama?" Squirrelly burst out.

"Also know as the Panchen Lama," Lobsang hissed. "He is and always has been a tool of the Chinese."

"Is he very powerful?"

"He is the reincarnation of Opame, Buddha of Boundless Light."

Squirrelly's eyes went wide. "Boundless light! Is he a bigger star than me? Am I outranked? How big is his trailer? Oh God, on top of everything else, I'm being upstaged."

"The Tashi comes!" Kula growled.

"Oh my God, the Tashi Lama is coming and my hair's a mess! And look at these clothes! I have to change. Where's my dressing room?"

"Hush. This is a moment of great importance."

The crowd parted, and a quartet of abbots in red-and-gold vestments glided into view. They approached with stately steps.

"Which one is the Tashi?" Squirrelly whispered.

As if on cue, the abbots separated, revealing a tiny figure in golden robes padding along, face soft and serene beneath his miter, eyes possessing an innocence and beauty that were beyond words.

"It's just a kid," Remo said.

It was. The Tashi Lama could not have been older than eight. His tiny face was suffused with glowing pride.

Squirrelly gasped. "But look at the size of that prayer wheel. It's humongous! And all I have is this crummy Oscar."

"That's the biz, sweetheart," said Remo.

The Tashi Lama padded up to Squirrelly Chicane with serene purpose. His guileless eyes never left her face, and he carried his great prayer wheel high, although with difficulty.

"What do I say?" Squirrelly asked nervously of Lobsang.

"Do not kneel!" Lobsang counseled.

"Is an air-kiss okay? He's so cute."

"Let him bow to you, Buddha Sent," Kula urged.

Squirrelly drew herself up to her full height and patted her hair into some semblance of order.

The Tashi stepped directly in front of her. He stood looking up with a face that was like a jewel made of perfect flesh. His eyes were unreadable. Squirrelly swallowed. She had never been very good with kids.

She hoisted her Oscar high so the crowd could see it. There was no reaction. What was wrong with these yokels? she wondered. Don't they know glamour when they see it?

Squirrelly closed her eyes and steeled herself. I'm not going to bow. No matter what. I can take this little squirt, even if I do look like a wreck. He probably wears rubber underpants. I can handle this. I know I can.

Minutes dragged past. The Tashi and the Bunji stood face-to-face at one end of the runway, surrounded by anxious-faced Tibetans, under a sky of impossible blue.

In this encounter, everyone knew, would be decided the question of the true spiritual leader of Tibet and the future of Tibet itself.

"How long does this go on?" Remo whispered to Chiun at one point.

"Until one acknowledges the other's karmic superiority."

"We could be here all day," grumbled Remo, his eyes sweeping the crowd. He noticed the minister of state security melting back into the crowd. He was walking backward, his eyes riveted on the tableau, wriggling behind a literal wall of oblivious Tibetans.

Something about that struck Remo as wrong.

Then he saw the man reach into a pocket and lift something small and black, and when he pressed it with his thumb, there was a nearly inaudible click.

THE SCRIPTURES RECORDED that on the momentous day when the Bunji Lama and the Tashi Lama met, their combined karma met, mingled and struggled in realms unknown to men. Their indomitable wills refused to relent. There could be no victory, no defeat and no outcome but stalemate.

There being no other possible outcome, the Bunji and the *tulku* simply winked out of existence, each knowing that they would return in the round of existence to vie with one another in their next life.

It was reported by all witnesses that after the two winked out of existence, there were great lamentations, and to appease their disappointed followers, a bright light was left in their place as a promise that they would one day return.

And miracle of miracles, strangely colored rain fell from a clear sky.

THE GIANT PRAYER WHEEL in the Tashi Lama's tiny fist detonated with a sound like near thunder. The concussion blew every witness back at least thirty yards in a tangle of human limbs. The flare of light burned a lingering afterimage into every retina.

Remo was the only one who saw it coming. Even then there was no way to stop it. The click of the radio detonator gave him time enough to shout "Bomb!" on the run, and then he, like everyone else, was thrown off his feet and slammed backward by a hot wall of moving air.

Airborne, Remo forced his body to relax. Dropping his heels, he created drag. When he was in control of his trajectory, he cartwheeled twice and snapped to a sudden stop on his hands and knees, uninjured.

The Master of Sinanju, also thrown backward, grabbed a passing electrical pole, whipped himself around it twice and alighted on his feet, his face scarlet with rage.

"It was a trap!" Remo shouted. "That Chinese guy had a detonator."

"The Bunji!" Lobsang cried, flat on his back. "I do not see the Bunji!"

The cry was taken up by hundreds of anguished voices. Others called out for the Tashi Lama. Then the rain came. It was red, bright red and very warm as it pattered on human skin. It fell from a completely clear sky.

All around, Tibetans scrambled to capture drops of the bright red rain. In later years there would be arguments as to whose life drops had been captured—the Bunji's or the Tashi's.

In the end it did not matter. Both had been erased from the sensual world.

Remo moved among the fallen Tibetans, searching. It was Chiun who found the minister of state security, stunned and still clutching the incriminating detonator.

The man groaned in his confusion. He looked up, his eyes beginning to clear. "I have saved face," he gasped. "Tibet will belong to China forever."

"There is more than one way to lose face," retorted Chiun, and his long-nailed fingers swept down like tiger's claws. Up and down on the man's exposed face they worked. When they came away, the bone mask of his skull lay exposed to the sun amid the red ribbons that had been his lying features.

The minister of state security obviously realized something was amiss. He clapped his hands over his face and found smooth bone instead of flesh. His eyes widened in their white sockets, and his mouth opened to scream.

Remo's hard boot heel drove the unborn scream back into the shattered mask of bone that was now no longer face or skull, but was instead more like a bowl filled with white gravel.

"Better luck next life, pal," Remo said harshly.

"One who would sacrifice a child to reach his evil aims does not deserve a next life," Chiun spat out.

"Okay," said Remo. "Let's get out of here."

No one tried to stop them. The Tibetans were too busy chasing raindrops. But when they reached the turboprop plane, two PLA cadres made the mistake of lifting rifles to shoulders.

Remo and Chiun hit them in concert, driving the rifle butts into their shoulders and breaking both. After that the guards lost interest in everything.

"Can you fly one of these?" Remo asked Kula as he held the door open for Chiun.

"We will find out," said Kula, clambering aboard.

The next minute the pilot came flying out, the top of his skull in one hand and his brain exposed to the light.

Remo had wondered what the popping sound was.

The engines were already running, so it was just a matter of finding seats as Kula engaged the throttles. The turboprop lumbered along, swung around, and the engines roared.

Tibetans scattered before them as the turboprop gained the air and strained toward the nearby mountain ranges.

No one tried to stop them. Not even after they had put Lhasa Valley behind them and were over the endless mountains of Tibet. No jets or helicopters scrambled to challenge them.

When it looked like they were out of the woods, Kula turned from the controls and shouted back, "I will put you all off in India."

"What are you going to do?" Remo asked.

"Lobsang and I must seek out the Bunji."

"What?"

"In the exact moment of her death," Lobsang said hollowly, "the Bunji's spirit entered the body of a child. The child must be found. As the last of the Worshipful Nameless Ones in the Dark Who See the Light That is Coming, it is my responsibility to seek out the Bunji's new body and guide him to the Lion Throne."

"And I will help because Boldbator Khan has decreed that China will surrender Tibet," added Kula.

"I will help, too," offered Bumba Fun.

"I will not walk with a Khampa," vowed Kula.

"The Bunji will not be found by a mere horse Mongol," Bumba Fun insisted.

"Don't you guys ever give up?" muttered Remo.

"We are Buddhists," said Kula. "We have only to be in the right place at the ordained hour, and glory and merit will shower down upon us."

"Sounds like you all have a full calendar," said Remo. He left them to their planning to rejoin the Master of Sinanju in the rear of the aircraft.

"Smith is going to have a lot to say to you," Remo warned.

"I appoint you official explainer of the House of Sinanju," Chiun said dismissively. "You may tell him what you will."

"But I don't know anything," Remo protested.

"At least you admit your ignorance," Chiun sniffed.

They sat in silence as the endlessness of Tibet rolled under their wings.

"So," Remo asked after a while, "who the hell was Gonpo Jigme?"

Chiun turned his face to the window. "I will tell you after we have escaped Tibet. And not before."

"Why not now?"

"I will tell you that later, as well."

And for the rest of the flight, Remo couldn't get another word out of Chiun. It was very strange.

But not as strange as the landscape below. It looked very familiar. Especially one rounded snowcap they overflew near the Indian border. A long scar ran down its face. Remo couldn't take his eyes off it. It looked most familiar of all.

After it was lost to sight, Remo caught Chiun looking at him strangely. Abruptly the Master of Sinanju looked away.

**39**

Three days later Remo Williams was speaking to Harold W. Smith by telephone from his Massachusetts condominium.

"The President has calmed down," Smith was saying.

"You mean the First Lady has calmed down," Remo corrected.

"Whatever, the crisis appears to have blown over. The Chinese had been accusing Washington of having interventionist designs, but once the President pointed out that Squirrelly Chicane perished under suspicious circumstances while being technically a guest of Beijing, their blustering abated."

"So that's it?"

"Pockets of Tibetan agitation have been put down. There have been summary executions. I'm afraid one of those was our contact in Lhasa, Bumba Fun."

"There's plenty more where he came from."

"It is fortunate that this incident did not erupt into open revolt," said Smith.

"Never happen," Remo said. "The Tibetans don't believe in fighting. Until they get a new attitude, they're stuck with the Chinese."

"Did you ever find out why Chiun intervened in Tibet?"

"No, he's being very closemouthed about it. And he's blaming me for wrecking everything."

"On the contrary," said Smith. "Your timely arrival may have forced the best outcome among the admittedly bad possible scenarios."

"Tell that to Squirrelly Chicane's survivors," Remo said flatly.

"I understand they have been hired as consultants for a new movie based on her rather, ah, colorful life," Smith said dryly.

"I'll wait for the video," said Remo. "Speaking of video, I found that episode of 'The Poopi Silverfish Show' that started all this on tape. It's an old episode. Looks to me like Chiun saw Lobsang coming." Changing the subject, Remo asked, "You find anything on your computers about that name I asked you about?"

"Gonpo Jigme?"

"Who else?"

"Unfortunately, no. It is Tibetan. My data base is curiously deficient in that language."

"Chiun promised me he'd explain what it meant, but so far he's avoiding the subject. What gets me is why Tibet seemed so familiar. I've never been there in my life."

"Déjà vu," said Smith.

"Huh?"

"A common delusion. Persons happening upon a new person or place sometimes experience false feelings of recognition. Behavioral scientists have theorized certain smells or scents associated with a person's past trigger the phenomenon. The brain recalls the scent, but the mind believes it is recalling the place."

"Yeah, well, Tibet smelled like nothing I ever encountered before," said Remo glumly.

Down below he heard the door open and close.

"Chiun's back," Remo said quickly. "I gotta run."

Hanging up, Remo ran down the stairs to greet the Master of Sinanju at the door. Chiun carried a paper sack from which the unmistakable odor of fresh fish wafted.

"Cod?" asked Remo, taking the sack.

"There was no haddock," said Chiun, closing the door. "And it is your turn to cook."

"I cooked last time," Remo pointed out as they entered the kitchen together.

"You cooked badly last time. The duck was greasy and the rice undercooked. Therefore, you will cook tonight in atonement for your past errors."

"Tell you what, you break down and answer my questions, and I'll cook gladly."

"I do not care whether or not you cook gladly so long as you cook well," sniffed Chiun.

"Deal?"

"If the food turns out to my satisfaction," allowed Chiun.

AN HOUR LATER they were basking in the afterglow of full stomachs high in the meditation room with the dying light of day pouring in through its four great windows.

"Okay," said Remo, laying down his chopsticks. "Answer time. First tell me why you tore off to Tibet without me."

"Because I was obligated to do so," said Chiun, laying aside his rice.

"Not according to Boldbator Khan. He paid you to find the Bunji Lama, not to see her through all the way to Lhasa."

"In truth, my journey to Lhasa was repayment of an old debt."

"I'm listening," said Remo.

"I have told you the many stories of the House of Sinanju, its masters, its emperors and its clients. Of these, one state Sinanju rarely served was Tibet. Now, you would think that with its ambitious abbots and its intrigues, Sinanju would have found much gainful employment there. So it was thought by Master Pojji, who on his first contract went to Tibet at the behest of an abbot who was in truth Chinese, not Tibetan. Now, this abbot was a regent of a certain Dalai Lama who was proving recalcitrant. He would not obey his *chela*, which is another name for teacher. It was decided that this lama must be done away with quietly, and another, more compliant one found to take his place."

Chiun closed his eyes as if recalling the event from memory.

"Master Pojji received his instructions from this skulking abbot in the shadow of the Potala along with a bag of gold. In the dead of night, Pojji slipped into the mighty palace and followed the directions toward the lama's sleeping room. Stealing in, he came upon the Dalai asleep, his bedclothes drawn up over his head as if in fear. In his heart, Pojji was glad, for this made his task much easier. Creeping up on the bed, he crushed the head under the blanket with a single blow. And all was well. Or so Pojji thought.

"The next day, as the body of the dead Dalai lay in state, Master Pojji received the balance of his gold. Novice that he was, he foolishly tarried to see the dead face of his victim."

Chiun's eyes grew heavy with sorrow.

"I think I can see what's coming," Remo said softly.

"The face was that of a child, Remo. Pojji had murdered a child. This, as you know, is the greatest crime a master can commit. And although Pojji was blameless insofar as intent was concerned, still it was his hand that had robbed the sweet child of his life. In his anger, Pojji slew the abbot, who was a tool of China, which coveted Tibet even then. And in his shame, Pojji vowed to one day atone to Tibet for this crime. But the opportunity never came in his lifetime. And so the debt was handed down from master to master until a suitable opportunity arose. I chose to repay that debt by going to the rescue of the Bunji."

"But she died."

Chiun made a face. "That is not my fault. Nor is it the point. The debt has been repaid. Besides, the Bunji did not die. She merely passed on to a new, possibly more worthy body."

"You don't really believe that crap."

"I do not wish to discuss my beliefs," said Chiun aridly.

"Fine. Let's discuss Gonpo Jigme."

Chiun nodded quietly. "You have told me you already know the meaning of the Tibetan name, Jigme," he said. "It means 'dreadnought'. A common name among Tibetans, strange as it may seem for such a peaceful race of men."

"Got it," Remo said impatiently. "What about Gonpo?"

Chiun eyed his pupil critically. "Can you not guess?"

"No."

"Not even after you told me that you found Tibet familiar to your eyes which have never before come to rest on its grandeur?"

"Déjà vu."

Chiun stroked his beard. "I do not know that name."

"Smith explained it to me. It means a sense of having been someplace even though you'd never set foot there. I had an attack of déjà vu. No mystery."

"No. No," Chiun said in exasperation. "Smith is wrong. Gonpo is a god known to the people of Tibet. He is also called Mahakala."

"Seems to me I've heard that name before," Remo admitted.

"There is yet another name for Gonpo. One far better known. Can you not guess this name, Remo?"

"I'm not up on Tibetan gods."

"Forget Tibet! I am speaking of Gonpo, who is also known as the Dreadnought."

"Yeah?"

"What is another word for dreadnought, thick one?"

"Sue me. I don't know."

"Destroyer. Destroyer is another word for dreadnought. He is Gonpo the Destroyer."

Then it hit Remo. "You mean Gonpo is another name for Shiva?"

"I mean exactly that. It is believed that Shiva the Destroyer lives atop Mt. Kailas. That is one of the reasons why although many make pilgrimages to its peak, none dare climb to the summit. What do you think of that, Remo?"

"Well, it proves I'm not Shiva or a reincarnation of Shiva. I grew up in Newark. Never heard of Mt. Kailas."

"No. No. It proves nothing of the kind. You were recognized as Gonpo by the Tibetans. And when you flew over Mt. Kailas, you could not tear your eyes from its awesome peak."

Remo frowned. "Was that that scarred mountain near India?"

Chiun nodded. "Does that not prove that Shiva's spirit rides you?"

"Rides? That's what that nomad girl said. 'The god rides you.'"

"Among Tibetans they have mystics called *powos* who go into trances and surrender their bodies to the spirits of certain gods who then speak through their mouths. No doubt this woman recognized the spirit of Shiva had manifested itself through you."

"Sounds like channeling. That's the kind of New Age bulldooky that Squirrelly Chicane believed in."

"Simply because a fool believes that the sun will rise each morn does not mean the sun will malinger simply to spite the fool," Chiun advised.

Remo folded his arms stubbornly. "Yeah? Well, I still don't buy any of it. Not reincarnation, Bunji Lamas, or Shiva or Gonpo or any of it."

"That is your privilege," snapped Chiun. "It was not I who pressed the matter but you. And now you castigate me for explaining it to you."

Remo was silent for a long time. In the lingering dusk, his hard face gradually softened. Chiun's did, as well. They relaxed.

"Maybe some day I'll climb Mt. Kailas and see if anything's really up there," Remo said thoughtfully. "Just to settle the question."

"Perhaps you will, my son," said Chiun slowly. "But before you do, consider this question—if Shiva truly dwells there, who will come down off Mt. Kailas wearing your flesh and bones?"

Remo had no answer to that. Instead, he said, "Well, one thing's for sure. Squirrelly Chicane wasn't the reincarnation of the Bunji Lama. She was just a starry-eyed dip with delusions of grandeur."

"You are very sure of yourself for one who professes belief in nothing other than his own stubbornness," said Chiun.

"If Squirrelly Chicane does come back," Remo said, "let her find *us* this time."

"Do not call down such unpleasant karma on our heads," warned Chiun. "One Squirrelly Chicane in one lifetime is too much."

And in the dying light of day, they both smiled.

# EPILOGUE

On the very first day of the third month of the Tibetan Year of the Earth Dog, Dra Drang lay on a bed of clean straw in a cow byre in the town called Burang, grunting and grimacing in the joyous labor of giving birth to her first child.

At last, after much effort, the baby came, sliding out in a slippery flood of blood and amniotic fluids.

The midwife took up the child, spanked a short bleat of complaint from the tiny lungs and cut the umbilical cord with her teeth.

Enveloped in the yak-wool wrap, the child, strangely serene of face and disposition, was handed over. Dra Drang took up the peaceful bundle to her gently heaving chest.

About to unwrap the cloth to see if she had just borne a boy or a girl, Dra Drang was astonished to see that there was hair on the tiny, throbbing head. And the hair was the red of rust.

She wondered what such a presentiment could signify.

NEVER. *Never play opposite children or dogs. Thanks to that little snot, I have the biggest bomb since* Heaven's Gate *against my name, and I have to go around all over again. Just when I had the perfect incarnation and my third-reel climax, too!*

The bitter thoughts echoed in the darkness of her mind where there was no thought, no fear, no pain. Only recriminations.

Suddenly she felt herself moving. Like a helpless cork, she was being violently expelled from the place of floating darkness. A sharp blow struck her bottom, and she breathed again. The air smelled like a stable.

Squirrelly Chicane opened her eyes and took note of her surroundings. She saw Tibetan faces. Good. This time she wouldn't have to wait sixty years to be found. This time she'd do it right. This time she would be the Bunji Lama first and *then* launch her glorious film career. It would be the comeback of all time.

She looked up into the broad face of her new mother. Not so good—pocked skin and teeth so rotted they couldn't be capped. Well, she wouldn't win any beauty contests but she *had* to be an improvement over the last one. And by the time they went to camera, a good Tibetan actress might happen along. But not too good. No one could be allowed to outshine Squirrelly Chicane, six minutes old and already scxellent.

The body warmth of her new mother was making Squirrelly sleepy, so sleepy, and the memories of her last body were already starting to slip away. But they'd come back, she knew. When the Wheel of Time clicked into the right karmic notch.

Just before the first slumber of her new life overtook her, Squirrelly felt her blanket being unwrapped. Curious, she looked down at herself and saw a tiny pink penis.

*Yuck. I'm a boy again. My public isn't going to like it if I turn up in drag.*

Still, there was one consolation. She had been born a Taurus again. And everyone knew they had the *best* karma.

Don't miss the next installment of

# THE Destroyer

## Infernal Revenue
### Created by
# WARREN MURPHY
## and RICHARD SAPIR

A fiendish artificial intelligence chip known as *Friend* boots up disaster for CURE....

*Friend* has covertly hijacked the new computer system at CURE and screws up the database so efficiently that both Remo and Chiun quit—just as *Friend* releases a stealth virus that will hold the world hostage to technoterrorism! Can a reluctant Remo and determined Chiun work to foil the greatest threat CURE has ever faced?

Look for it this September, wherever Gold Eagle books are sold.

**BATTLE FOR THE FUTURE IN A WASTELAND OF DESPAIR**

## AURORA QUEST

### by JAMES AXLER

The popular author of DEATHLANDS® brings you the gripping conclusion of the Earthblood trilogy with AURORA QUEST. The crew of the U.S. space vessel *Aquila* returns from a deep-space mission to find that a devastating plant blight has stripped away all civilization.

In what's left of the world, the astronauts grimly cling to a glimmer of promise for a new start.

Available in July at your favorite retail outlet.

A biochemical weapons conspiracy puts
America in the hot seat. Don't miss

# STONY MAN™
## S E C R E T
## ARSENAL

With a desperate situation brewing in Europe, top-secret
STONY MAN defense teams target an unseen enemy.
America unleashes her warriors in an all-out counterstrike
against overwhelming odds!